Edeet Ravel was born on an Israeli kibbutz and now lives in Canada. *Ten Thousand Lovers* is her first novel.

Praise for *Ten Thousand Lovers*:

'Ravel is a shrewd and compassionate storyteller'
Sunday Herald

'Compusively readable . . .[Ravel's] seemingly simple and direct sentences often resonate with myriad meanings, possibilities and ironies . . . fascinating, insightful . . . this is a brave and beautiful book. It is a heartbreaking book' *Globe and Mail, Toronto*

'Stunning . . .a must-read for anyone who likes a love story and who cares about justice, humanity and the state of the world' *Quill and Quire*

'This is a powerful, provocative and poignant debut novel. A love story haunted by the endless tragedy of day-to-day living in the world's most intractable trouble spot' *Canberra Times*

'A powerful love story' *Mslexia*

Ten Thousand Lovers

Edeet Ravel

Donated by

review

First published in 2003
by REVIEW

An imprint of Headline Book Publishing

First published in paperback in 2003

10 9 8 7 6 5 4

ISBN 0 7553 0371 7

Typeset in Perpetua by Palimpsest Book Production Limited, Polmont, Stirlingshire
Printed and bound in Great Britain by Mackays of Chatham plc, Chatham Kent

Papers and cover board used by Headline are natural, recyclable products made from wood grown from sustainable forests. The manufacturing processes conform to the environmental regulations of the country of origin.

Headline Book Publishing
A division of Hodder Headline
338 Euston Road
London NW1 3BH

www.reviewbooks.co.uk
www.hodderheadline.com

For my daughter Larissa
and my friend Mark Marshall

'What country, friends, is this?'

—*Twelfth Night*

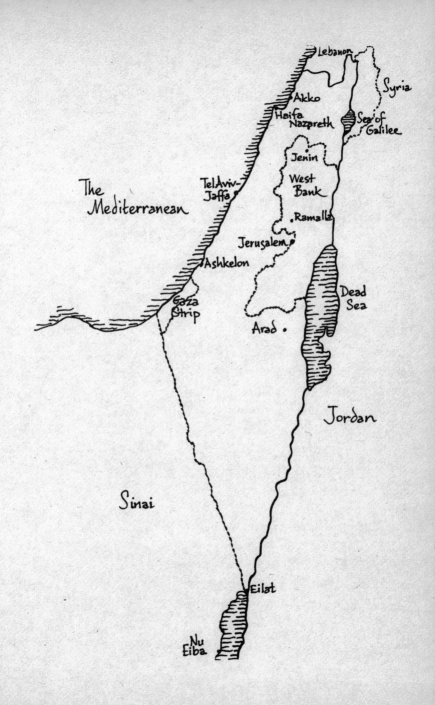

A long time ago, when I was twenty, I was involved with a man who was an interrogator.

I met him on a Friday morning while hitchhiking from Jerusalem to Tel Aviv. I was studying at the university in Jerusalem but I always spent weekends in Tel Aviv because Jerusalem shut down at weekends and there was nowhere to go and nothing to do. Tel Aviv, on the other hand, was at its liveliest on Friday nights and Saturdays. That was the weekend: Friday night and all day Saturday. Sunday was an ordinary working day, and I had to be back for an early class.

I was hitchhiking from the soldiers' hitchhiking booth, and I was embarrassed. The booth was supposed to be for soldiers only; a student with waist-length blonde hair and wearing a short skirt would always get picked up before the soldiers did and they resented it. But that was the only place you could hitchhike from, because right after the booth the road began winding wildly around the dark green mountains of Jerusalem.

Usually I took a shared taxi to Tel Aviv on Fridays. The shared taxis were seven-passenger Mercedes sedans and were fairly comfortable if you had a window seat. But I was short on cash that morning. My roommate, a Russian immigrant, had asked me for a loan, and I had just enough left to get me through the weekend, so I walked to the booth, stationed myself as far from the soldiers as possible, stretched out my arm and pointed at the road with my index finger. Hitchhiking in Israel isn't deductive. It's not about letting the driver know what you need (which is what an upturned thumb would indicate) but about telling the driver what to do (which is what a finger pointing to the road indicates).

The soldiers began to mutter and grumble. I tried not to listen to them. I wanted to be liked.

A car stopped almost immediately, pulled up next to me. Three pissed-off soldiers left the booth and walked defiantly towards us.

'Tel Aviv?' I said.

The man in the car said, 'Tel Aviv.'

'You're sure?' I asked. Because the last time I'd hitchhiked, the driver lied about where he was going and left me stranded in the middle of nowhere.

'*Ya-allah*, what a paranoid. Hurry, get in before they kill us.'

Behind us the soldiers were cursing. '*Kusemak*,' they said.

'Let them in,' I said, getting into the front seat.

'Well, unlock the back door.'

I pulled up the lock and the three soldiers, two men and a woman, slid in gloomily. They all needed to get off at different places. One was headed for Petah Tikvah, one for Shfayim, and one for Hadera. They were still pissed off, but they couldn't really say anything now that they had what they wanted.

᠙ ᠙

Ya-allah is Arabic, of course. _Ya_ is an Arabic particle, similar in usage to 'O' in English (as in, 'O Pyramus' or 'O wall'). Placed in front of a name in everyday speech (e.g. *ya-Asaf*) it's emphatic and means something like 'Yes, you, my friend, I'm talking to you.'

You wouldn't think *ya-allah* would be a favoured phrase among Israelis, but it is. You use it the way you'd use the expletory 'God' or 'Christ' in English.

Kusemak is Arabic too. There aren't a lot of swear words in Hebrew because for 1800 years Hebrew wasn't really a spoken language. When Hebrew was (artificially) revived, some swear words had to be borrowed. *Kusemak* means 'cunt of your mother' in Arabic, but it isn't used as an insult in Hebrew:

3

it's just used to express annoyance. In Arabic you wouldn't use that phrase lightly, but in Hebrew it's no big deal, because native Hebrew speakers don't really think about what it means.

─∽──∽─

The man said, 'Ami,' and I said, 'Lily,' and we shook hands sideways and said, 'Pleased to meet you,' or, literally, 'very pleasant,' which is what you say when you shake hands in Israel; you can't shake hands without saying *na'im* (pleasant) *me'od* (very). Everyone in Israel shook hands when I was there, even young people, even very cool young people. It was cool to shake hands (with a grim look on your face, though) when you met someone. I wonder whether it's still like that today.

It was a little awkward shaking hands in the car, and I could feel the contempt of the soldiers in the back, thinking they were watching a pick-up.

But Ami didn't say much after that. He only asked me whether I was in a rush, because he wanted to drive the soldiers as close as possible to their final destinations, which meant a lot of detours. I didn't mind. I liked going on drives, especially in expensive cars with bucket seats.

He dropped off the soldiers one by one: one at her home in Petah Tikvah, one at his home in Shfayim and the third at the turn-off to Hadera. The soldiers were no longer angry; they were grateful to be taken right to their door or to a convenient intersection. They thanked Ami enthusiastically and one even placed his hand on Ami's shoulder before he got out.

After the soldiers had gone, Ami said, 'Student?'

'Yes.'

'What are you studying?'

'Literature. Linguistics.'

'Chomsky?'

'Yes, he's hot now.'

'Our good friend Noam.'

'Uh-huh.'

'You're Canadian.'

'How did you know?' Usually I was taken for an American.

'I'm good at accents.'

'Canadians have the same accent as Americans.'

'Not exactly.'

'I don't believe you. You just guessed.'

He laughed. 'OK,' he said.

'What do you do?' I asked him. In Israel it isn't considered rude to ask questions like that. It's expected.

'I work for an interrogation department.'

Since the Hebrew word for interrogation is the same as the word for investigation, I thought for some reason that he was an accountant. I said, 'You check people's income-tax returns?'

He seemed amused. 'No, I interrogate people.'

'You mean you go to people's houses?' I still thought he was referring to income tax. I had recently been babysitting in Jerusalem when two extremely stern-looking men from the income-tax bureau had knocked on the door and asked to see the child's father. I told them he wasn't at home and they left, promising to return in the evening. When the father heard about the visit he turned pale.

'I interrogate war prisoners.'

'War prisoners!'

'Yes.'

'That's a real job?'

'So it seems,' he said. 'Did you think they take people off the street? Excuse me, we just need an interrogator for a few hours, how about it?'

'I never thought about it one way or the other. How many war prisoners are there anyway? We don't have a war every day.'

'The word is used loosely.'

'Loosely, how?'

'Loosely to refer to the enemy,' he said. He said it ironically, but Israelis are ironic a lot of the time and you can't always tell what lies behind the irony.

'Still, how can that be a full-time job?'

He laughed again. He was a little stoned, though I didn't know it then. 'It's full-time, all right,' he said.

'I can't believe it. I can't believe I'm sitting in a car with someone who does that for a living.'

'Believe it, Canadian woman,' he said.

◦——◦

My daughter is visiting from Belgium. She has brought a boyfriend, one of the musicians from her contemporary dance troupe Piesas. He loves her but she is still wavering.

I offered to pick them up at Victoria station but my daughter said they weren't sure when they'd be arriving. I waited impatiently, looking out of the window every time I thought I heard a car stopping on our street. I live on a quiet street in North London, a cul-de-sac with very little traffic.

I haven't seen her for four months. She's been in rehearsal since early autumn. At first she phoned every day, brimming with enthusiasm: the dance is brilliant, the director is brilliant, everyone is nice. Now that she's involved with Keys, her boyfriend, the phone calls have become less frequent, though they are just as intense, and twice she's called me for advice about contraception.

They finally arrived at eight in the evening. Keys is sweet and open and polite. He has a thin, kind face, an easy smile. They were both exhausted and went straight to bed. I've given them my bedroom and have settled in my study, previously my daughter's room. Her bed is still here, in the corner by the window, and I've taken down her old ballerina blanket.

~⌒~

He didn't ask me where I wanted to be let out. He drove into the city, parked along a boulevard near Dizengoff Street, and said, 'Come, I'll buy you lunch at Mandy's.'

'I don't know,' I said. I stared out of the window at the palm trees that lined the boulevard. On a park bench a woman wearing white gloves and a hat was blinking and nodding at imaginary passers-by.

'Come on,' he coaxed. 'As a reward for putting up with all the extra driving.'

'I like driving around.'

'Well, then, for no reason at all.'

'No, I can't,' I said. My voice was shaking, I had tears in my eyes.

'Please say yes.'

'I don't want to. But thanks for the lift.' I didn't move.

He sat there waiting for me to make up my mind. It was a beautiful day in October. Ordinary sunlight had replaced the blinding white glare of the summer season and an ocean breeze carried the friendly smell of damp salt through the city.

'All right,' I said finally. I was hungry; I was curious; he was handsome. I don't know what else to add to that list.

Mandy's Drug Store was a restaurant on Dizengoff Street. It was named after Mandy Rice-Davies, of the Profumo scandal. When the scandal was over she married an Israeli, and he named his restaurant after her. We sat at a polished wooden table and waited for the waiter. It was still early for lunch and only three tables were occupied, but the waiter was reading the sports section of the paper and didn't want to be interrupted. Ami sighed. Finally, he rose from the table, went over to the waiter and said, 'I know it's nice to be out of the army, but we really would appreciate some help here.'

The waiter laughed. 'Sorry,' he said.

We both ordered the same thing, breaded chicken.

'Where are you staying?' Ami asked me.

'I have a relative here, on Sokolov Street. My mother's fourth cousin or something. A widow with a daughter, Noga. Noga's in the army so I sleep in her bed. I used to change the sheets before and after I slept there – I had my own sheets in the cupboard. Then one time Noga came home unexpectedly at midnight and we had to share her bed. So now I don't bother changing the sheets, and neither does she. Everyone showers all the time here anyway. The first time Bracha offered me a shower I thought maybe I smelt. I didn't know it was like offering someone coffee.'

'Women think about things like that. Sheets. Whether to

change them or not. Who to change them for. I love that about women.'

'And I have a party tonight.'

'Where?'

'This guy Ibrahim.'

'Which Ibrahim?'

'Ibrahim who lives with David and Michel.'

'Great. I'll come with you.'

'I can't take you.'

'I'll take *you*. Ibrahim and I go way back.'

'You're making that up.'

'You're a very suspicious person, Lily, do you know that? First, you don't believe that I'm really going to Tel Aviv. Then you don't believe that I can tell you're Canadian. And now you think I'm inventing my friendship with my old and excellent friend Ibrahim.'

'Well, the last time I hitchhiked the driver tried to stick his hand inside my shirt so I made him stop and I had to walk to an intersection. The next driver left me stranded in some village in the middle of nowhere and it ended up taking me four hours to get to Tel Aviv.'

'You shouldn't be hitchhiking, maybe.'

'I don't usually, but sometimes I run out of money. Today my roommate needed a loan. And if you're so good at accents, you should know something else about me.'

'You spent part of your childhood in Israel?'

I couldn't help being impressed. He wasn't conning me, after all. 'Yes. First seven years. I'm an Israeli like you.'

'Your *resh* gives you away, and your perfect *het*,' he said. 'Perfect stoppage on the *aleph* too. But your vowels have taken the Canadian route, although they're struggling to recover. So where were you born?'

'Can't you tell that too?'

'Not a clue.'

'Kibbutz.'

'That explains everything.' He smiled at me. He had a beautiful smile, dimples, perfect teeth.

'Such as?'

'Well, your sensitive soul, Lily. Don't look at me that way, I'm not patronizing you. You remind me of my brother Ronny, of blessed memory. What are David and Michel up to these days?'

'I don't know, they're both in Argentina, according to their mother. I ran into her last week.'

'Still selling carpets?'

'I have no idea what they're selling. I don't think anyone does, not even their mother. Especially not their mother. It seems to pay the rent, though.'

The waiter brought our food, breaded chicken in woven baskets. We dug in. I was famished. I was always famished in those days.

'Where are you from?' I asked. 'I mean, were you born here?'

'Yes, but only by a two-day margin. I came forth from my mother's womb two days after she landed in Haifa.' Israelis sometimes get a kick out of using old biblical or rabbinic phrases ironically.

'Landed in Haifa from where?'

'From France. She was born in Lyon.'

'How can you be friends with Ibrahim? Doesn't it bother him, what you do for a living?'

'We go way back,' he said.

'In the Middle Ages torturer was a profession. I came across that recently, when we were doing the mystery plays,' I said. 'There was a list of professions and salaries. Magistrate, beadle, torturer.'

'Who was paid the most?'

'The magistrate. The torturer was in the middle. Beadle was at the bottom but he got free room and board in the church.'

I pictured Ami in a room with a prisoner, the prisoner sitting on a chair, Ami standing over him; then the picture went blank. I felt sweat gathering at the roots of my hair and under my arms.

'I'm surprised you're not a vegetarian,' he said. 'You have a tough side, after all.'

'One of these days I'm going to become vegetarian. Maybe even today. Maybe this is my last non-vegetarian meal.'

'Yes, you're a bit picky, aren't you? Look at the way you

examine every piece of chicken before you eat it. I should bring a microscope next time we eat together.'

'You're right, I like to see what I'm eating. What if there's a vein, or blood, or fat? Or something gross?'

'Your Hebrew is excellent,' Ami said.

'I make mistakes in conjugation. And my vocalization of conjunctions is pure guesswork, I don't know the rules.'

'Now you've really shocked me. We'll have to notify *A Hebrew Moment.*'

He was referring to a radio programme that addressed common language errors. A man (usually) would make a grammatical error and a woman (usually) would correct him. *It's more elegant to say . . .* she'd tell him. They didn't want to offend the listeners, so they used the word 'elegant' (*yafeh*) instead of the word 'correct' (*nakhon*).

'I envy people who know all the rules.'

He laughed. He had a charming laugh. 'And now, for all our new immigrants and the more ignorant, boorish members of our population, we bring you this reminder of your inferiority.' He mimicked the tone of the obnoxiously gracious radio announcer and I wanted to laugh too, but I didn't.

'I like to know if I make a mistake,' I said. 'Correct me if I make a mistake.'

'There's no such word as *oneh*.' He was referring to the word I'd used for 'torturer', which I'd constructed from the verb. 'There should be, I agree, but there isn't.' He was trying not to smile, and I knew why. When second-language Hebrew speakers garble verbal constructions the results aren't jarring the way they are in English. They're usually comical or heartbreaking or both.

'What's the right word?'

'There isn't any word, really, though you could say *me'aneh* if you got desperate.'

'Interesting.'

'On the other hand, English doesn't have any word for the person who's being tortured, and Hebrew has two.'

'I like to think about things like that.'

'So do I.'

We didn't speak for a while after that, although we stared at each other. I liked that about Israelis. I liked that there wasn't any pressure to keep making conversation. You could be silent and it was OK, it wasn't rude or awkward or significant. Even in groups there would be moments when everyone suddenly sank into thought. It was almost a group activity, sinking into thought. There always seemed to be a lot to sort out.

Neither of us wanted dessert. Ami asked for the bill, and then he said, 'Come to my place, Lily. I want you.' That's another thing about Israelis: they're direct. And even if you're not Israeli, as soon as you start speaking Hebrew you're forced to be direct too. Hebrew doesn't have a lot of detours. You've only got a limited supply of words to choose from, a limited number of ways to say whatever you need to say. There aren't a lot of tenses either. Hebrew doesn't offer endless evasions the way English does.

'Want me how?'

'Want you as in want to be with you. Are you involved with someone?'

'Not at the moment.'

'Come over just for a visit.'

'A visit?'

'Yes, just a visit. We'll have coffee, listen to music, smoke. I have some high-quality grass at home.'

'I don't smoke.'

'I have some good hashish, too.'

'Oh, let's face it. If I come over we'll end up in bed. And I don't want to. I'm bothered by your job.' My voice began to shake again.

The waiter brought the bill and I tried to split it with Ami but I didn't succeed. He paid and we went back to his car. I gave him my mother's cousin's address on Sokolov Street, but he drove us to his place instead.

〜

The Hebrew noun *rehem,* **which means womb, may be related to** the verb *rhm,* which means to feel compassion. The same applies to the respective Arabic cognates, *rahim* and *rihm.* Both words (in Hebrew and in Arabic) seem to derive from the same Akkadian word *remu*.

The Hebrew word for torture, *inui*, is a cognate of the Arabic *'ana*. The word *inui* can also refer to oppression in general, as in the biblical warning, 'You shall not afflict [*te'anu*] any widow or orphan.' Sometimes the word is associated with rape, as in 'He would not listen to her; and being stronger than she, he forced [*ina*] her and lay with her.'

The reference there is to Amnon, David's son, who fell hopelessly in love with his half-sister Tamar. He didn't think there was much chance of having her legitimately (Tamar thought they should at least try asking for permission to marry, but he wouldn't listen to her) so he took her by force. After which the very sight of Tamar filled him with disgust ('Then Amnon hated her with very great hatred, so that the hatred with which he hated her was greater than the love with which he had loved her') and he told her to go away and never return.

The use of the word *inui* to refer to methods used during questioning makes its first appearance in Hebrew in the Middle Ages, during the Crusades.

The word for interrogation is *ḥaqira*, from the root *ḥqr*. Hebrew is a sparse language but Hebrew words often resonate in complex ways because of their history in ancient biblical and mystical and exegetical texts. The verb *ḥqr* is an example of such a word. It means to investigate, ponder, cross-examine, research, interrogate and look closely at a text with a questioning mind in order to discover its hidden meaning.

Like the word *inui*, the word *ḥaqira* first appears in reference to interrogation at the time of the Inquisition.

The Arabic (and now international) word hashish also acquired new meaning at the time of the Crusades. A twelfth-century sect of hashish users who lived in the area of the Golan Heights and who were in the habit of toking up before they set off on secret missions to assassinate their various enemies came to be known as *ḥashshashin*. Hence the word 'assassin'.

◦──◦

His house was in Neve Avivim, near Tel Aviv University, and, incidentally, a five-minute walk from the home of Shimon Peres. It was a beautiful house, made of white stone, wrapped in vines, and surrounded by trees and hedges and flower-beds. The flowers were very elaborate: some were tall and exotic; others made me think of the surprising patches of small wild flowers one comes across in a forest.

'Is this house yours?' I asked. Only rich people had houses of their own in Israel. It was more common to own a flat in a building. Shimon Peres lived in a flat.

'Yes, it's all mine.'

'Your job must pay well.'

'It's me. I get paid well.'

'You get more than others?'

'Yes.'

'How come?'

'Because I'm so good at it.'

'Who does all this gardening? It's beautiful. I've never seen anything like it.'

'Thank you, Lily. I like gardening, it relaxes me.'

'Maybe you should go into gardening.'

'It's no fun planting flowers for other people. Planting is such a personal thing, don't you find?'

He unlocked the door to his house. 'Coffee? Tea? Beer?' he asked, as soon as we were inside. I stood with my back against the door and looked around. The ground floor was a single large room, which included a kitchenette, dining area and living room. French windows led to a tiled patio that ran along the side of the house. The walls were bare, and there was very little furniture: apart from a white sofa, a television set and stereo in the corner and a small kitchen table and two chairs in the dining area, the room was empty. The effect wasn't Spartan, though, but rather cosy and inviting, maybe because of the Oriental rugs and pillows scattered on the living-room floor.

'Tea.'

'Don't be so angry.'

'You were supposed to drive me to Bracha's house. I have to ring her at least to say I'll be late.'

'There's a phone in the bedroom,' he said.

There were three rooms at the back of the house, up a short flight of stairs: a bedroom, a study filled with books, and a storage room. The storage room was a mess, crammed with boxes and pieces of old furniture stacked one on top of the other, like something out of *Adventures in the Skin Trade*. It was the only messy room in the house.

I entered the bedroom, sat on the green and white quilt that covered the bed. I wondered whether I would come to know that quilt well and whether one day it would be hard to remember seeing it for the first time and not associating it with anything. I phoned Bracha. 'I've met someone,' I told her. 'I may go straight to the party with him, so I might not come over until late.'

'Any time, any time at all,' she said. 'You have the key. I made that apple cake for you.'

I felt bad, of course. 'I can't wait,' I said. Bracha acted like an old woman, and that's how I thought of her then, although she was only around fifty.

When I came back Ami was sitting on the floor rolling

joints. There were two cups of tea on a tray, along with a bowl of sugar cubes, slices of lemon and a plate of imported chocolate biscuits.

He lit up and offered me a drag but I shook my head. 'Did you really buy this house just with your salary?' I asked.

'Yes.'

'Your parents didn't help you?'

He laughed. 'No.'

'What's funny?'

'The idea of my parents helping me.'

'Why?'

'Even when he was alive my father struggled to keep us going. And my mother's in an institution.'

'An institution?'

'Yes. Both of my brothers died in the same week and she tried to jump off the balcony, but someone caught her. Or, at least, softened the landing. A fat man. He ran under her, acted as a cushion. Now it's not clear whether she's just lost her mind or whether her brain was damaged by the fall.'

In Israel it isn't unusual for people to give you this sort of biographical information straight away. Even strangers tell you who died in their family and how they died. Israelis wouldn't understand why people don't do that in other places. They wouldn't see a reason for reticence about tragedy and personal disaster.

'How did your brothers die?'

'One died in an accident during training, and the other in a motorcycle accident five days later. He shouldn't have been driving, and if I'd been around I'd have kept him at home but I wasn't around, I was in a show.'

'A show?'

'A play. I used to be an actor. Long ago.'

'You were an actor?'

'Yes.'

'You're not making all this up, are you?'

'Do you trust anyone at all?'

'I trust people once I get to know them. I don't just trust them automatically, especially now. I mean I used to, but I got smart.'

'Who lied to you?'

'Several people.'

'Guys?'

'Yeah. Well, I was naïve. So now I'm careful.'

'Like married and said they weren't?'

'Yes. Among other things.'

'Here's the deal, Lily. I promise never to lie to you.'

'You say that like we're going to be friends. We're not. Anyway, what's my part of the deal?'

'You decide that, not me.'

'I still don't know whether to believe you. Maybe you're not even an interrogator. Maybe you were pulling my leg. I need the bathroom.'

'You just went at the restaurant.'

'I go a lot.'

'There's one off the bedroom and one down the landing from the bedroom.'

I used the bathroom on the landing. It smelt of cinnamon perfume and I wondered whether a woman had been there recently. I also wondered whether Ami had a cleaning woman or whether he kept the house clean himself. Even the hand towels were newly laundered and neatly folded on the towel rack.

After I had used the bathroom I peeked into the storage room. There was a scroll pinned to the wall and I pulled it down. I thought it might be a Purim scroll, illuminated with tiny Persians wearing billowy trousers and blue and gold tunics. But it wasn't a Purim scroll. It was some sort of map.

I didn't know Ami was behind me and when he touched me I jumped and made that frightened sound people make when they're startled. He drew his arm round my waist and pulled me away from the scroll, which bounced back to its rolled-up position like a window blind.

'That's not for you,' he said, releasing me. He was much taller than me. I'm five-three; he was five-eleven.

'What is it?'

'A military map. I couldn't care less personally, but this way if you get asked you won't have to lie. You can say you never saw it.'

'Asked by whom?'

'No one right now. But if we do end up in a relationship, which is what I'm hoping, I'll get you security clearance. So, no more snooping until then. Come and drink the rest of your tea.'

I returned to the living room and sat down on a cushion. 'It's so clean here, do you have a cleaning woman?'

'No, I clean the house myself.'

'Why does everyone in Israel wash the floor a hundred times a day? And how come everyone's into clean feet? You know, I constantly see Israelis washing their feet in the little sink in their rooms. They lift their foot up – it's really awkward but they lift their foot right up and wash it, first one, then the other. And they're not embarrassed if you're there, they go on having a conversation with you while they're doing it.'

'Feet are important. What are you living on, Lily?'

'I have a scholarship. And my parents send me money now and then. In the summers I work at a daycare centre, I'm an expert biscuit distributor. It took me a while to get used to the way children talk here. Like they're the ones running the world. And no one seems to mind . . . Was there a woman here recently?'

'Yes.'

'I smelt her perfume. Cinnamon.'

'Very good.'

'So how come now you're asking me out?'

'Because that woman was not someone in my life. She drifted in for the night and drifted out in the morning. She's married, anyway. But that's not the point. If I had you, there wouldn't be any women wearing cinnamon perfume in this house. With you it's different.'

'"With you it's different. With you it's different." Why?'

'This is going to be an uphill battle, I see.'

'Yes. I'm not as stupid as I was.'

'When you were young?' He laughed. He was getting very stoned. 'Long ago when you were young?'

'When I was seventeen and eighteen and nineteen. How old are you?'

'Twenty-nine.'

'What do you do? In your job, what do you do to the men you interrogate? Or women?'

'I don't interrogate women.'

'How come?'

'There aren't a lot of women coming in, for one thing.'

'And for another?'

'And for another, women intimidate me.' I couldn't tell whether he was serious.

'What do you do to the men?'

'I chop them up into little pieces and eat them for dinner.'

'Do you like your job?'

He laughed again. 'You must be joking. You *must* be joking.'

'Well, then, why don't you leave?'

'I keep leaving all the time. I've left a hundred times. Whenever I leave they offer me more money. Like Faust, I go back.'

'Why? How come they want you back so badly?'

'I told you, I'm very good at it.'

'How much do you make?' I asked him. Asking people how much they earn is common practice in Israel. Money isn't a taboo subject: Israelis like to compare and see who's getting the best and worst deal.

'Most of my income comes from bonuses. Last year I made about two hundred thousand lirot in bonuses. And they gave me the car.'

'So, you just do it for the money?'

'Nothing's that simple, Lily. Especially questions beginning with why.'

'I don't want to think about this any more. It's exhausting. I think I'll have a joint after all.' I picked up one of the joints and lit it. I coughed a little, but not as much as the last time I'd tried to smoke.

'I think I have to kiss you,' Ami said.

'OK,' I said.

~~~~~~~~

My daughter wants to know what I'm working on. She drifted into my room early this morning, while Keys, her boyfriend, was in the shower. She had draped Ami's green and white quilt around her shoulders and was trailing it behind her like a queen. Our flat is chilly on winter mornings.

'The history of our quilt,' I told her.

'Is it a sad story?' she asked, sprawling on the bed.

'Some parts.'

'Which parts? The ending?'

'Yes.'

'I don't like sad endings.'

'I know.'

She invited me to join her and Keys on a trip to Brighton, but I declined. She has to sort this one out herself: I would only be in the way.

'Please, please, darling Mummy.'

'Next time, I promise.'

At breakfast she did imitations of the other dancers in her troupe, made fun of their neuroses. Keys is cautious with her, and also protective, full of hope for the two of them.

I enjoy having someone to share the cooking again. I also

enjoy being the object of affection: my daughter reaches out continually to stroke my arm or touch my shoulder, as though she wants to make sure I have not vanished now that she's started forming other attachments. I am a little shy about these gestures in the presence of her boyfriend. My daughter doesn't seem to have any difficulty, which is not surprising given that in the latest Piesas piece — a two-hour dance based on a play by Peter Handke — she has to strip altogether at one point. Dancers need to be generous with their bodies. My daughter's boyfriend and I are more ordinary souls, not quite so brave.

⌒～⌒

He told me he'd lived with a Norwegian woman for two years; they were engaged to be married. But she had allergies; she was allergic to Israel, to Israeli vegetation. It gave her asthma, which she'd never had before, and which stopped the minute she left the country. In the end she couldn't bear it any longer, and even though she loved Ami she went back to Norway. She begged him to go back with her but he couldn't see himself in Norway.

A week ago she'd sent him a photo of her new baby. She was married to an obstetrician; she was happy.

He showed me the photo of his former Norwegian girlfriend holding her baby. The baby wore a sky-blue cap made of soft mohair and a matching sweater. The Norwegian girlfriend looked puffy and tired. Ami said that for a long time after she left he hadn't wanted to get involved with anyone. Maybe he simply hadn't met the right person.

But I was the right person, finally. He said this after sex. We were eating cake on the bed, getting crumbs on the sheet. I'd put on one of his shirts but he was still naked, reclining on the bed, showing me photos. 'You I could love,' he said.

'You've only known me since ten this morning. That's a total of eleven hours.'

'You don't need a lot of time for some things.'

'I'm not going to have a relationship with you. I can't. What you do is just too weird.'

'You're weird too, Lily.'

'Yes, but not in the same way.'

'We're a very good match.'

'Only in bed. Not in other things.'

'In bed because of other things.'

'I refuse to be like you.'

'How come you're not in the army, by the way?'

'I have a deferral. Which is over at the end of the year, when I graduate. They've already called me in twice. They gave me an eye test, urine test, blood test, foot-arch test, chest X-ray, they measured my blood pressure . . . I'm surprised they didn't look at my teeth.'

'They'll get round to it.'

'It was the first time in my life that someone was giving me a check-up not for my benefit but theirs. To see what needed to be repaired, or to see how useful I was. It was so strange, I can't describe it. Like being a car suddenly.'

'Lily, Lily, where's your patriotism?' he said.

'Actually, a part of me liked it. I could see the attraction, you know. You could be a little kid again, someone else was going to make all the decisions for you. You could relax.'

Ami didn't say anything but his eyes narrowed, and I could see he had retreated to a place that excluded me, although at the same time he seemed to be looking right into my soul.

'And I took the psycho-technical exam,' I said, flustered. 'Which by the way, I flunked. I think I came out with an IQ of sixty-five. I was never good at stuff like that. "What shape comes next?" How would I know? That part of my brain doesn't function at all. Anyway, they're getting ready to draft me. With my test results, I'd end up in the kitchen, peeling potatoes.' I was rambling, because the way he was looking at me made me nervous.

'When's your induction?'

'August. You know, I think I was there on misfit day. I think they do all the misfits at the same time. Because there were all those guys with tight clothes, hitting each other and acting crazy and being bad. What happens to them? Does the army take them?'

'Yes. They go in, and then they misbehave and go to prison,

and they misbehave in prison and get put into solitary. After four weeks in solitary they usually decide to behave themselves, though sometimes it takes two or three sentences until they give up. Or if they're authentically disturbed they get a low profile and go on a special training course for low profiles.'

'Someone told me you can't get more than a ninety-seven profile if you're circumcised. They take three points off for circumcision, is that true?'

'Yes. What will you do, Lily? About the army?'

'I'm not going, of course. I'll get out of it somehow. I'll say I'm unfit. Or else I'll get someone to marry me for the benefits. I have new-immigrant status.'

'You're right, it would never work. You'd last exactly a week. If that long. You'd be one of those girls they send home in disgrace.'

'Noga says I'm lucky. She says she's bored.'

'Shall we go to Ibrahim's?'

'Yes, I'm really in the mood. But . . .'

'Don't worry, I'll be discreet. I'll pretend I barely know you.'

'How do you know Ibrahim?'

'We go way back.'

'Does he know what you do?'

'Yes, Lily, he knows.' He got up, went to the kitchen, found a small plastic bag, and filled it with marijuana.

Then we got dressed, and left for the party.

My daughter decided to have a small party before she and Keys head
off for Brighton. They spent the day making elaborate cakes
and asked a few friends to drop by. They insisted I join them,
and thoughtfully invited another parent and an aunt. We sat in
the living room and watched a short film one of my daughter's
friends made, a film about doors. Bottles of wine were opened,
everyone relaxed, and Keys played the flute for us, one of his
own compositions. A mesmerizing piece, after which no one
wanted to move at all. 'He's put a spell on us,' my daughter
said, and so it seemed.

Now I am back at my desk, back inside the bedtime stories I
used to tell my daughter, with the ogres and dragons carefully
removed. Once upon a time there was a young man who lived
in a house with a garden. One day—

Ami, by the way, is a modern Hebrew name. It's close in
pronunciation to Sammy, except that the initial vowel sound
resembles the sound you make when the doctor tells you to
open your mouth and say *ah*. There are lots of biblical names
beginning with Ami (Amiel, Aminadav, Amishadai), but Ami
by itself is a new name.

The word *am* means nation, and *ami* means 'my nation',
but Ami's mother liked the name because she was French.

Actually the French word for friend, *ami*, is close to a Hebrew word for friend, *amit*, and Ami was almost called Amit, but a nurse at the hospital made a mistake and wrote Ami on all the documents. By the time Ami's parents discovered the mistake, it was too late.

The word for 'weird' is *muzar*, from the word *zar*, which means alien, strange, foreign, removed, unholy.

My favourite phrase in this context is *muzar hayiti le-ahi*, I became alien to my brother. Or from my brother.

∽——∾

The flat Ibrahim shared with David and Michel was on Edelson Street. The three of them had a party every Friday night, and it usually lasted until Saturday afternoon. You didn't need an invitation, but you had to know someone who was a regular until you became a regular too. Sometimes it was so crowded and loud you could barely move or hear yourself think, and at other times we were only a few people, and the mood was mellow and relaxed.

That night, the night Ami came with me to the party, was quiet, partly because David and Michel were away and partly because of Mary Jo, Ibrahim's new girlfriend.

Although he had a wife and children in a village in the

north, Ibrahim lived in Tel Aviv. He worked at a garage as a mechanic, and he was famous, among other things, for his romantic liaisons, which were intense and full of high drama, and usually ended up with the women locking themselves in the bathroom and threatening suicide. That was because he went out with a certain type of woman: volatile, neurotic, usually an artist with frizzy hair, usually from Europe or South America. He wanted to go out with me too, even though I was Canadian and didn't have frizzy hair, and I was tempted, but in the end I said no because I knew I'd have a hard time with Ibrahim's jealousy problem. His women weren't allowed to talk to anyone else or look at anyone else, and he never believed that they were loyal to him. That's why most of them ended up in the bathroom having hysterics. He was hard to live with.

On the other hand, he was an extremely cheerful person. And this amazed me, because every now and then he said he planned to open a car-parts factory one day in his country. Which I found depressing, because (a) he didn't have any money and (b) he didn't have any country. In those days I thought that if you had a dream that was not in your own hands, not something you could count on, it was unbearable. It didn't occur to me then that dreams in general are subject to any number of obstructions and that most people knew this.

It turned out to be a good thing that I said no to Ibrahim, because just after that Mary Jo arrived on the scene and Ibrahim's romantic life took a definite turn for the better. It was a surprise to everyone, including me. I knew Mary Jo from the halls of residence. She was a Mennonite, her father was a minister, and she was quite religious. She played the guitar and between the Dylan tunes she'd always insert a little God song. She didn't date and she rarely went out. She had dark red hair and pale watery blue eyes and a delicate nose.

I have no idea how she ended up at one of Ibrahim's parties. It happened in August, while I was in Canada visiting my parents. By the time I returned, Mary Jo had transferred from Hebrew University to Tel Aviv University, and she had moved in with Ibrahim, who seemed far happier with his romantic life than he'd been in a long time.

They were considering getting married, if they could find a way to do it without Ibrahim divorcing his present wife.

Ibrahim wasn't paranoid with Mary Jo, partly because Mary Jo had been a virgin when they met. This seemed very significant to him. He sometimes referred to her (affectionately) as 'my virgin', *ha'betulah sheli*. 'Meet my virgin,' he'd tell people, and Mary Jo would look down at the floor and smile.

Apparently Mary Jo's parents were happy with her choice. She sent them a photo of Ibrahim in the garage, holding a fuse and grinning into the camera. She didn't tell them about the drugs, of course, or the several children Ibrahim had fathered.

The minute Ibrahim saw Ami he jumped on him and they hugged. Unlike most Middle-Easterners, Ibrahim was huge.

He was very tall and very broad. And he was extremely good-looking. 'Where have you been?' Ibrahim asked Ami, and Ami answered in Arabic and the rest of the conversation was in Arabic so I have no idea what they said, although it was clear that Ibrahim was pleased with the grass.

There was a belly-dancer that night. She'd brought a cassette with her and she put it on and started dancing. She was spectacular. The music seemed to have been written specifically for belly-dancing; it was almost impossible to listen to it and not feel an urge to do some belly-dancing yourself.

We all sat on pillows and watched her. I looked at the cassette case; the label was in Arabic script. I asked Ami what it said.

'You expect me to know Farsi, too?'

'What's the difference?' I asked. I was very ignorant about some things.

'I thought you were in linguistics. Farsi isn't even in the same family as Arabic. They just use the same alphabet.'

'How do you know Arabic?'

'I grew up with Iraqi immigrants,' he said.

'It's so strange to me that Ibrahim speaks fluent Hebrew. Such a historical oddity.'

'Yes, the whole concept of an Israeli Arab is surreal.'

'Would he leave Israel if he had somewhere to go?'

'He's attached to his village.'

'I'm going to ask for a copy of this tape. I love this song. I love this type of music.'

I leaned my head on his arm and he drew me towards him, drew his arm around my shoulder. The belly-dancer moved to where Ibrahim was sitting and she curved her spine backwards until her hair flowed on to Ibrahim's lap. Ibrahim smiled happily. Mary Jo was delighted.

We stayed at the party until two. I talked to Mary Jo and some of my other friends, and then there was dancing and a few of us climbed up to the roof of the building and another group of people headed for the beach. I would have gone to the beach too, but it was getting late. Ami and I stood on the roof and looked out at Tel Aviv. During the day Tel Aviv was a museum of its own hectic and determined past: layers of stained walls and small balconies in intimate proximity. But at night the view changed and the city became uniform: sultry and decadent.

Several people at the party seemed to know Ami well. Alex, a saxophone player with shoulder-length white-blond hair and transparent blue eyes, came up to us and said, 'I didn't realize you two knew each other. Ami, where have you been, what sights have your eyes seen?'

'How's it going, Alex?' Ami said.

'Look around you, Ami. Look around. We are headed for dark times, my friend. But who in this madhouse known as a state gives a fuck? Tell me that.'

'What happened with your recall?'

'My recall? Oh, that. You really haven't been around for a while. I managed to keep my twenty-four. They made me wait six hours in the sun, and by the time I went in for my examination I really was half dead. You wouldn't happen to have any mushrooms, by any chance?'

'I think Miki is your man for hallucinogenics.'

'Hey, listen, I'm trying to get *out* of the hallucination I'm in. Tell me I am not dreaming. Tell me I am not dreaming.'

'You are definitely not dreaming.'

'Rumour has it that you've infiltrated the *Shabak*. Impressive.'

Ami smiled, reached out and ruffled Alex's hair. 'Take it easy, Alex,' he said.

Alex sighed. 'If my grandmother were alive, I wonder . . . I wonder what she would be now. Maybe another Geula Cohen, who knows? Lily, it's lovely as always to see you. You lift the weary heart.' And he wandered off, possibly in search of Miki.

'Who was his grandmother?' I asked.

'A famous spy. She was caught and executed.'

When we were ready to leave, Ibrahim saw us to the door. 'You're together,' he announced.

Neither of us said anything.

'Ami's a good guy,' Ibrahim told me. 'In spite of everything.' He was quite stoned. 'We're all good, in spite of everything,' he added with conviction.

Ami drove me to my mother's cousin on Sokolov Street. He double-parked and walked with me up the narrow stairs to Bracha's small flat. Corridors of buildings in Israel have automatic lights that only come on for a few seconds when you press a switch, partly (I assume) to save energy and partly because during war-time everything has to be dark. When the lights in the corridor of Bracha's building went out, immobilising us, Ami didn't grope for the switch, although he was closest to it. Instead he held me and said, in the dark, 'I want to see you tomorrow.'

'I can't. I promised Bracha I'd go to the beach with her. But I'm free on Sunday – our teacher's on reserve duty, class is cancelled.'

'Great, you can meet my sister. I'll pick you up before lunch.'

'After lunch. Bracha likes to feed me. Turn the light back on.'

'Are you afraid of the dark?'

'Yes. I can't see you. It could be anyone holding me.'

He switched on the light, but didn't want to let go of me. I had to pull myself away.

⌒~⌒

Through a mysterious semantic process, the word *zayin*, which means

weaponry, and which is also the name of the seventh letter of the alphabet, came to mean 'cock' in modern Hebrew.

Maybe it was inevitable: the somewhat phallic shape of the letter *zayin*; the somewhat phallic shape of most weapons; the association of arms in general with sexual gear; the influence of the verb *zyn*, which means to feed or provide sustenance; and the alliterative link of *zayin* with the entirely unrelated biblical (and modern) word *zona* (prostitute).

These factors must have all conspired to create the modern Hebrew slang word *zayin* (and the related verb, *le-zayen*, to have sex). When Alex said no one gave a fuck, the phrase he used was *mi bekhlal sam zayin*, from the idiom *lo sam zayin*, which literally means 'not putting your cock (into something)' and which is a variation, I think, on *lo sam lev*, 'not putting your heart (into something)'. Not putting your heart (into something) means you aren't paying much attention. But not putting your cock (into something) suggests fierce apathy. It isn't only a matter of the heart. Even that most primitive and potent instinct, the sexual one, has ceased to function.

‧‧‧‧‧‧‧

Now I understand how lonely Bracha was, and how happy she was to see me at weekends. Her husband had died of stomach cancer, and Noga, who was her only child, was away in the army. She worked mostly at home; she was a freelance accountant.

Bracha was asleep when I came in after Ibrahim's party, but the following morning at breakfast she asked me who I'd met.

'Just some guy,' I said, pigging out on the apple cake she'd baked for me. 'You'll meet him – he's coming tomorrow to pick me up after lunch, he wants me to meet his sister. The cake's amazing, Bracha. Thanks.'

'What's his name?'

'Ami.'

'What does he do?'

'Something in the army.'

She nodded absentmindedly. 'Any news from home?'

'My parents don't write that often. And when they do, they don't tell me much.'

'No news is good news. We have way too much news in this country.' She sighed. 'How about your sister?'

'She writes even less than my parents.'

'I wish my Noga'le would call me more often. She says there's always a queue for the phone, or else she's too tired, poor thing.'

The rest of the conversation bored me. I hope I managed to disguise my boredom. Or if I didn't, I hope she didn't mind.

On Sunday, when Ami came to get me, Bracha invited him

in for coffee and cake. She liked him. 'You work for the army,' she said.

'Yes.'

'And you live in Afeka?'

'Yes, around there.'

'I hear you have a house. Good for you!'

'Thank you.'

'Lily's a sweetheart,' she plugged for me.

'Yes, I already know.'

'If she starts staying with you, I'll never see her.'

'We're not going out,' I said. 'We've only just met.'

'But he's such a nice man!' Bracha plugged for him. 'Works for the army, already has his own house, handsome, polite, obviously well educated.' She turned to him. 'You look very, very familiar to me. Very, very familiar. Why is that?'

'I used to be in the theatre.'

'Hamlet!' she exclaimed. 'I remember you! Why did you give it up?' she said angrily. 'You had no right to do that, with a talent like yours . . . Or was there some personal tragedy?' Her tone softened. 'I seem to remember, I'm very sorry. Very sorry. So, where are you off to now?'

'A family visit. My sister and I are going to visit one of my brothers.'

'I didn't know,' I said. 'I didn't know you had another brother.'

But what he meant was his brother's grave. We thanked Bracha and got into Ami's car and he drove us to a cemetery outside Tel Aviv. On the back seat of the car lay flowers wrapped in newspaper and a bag of potting compost and two flower-pots. Ami carried the flowers and the compost and I helped him with the pots.

I'd never been to a military cemetery before. I stared at the dazzling rows of identical white stone beds, each with its own massive white stone pillow. The oversized pillows, I realized, were the tombstones. The beds were raised about a foot from the ground and set only inches apart; bed after bed, in perfect symmetry, row upon row; and the paths between the rows were also paved in bright white stone. The effect was dizzying. It was like being in a dormitory on another planet, where everything is orderly and symmetrical and beds are made of white stone and covered with flowers.

We walked down the paved path towards Ami's sister. She didn't greet us and Ami didn't introduce me. He only said, 'Act one, scene two.'

Ami's brother's white stone bed was lined with clay pots of pink and blue flowers that seemed to be breathing softly in the still air. Ami's sister handed out biscuits. She was only in her early twenties but she had the serious, unsmiling look one often sees on young Israeli women, which makes them seem older than they are. She had pulled back her hair from her forehead with a red kerchief twisted into a band.

After she had given us the biscuits she took a notebook out of her handbag and read aloud to her dead brother. What she read was a diary of the week's events followed by a poem. I didn't know whether she'd written the poem herself or whether she'd found it in a book.

Then she left, without saying goodbye.

Ami began potting the new flowers he'd brought with him and tending the ones that were already there.

'"Died while fulfilling his duty",' I read.

'We didn't have much choice in the inscription,' Ami said. 'Though "died in a stupid accident" would have been more accurate. He shouldn't even be here, in the military cemetery, he should be with Ronny.'

'What happened?'

'He was doing guard duty and the batteries in his torch ran out. He fell into a ravine and lost consciousness and no one knew. There was supposed to be someone with him but there wasn't – the other guy didn't show up – and by the time they found him he was dead.'

'Do you visit Ronny, too?'

'Yes, we alternate. These need more water . . . Well, I guess the rains will be starting soon enough.'

'You do this every week?'

'Yes, unless something comes up – you know, if one of my

sister's kids gets sick or I have to work.'

'Is she OK, your sister?'

'Yes, she's OK, Lily. She's fine.'

'She didn't seem to notice me.'

'She noticed you, all right. You remind her of Ronny.'

'How do you know? How do you know I remind her of him?'

'I know her. I can read her.'

'This is getting creepy. I'm sorry, I have to leave this place. I don't like it here.' I started crying. I was very angry. 'Why did you bring me here? And why didn't you tell me where we were going? You're assuming we're close, you're acting as if we're close, but we're not. I don't know anything about you. You're trying to manipulate me.'

I said that last part in English, because there isn't really a word for 'manipulate' in Hebrew: you just use the English word and give it a Hebrew construction.

He didn't answer. He got up and we walked back to his car.

We didn't talk in the car, but he didn't seem at all upset.

At his place he put on Bach's Goldberg Variations and made coffee. There was a packet of cigarettes on the kitchen counter, Camel cigarettes in European-style wrapping. He pulled one out and lit it, but he only took one drag, then left the cigarette burning in an ashtray.

He said casually, 'Already we're fighting.'

'What do you do in your job?'

'It'll be better for you if you ask me that question after you're cleared. If you're still planning to see me, that is.'

'Why did you take me to the cemetery?'

'I like it there. It's peaceful. I wanted my sister to meet you. I didn't realise it would be such a heavy thing for you. We forget in this country, we get used to things. Forgetting is one of our biggest problems.'

'I have to go back tonight. I have an early class tomorrow.'

'I'll drive you back to Jerusalem.'

'Jerusalem! That's way too far.'

'I like driving. I have tomorrow off. I get a lot of time off. And next Friday I have to go to Jerusalem to visit my mother at Ezrat Nashim. You can come with me to see her, if you want, or I can pick you up afterwards. If you're not busy. If you don't have other plans.'

I didn't answer but I felt my anger dissolving, and we spent the rest of the afternoon listening to music. Ami had a large collection of jazz and blues records. We lay on the carpet and he asked me about my family and my life in Canada.

'There isn't much to tell,' I said. 'We aren't close. We're not a close family.'

'Why?'

'I don't know. I guess it's just the way my parents are.'

'Who were you close to, growing up?'

'I liked visiting my grandmother. We used to discuss Dostoyevsky and eat over-salted pretzels and drink tea made with about a hundred lemons and half a ton of sugar. She tried to teach me Russian, but I couldn't get all those *ch* sounds straight, so I gave up. And I had a best friend, Sheila. She's in Israel too, but she's become sort of right-wing.'

'And now?'

'I have lots of friends.'

'Yes, I noticed.'

'I feel close to them in a way.'

'You connect quickly to people.'

'I guess. People interest me.'

He touched me as I talked. My ears, my fingers, my belly. We made spaghetti sauce for supper and while it simmered Ami switched on the television for the news. 'Let's see what they want us to be scared of today,' he said. But after only a few minutes he'd had enough, and he turned it off. 'That's my favourite part,' he said, meaning the return of the blank screen.

'Well, are you scared?'

'Yes, but of what they didn't tell us . . . I was thinking, Lily, maybe before we leave for the Holy City I could see you naked again.'

'Yes, but not in your bed, otherwise I'll get too cosy and I won't want to go back afterwards.'

'We'll aim for maximum discomfort.'

'It's just that beds are hard to get out of.'

'Are sofas OK?'

'I think the floor is best.'

'Floor it is, then. I'll just get a blanket.' He dug around in a cupboard, pulled out a folded woollen blanket with the army's stamp on the corner, and spread it on top of the Oriental rugs. It had a faint metallic smell.

'You stole this?' I said.

'No, no, nothing like that. Just somehow . . . it ended up not getting returned . . .'

'I used to go camping with these Israelis. They always had canned food they'd stolen from the army. With the labels removed, of course. That's so weird, it wasn't as if they couldn't afford canned food.'

'People like to pick up souvenirs. Especially from places where they've had such a good time. I love your hair, Lily.'

'It gets all tangled, I should probably plait it.'

'The Zionist plait! I'm afraid if you do that I'll be forced to hand you over to the local branch of one of our youth movements.'

At midnight he drove me back to Jerusalem, to the Mount Scopus halls of residence. Before I got out of the car he asked for a list of all the places I'd stayed at in Israel and people who knew me at each place. The list was short: the halls, Bracha, a penpal I had visited in Ashkelon.

When I got back to my room I realized I still had all the money I'd taken with me before the weekend began.

❧ ❧

The house is quiet again. My daughter has left with Keys for Brighton; they won't be back until tomorrow. The old man in the flat next door came and asked for help with a complicated form from the tax bureau. He's having trouble with his eyes, and I do these things for him now and then; he seems to be alone here in London, although apparently he has a large family 'back home', wherever that is.

❧ ❧

I phoned Ami in the middle of the week and he said he'd pick me up at Mount Scopus on Friday. I told him not to come until late afternoon, because I had to finish writing an essay. I wanted to get it out of the way before the weekend started.

And so at five o'clock, after his visit to the psychiatric hospital, Ami came to pick me up at Mount Scopus. He parked illegally on Martin Buber Street and came up to my room. I was sitting at the desk, putting the last touches to my essay on Lear. My topic was 'unaccommodated man'. I was looking at the passage in which Lear says, '. . . thou art the thing itself: unaccommodated man is no more but such a poor, bare, forked animal as thou art. Off, off, you lendings! Come unbutton here.' At which point Lear tears off his clothes, even though he's homeless and it's raining. I was looking at the many references to clothes and nakedness and accommodation in the play, and at the various meanings of the words 'accommodated' and 'unaccommodated'.

My heart began beating rapidly when Ami walked into the tiny room and I didn't get up from my chair. He looked around and smiled, as though amused by the entire set-up: university, halls of residence, underwear drying on the back of a chair, the poster of John Lennon above Nadya's bed.

I had decorated my side of the wall with drawings and cartoons, and he went over to read the cartoons and take a closer look at the sketches.

'You drew these?'

'Yes, but I'm a complete amateur. A real artist was here and he said they weren't any good.'

'I find that hard to believe.'

'He said I was going about it all wrong. I don't care. I'm not planning to be an artist, I just do it for fun. He offered to give me lessons, but I said no.'

'Oh, lessons . . . that explains it.'

'Maybe I'll try to draw you some time. You know what I'd really like to paint? If I could paint?'

'No.'

'Shabazi. Those really old houses in Shabazi, the ones that look as if they're going to float away, because the colours of the walls and windows are so faded.'

He stared at me when I said that. He stared right into my eyes and I stared back. One thing was striking: he wasn't afraid of intimacy. All the men I'd been with before Ami had distanced themselves when the atmosphere became charged. But Ami liked being close to me. He wasn't holding back at all.

He sat down on the bed. 'How's your essay going?' he asked.

'I've finished. It didn't take that long, most of it was already done.'

'Where's your roommate?' he asked.

'Gone for the weekend.'

'Let's rest together,' he said.

'Rest?'

'Yes, come rest with me.'

We lay down on the narrow bed. Rooms in the Mount Scopus halls are small, and the beds are narrow. He slid his arm under my shoulder and smiled. 'Good,' he said ambiguously. The word for 'good' in Hebrew is *tov*. It can mean any number of things. It can be an existential comment to the effect, 'So here we are, for whatever it's worth.'

It can also mean, 'This is good.'

We lay on my bed quietly for a while. 'Are you OK?' he asked me.

'Yes. But my heart's beating fast.'

'Mine too.'

Then he told me that he'd arranged an appointment for me on Saturday morning with someone from Security. He'd had to pull strings to get my check done so quickly, he said. A security check involved interviews with people who knew you and usually took a few weeks. But they'd already completed the interviews.

'Who did they interview?'

'Probably Bracha, and Nadya, and maybe one or two of your teachers.'

'Nadya didn't mention anything.'

'Maybe she was embarrassed.'

'She's just secretive. She's an introverted person. I don't know anything about her, really.'

'Except that she likes John Lennon,' he said. We looked at Nadya's poster of Lennon, and he looked back at us, reluctantly modest behind his round glasses.

'Yes . . . he looks a bit Russian, don't you think?'

'Russian? I don't know. Apart from the Trotsky glasses . . .'

'Maybe I just think that because of his working-class hero song. Speaking of which, I'm hungry.'

'Let's go, then.'

I got up and packed my things. Ami remained on the bed,

but he followed every move I made with his eyes. I collected my things and stuffed them into my knapsack. Then we went down to the car.

'I haven't been to this part of Mount Scopus before,' Ami said, as we drove away. 'I didn't really know about all these new buildings. What's it like, living here?'

'I like it. I get to meet a lot of people, from all over the place. We have the daughter of a famous person on our floor, a man who owns one of the big record companies. He flies in on his private plane to see her sometimes. When she was a kid all the famous rock stars came to her birthday parties. She met everyone, Bob Dylan, Janis Joplin, Crosby . . . She has a photo of herself at seven, sitting on Dylan's lap.'

'She has short blonde hair, big puppy eyes, pale skin?'

'Yes, do you know her?'

'I passed her walking up the stairs.'

'How did you know it was her?'

'It's pretty easy to tell. Highly-strung, with so much privilege it's driven her crazy.'

'It's amazing you can tell that. We all like her — she's generous and funny. But she's already tried to kill herself twice. The first time when she was thirteen.'

'You can just imagine what her home life was like.'

'"Oh, my parents don't like him, they say he's too poor; they say he's not worthy of entering our door",' I sang.

'Have you been to the amphitheatre?' He meant the outdoor

amphitheatre overlooking the billowy mauve and pink dunes of the Judean desert, dunes that resembled waves or the slightly rumpled bedspread of a giant.

'Yes, it's beautiful. I pass it when I walk to the Old City.'

'You walk behind Mount Scopus to the Old City?'

'Yes, someone told me about that route – it's a short-cut.'

'That's extremely inadvisable, Lily.'

'Why? No one bothers me.'

'For one thing it's rude: you're inappropriately dressed. And it's dangerous.'

'It seems perfectly safe. I only go during the day.'

'It isn't safe. It's stupid. Don't do it.'

'OK, OK.'

'We think this is the end of the story. We came, we saw, we conquered. Now we can barge in on everyone, trample over everything, because we're the rulers.'

'I wasn't barging. And I certainly wasn't trampling. I was walking on the road. I thought I was being friendly. You're telling me to stay away, be suspicious, be scared.'

'There's nothing friendly about the situation. Just use your intuition, Lily. Think back to your walk. What was it like?'

'Well, a bit spooky, I suppose. Everything dilapidated. No one around, not even kids, just a few old men here and there, sitting on the ground or a box or something. I guess everyone was indoors.'

'Who told you to take that route, anyhow?'

'I don't remember. Don't worry, I'll go the regular way

next time, I'll take the bus to the centre of town. Look, here's where you picked me up. Should we give those guys a ride?'

'Not today, Lily. I've had a hard week.'

'You want to hear something funny?'

'Yes.'

'When I first got here, and I saw all those signs in Hebrew, "Watch for suspicious objects", I just couldn't work out what that meant. I thought maybe it meant stolen objects, but that didn't really make sense. So then I started asking Israelis, but they couldn't explain it either, because they thought it was so obvious. I mean, they kept saying, "Suspicious objects, you know, suspicious objects," until finally I said, "Suspicious *in what way*?" and the person looked at me as if I came from Mars and said, "In the way that it could be an explosive." I knew about bombs, of course, but I didn't think you could prevent them like that.'

'What is it, Lily?'

When he said that I realized how frantic I sounded, how frantic I felt. 'I'm scared.'

'Why?'

'I'm remembering how we met. I don't know you. I'm afraid.'

'You walk fearlessly through a deserted Arab neighbourhood, you fearlessly hitchhike, you fearlessly ward off the unwanted advances of drivers, you fearlessly hitchhike again . . . and now suddenly you're scared? Of what?'

'I don't know. Of you. I don't know who you are.'

'Let's put on some music.' He inserted a Muddy Waters tape into the cassette deck in his car. I relaxed at once.

'If you want, I can take you to Bracha first,' he said. 'We can get together later.'

'No, it's OK.'

And so we had supper at Mandy's again, and I spent the night at his place.

❧

Keys and my daughter are back from Brighton, and more sure about their relationship, I think, than when they left. They seem to have had a meaningful experience on the pier. Good thing I didn't go.

But last night my daughter came to my bed, slid under the blankets, and cried. Something she used to do regularly, but hasn't done for a while: she climbs into my bed, faces the wall, and cries. She cries, I hold her, then it's over. She returns to her bed and I go back to sleep. In the morning she's as cheerful as always, no sign that anything is amiss. And I say nothing, because the few times I asked her about her nocturnal visits she laughed and told me I must have been dreaming.

This morning was no exception. She was sitting on Keys's lap when I came into the kitchen for my coffee, and they were both whispering and giggling. 'Sorry, Mum,' my daughter said, when she saw me. 'We were just keeping our voices down so we wouldn't wake you.'

'You're allowed to have secrets,' I said.

'We have no secrets from you,' Keys said politely.

'Our life is an open book,' my daughter added slyly, and giggled again. 'I'll make your coffee.' She jumped up and insisted on serving me.

'You were sleepwalking last night, I think,' I said.

'I did have an odd dream! All about Chinese lanterns. And little people dancing inside a box. Like those old theatre boxes. Here you go. Two level teaspoons of brown sugar, three drops of milk, steaming hot, full to the top. Mum's fussy about these things,' she informed Keys. 'We're going shopping today, will you come?'

'No, honey, thank you.'

'Staying at home to write?'

'Yes.'

'What are you writing about today?'

'About the Hebrew word for suspicious.'

The Hebrew word for 'suspicious' (ḥashud) buzzes through life in Israel like an insistent fly that won't leave you alone. Suspicious objects and suspicious people who need to be taken aside and checked out are only part of the problem. A bigger problem is the military problem of suspicious movement or a suspicious figure when you're in fighting mode. If the principle is (as the spokesman says) to shoot only when in danger, how deep does the suspicion of danger have to be before you shoot? That would be the difficult question.

∽──∾

On Saturday morning Ami drove me to a residential part of Tel Aviv and pulled up in front of an ordinary-looking block of flats. He told me he'd wait for me in the car; all I had to do was ring flat six and I'd be let in. 'Don't let anyone harass you,' he said.

The names of the residents had been written by hand on slots next to the buzzers: Gruenstein, Morris, Gal. The slot next to flat six was blank. I rang the bell and waited. I had to ring twice, and I was about to give up and leave when the buzzer released the door. I entered the building and climbed up the dark, narrow stairway. I might have felt like a mysterious character in a spy novel, but the strong odour of fish frying in oil succeeded in dispelling any romantic fantasy. Instead, I was reminded of my grandmother, and I suddenly missed her.

Flat six was on the third floor. The door was open and a man stood in the doorway. '*Shalom,*' he said. I followed him inside.

The flat appeared to be empty, apart from a few filing cabinets. In the kitchen a small battalion of cockroaches scurried among the unwashed coffee mugs and empty biscuit packets that lay on the counter. The only decorative item in the flat was an aquarium on the hall table. It was pretty, with black and orange fish darting around a tall blue castle. Two tiny figures, a boy and a girl, stood guard on either side of the castle's drawbridge.

The man who greeted me wore a short-sleeved shirt and his belt was buckled under his pot-belly. He was breathing heavily; he didn't appear to be in the best of health. We were alone in the flat.

He shook my hand without smiling. His handshake surprised me: it was warm and pleasant, and I almost wished he'd hold my hand a few seconds longer. He led me to a door at the back of the flat. A cartoon had been tacked on the door. It showed God presenting Canaan to Moses; in the distance a large Canaanite army stood in readiness. Moses was saying to God, 'May I suggest Plan B?'

There was a heater inside the room, and the man shut the door after us to keep the heat in. He sat at one of three identical desks and I sat down facing him. There was a framed photo of an attractive blonde woman on the desk.

'Is that your wife?' I asked him.

He looked at the photo, as if weighing his reply. Then he lifted it and put it away in a drawer without answering.

He began with a series of very boring questions. It was hard to tell who was more bored, him or me.

After he had written down a lot of basic facts about me, he said, 'Now, on the sixteenth of April 1974, you participated in a demonstration protesting against Israel's acceptance of the Chilean Ambassador's credentials.'

'I can't believe you know about that. I've almost forgotten it myself. Do you keep files on everyone?'

'Well?'

'Yes, I was there. That was some wild demonstration. We made quite an impression, all twelve of us.'

'More worrisome, we were told that you're promiscuous and unruly.' The word he used for promiscuous, *muphqeret*, was a word I'd never heard before.

'*Muphqeret*, what's that?'

'Easy, loose, sleeps around.'

'Who said that?'

'We spoke to the halls supervisors.'

'How would they know?'

'They said you had men in your room on a regular basis. And recently you and your friends created a disturbance in the middle of the night, tumbling down the stairs, apparently drunk.'

'They tumbled, not me. They were drunk. I was sober.' Actually they'd taken Quaaludes, but I didn't think it would be a good idea to mention that.

'Well, what were you doing hanging out with them at three in the morning?'

'We came home together from a party. We all shared a taxi. I was stuck with them.'

'What were you doing at a party with people like that?'

'They're just my friends from the halls. Having a good time.'

'Why are you sleeping around?'

'I'm not. Not really. I'm sure whoever you spoke to exaggerated.'

'Your teachers like you, you're clever, you're doing well at the university, but you aren't behaving like a clever person outside it.'

I sulked when he said that. I hadn't expected a lecture.

'Now, what about Salim Assad?'

'What about him?'

'You went out with him?'

'We went out for three weeks, then he left me.'

'How come?'

'How come, how come. I don't know.'

'And you cried when you broke up.'

'Yeah, well. I always cry when men leave me.'

He sighed.

'Speaking to you as a father, you seem like a nice girl. Why this deviance?'

There was a word I did know, *stiya*, and it seemed harsh, it hurt me, and I had to fight tears.

'It's not deviance.'

He sighed again. 'Well, Ami seems to think you're reliable.' He could see he'd upset me and he wanted to make me feel better.

'I *am* reliable.'

'What about the army?'

'What do you mean?' I'd already told him I had a deferral.

'Your induction is in August.'

'Yes. But I'm not going. I'm a pacifist.'

'Yes? And who exactly is going to defend your country from the enemy?'

'We should try a little harder to make peace. We should withdraw unilaterally from the territories for a start. It's the least we can do. A Palestinian state would solve everything, it's only fair.'

He threw down his pen. He'd given up on me. 'I don't know how I'm going to clear you.'

'Well, what harm can I do?'

'What did Ami tell you about his job?'

'Not much. Nothing.'

'You didn't ask?'

'I did ask. I asked him what he does to the prisoners. He said he cuts them up into little pieces and eats them for supper. Or lunch, I forget.'

'You know, this interview is not going very well.'

'Sorry.'

'In your favour, your teachers think you're stable, mature,

responsible. Ditto, your cousin Bracha and her daughter, and your roommate Nadya. But the halls co-ordinator thinks you're unstable, immature, irresponsible. And for an Israeli you have some very disappointing views. What do you say?'

'I'm not a spy — isn't that the only thing that counts?'

'Well, of course you're not a spy, but the question is, are you discreet? Or are you prone to hysterical, irrational outbursts?'

'I'm discreet.'

'Why do you sleep around?'

The truth was that I slept around because I felt like it. But it was also true that several times I'd let myself become emotionally involved out of sheer stupidity. So I said, 'I'm easily conned. Men lie to me and I believe them. Or they've lied in the past. Now I'm more careful.'

He was pleased when I said that. 'OK, that's it. Goodbye.'

He wanted to end the interview on a positive note, before I screwed up again.

'I don't think I passed,' I told Ami, when I got back to the car.

'Of course you passed. It's only a formality. It's not like you're applying for a job.'

'So why did I need to do this?'

'I asked for it. To protect you. Now it's on paper, everyone's happy.'

'They knew I was in a demonstration in 1974.'

'They like to feel they're on top of things.'

'The halls co-ordinator said I was unstable, immature and irresponsible.'

'That's a relief.'

I laughed.

'This is the first time you've laughed in my presence.'

'Really?' I was surprised.

'Yes, really.'

'Well, I'm still nervous about this, about you.'

'Maybe one day I'll show you my torture pamphlets.'

I thought he was joking, but he wasn't.

～——~

The word for (sexually) promiscuous, *muphqar* or *muphqeret* (depending on gender), has a dizzying etymology. You could probably write a small book on that word.

This is because there appears to have been some semantic drifting over the centuries among three distinct roots:

1. *kpr* (rejection of the principle of God and the concept of Israel; related to the Arabic *kaphara*);

2. *pqr* (detachment from what is good, association with bad company, descent into prostitution or sexual promiscuity, absence of order or the rule of authority, possibly derived from Epicurus);

3. *prq* (removal of a burden, whether worn or carried or
   experienced, separation of a whole into parts; origin
   unknown).

In modern Hebrew one of the most common words derived
from these roots is *hefker*, which refers to a general sense of
lawlessness, chaos and disorder, and is generally used with
ironic detachment.

Enemy in Hebrew is *oyev* and 'the enemy' is *ha-oyev*. When I was
a child in Israel we used that word, *ha-oyev*, all the time. We,
who must fight the enemy. There, where the enemy sits.

I've always found the effect chilling. The enemy is, first of
all, faceless and nameless, a dark force hovering in the distance.
Apart from that, it's an eternal force, like 'the night' or 'the
sky'. The enemy is always there, no matter what. It's something
you have to learn to live with. If the enemy had a name, you
could ask why you had that particular enemy, and whether there
was any way to turn that enemy into an ordinary neighbour,
but 'the enemy' is your enemy without rhyme or reason. It's
just a matter of bad luck.

On the other hand, the common inflection *oyveynu*, our
enemy, was somehow reassuring. You weren't alone facing
the enemy. Everyone was in this together.

◦——◦

We had lunch at a wonderful garden restaurant in Yafo. Ami spoke Arabic to the waiters, who all seemed to know him, though maybe it just seemed that way because they were joking so much. I asked Ami to translate the jokes, but he said they weren't translatable.

I had decided during the week to become a vegetarian. I stuffed myself with pitta bread and salad and dips and falafel and fried potatoes and breaded aubergine and I was still hungry at the end of the meal. I wondered whether I would finally put on weight. For some reason no matter how much I ate back then I didn't put on weight.

'Are you going to the cemetery tomorrow?' I asked Ami.

'Yes.'

'I don't think your sister likes me.'

'Of course she likes you. She likes you very much.'

The waiter brought us the bill and Ami said something and they both burst out laughing.

'What did you say?' I asked.

'I complimented him on the service.'

'You're leaving something out.'

'I just put on an accent.'

'What kind of accent?'

'Hebrew. Don't forget your bag, Lily.'

In those days waiters didn't get tips (I hear it's changed now); you just had a 15 per cent service charge added to your bill. But I couldn't get out of the habit of tipping. Ami paid for the meal, and I left a tip on the table. 'American-style,' Ami said.

I noticed when we got back to the car that he'd parked illegally again. It occurred to me that he never bothered with parking regulations. 'You're lucky you didn't get a ticket,' I said.

'I'm coded,' he said. 'I don't get tickets.'

'That's convenient.'

Ami suggested a drive up north to visit some friends of his near Ein Hod, but I wasn't in the mood for running all around the country. I wanted to go to the beach. So we drove south towards Ashkelon, to a beach near Nitzanim that I'd never been to or even heard of. It was much nicer than the beach at Tel Aviv and nowhere near as crowded.

'This is still tentative between us,' I said, as we walked barefoot along the shore. I was wearing a skirt and Ami was wearing shorts. We didn't hold hands.

'OK,' he said. 'I'm a patient guy.'

'Patient and persistent.'

'Yes.'

'Tell me about your acting career.'

'There's not much to tell,' Ami said.

'But Bracha remembers you.'

'I'm amazed. She must have a very good memory.'

'Were you famous?'

'In local terms, I suppose. But that was ages ago.'

I kept pressing him, and he finally told me that he'd wanted to be an actor all his life and that when he was only sixteen he was accepted into Nissan Nativ's acting school in Tel Aviv, which had just then opened. It was a school for adults, not kids, but they made an exception for Ami. He studied there for two years, until he was drafted, and as soon as he came out of the army he got the part of Lenny in Pinter's *Homecoming*.

Right away he was a big hit. Everyone started talking about him, people came to the play two or three times just to see him do Lenny. The run was extended.

But it was all a gimmick, he said. He wasn't acting, he was just pulling a bunch of tricks out of his pocket. He couldn't believe people fell for it.

After Lenny he played Hamm in *Endgame*. He had the audience in stitches. It was the same story, though: nothing but gimmicks, and nobody noticing, not even the reviewers who should have known better.

He insisted on doing something different after that, something that would expose him for the sham he was. So he auditioned for *Hamlet* and of course they took him: he was already a star by then. But even as Hamlet all he did was charm the audience, and they lapped it up, they gave him standing ovations, praised him to the skies.

He kept hoping he'd get better, and he didn't give up. He went on acting until Ronny died. He was in an Israeli play at the time. And even though he was supposed to be mourning his other brother, the one who was killed during training, he didn't want to ruin the play for everyone so he went on performing. It was a play by an unknown playwright about an army commander whose disciplinary tactics get the better of him, and also about homosexuality. They were performing in a small rented room somewhere, not even a real theatre, but people who normally would not have seen that play were coming in order to see Ami. And so he went on performing. Anyway, it was an escape. Anyway, it was only in the evening: he spent the rest of the day with his family. But had he been at home he would have noticed that Ronny was in bad shape and prevented him going out on his motorcycle at eleven at night.

So he stopped acting altogether.

'How did you get into interrogation?' I asked.

'It was entirely by chance. I was doing reserve duty, and I was sent to deliver a package. And while I was there, just after I'd made the delivery, someone grabbed me and told me to come with him. He said he needed a last-minute replacement. I went along, I had no idea what it was about. I was amazed when I realized I was being asked to be present at an interrogation. Apparently someone had had to leave at the last minute and they wanted three people in the room, and they only had two.

They just needed me to stand there and not do anything. I don't know what the story was, probably some directive that had just come in.

'You'd think you were watching the worst play ever staged. It was hard to believe it was real, I almost wanted to laugh. Anyway, they bungled it, of course. Afterwards we went to the officers' mess and I told them what I thought of the whole thing. I told them only retards would conduct an interrogation like that. They were interested in what I had to say, which surprised me. I didn't think they'd be interested, I thought they'd tell me to fuck off. But they didn't. Maybe it's the actor in me. Very persuasive. Or maybe it was because they were in some sort of transitional stage, trying out different things. Who knows?

'They asked me to give it a go, just once, demonstrate my ideas. I said I wanted to be alone with the prisoner, and they didn't agree at first, but finally they gave in. And it went well, although I was just improvising. I got everything out of that guy, just by talking to him. He wasn't a hard case, though. They gave me an easy one. A kid, really, and they didn't need much from him. But it took five hours. I was wiped out.

'A week later I got a call and they offered me a job. So here I am. Now I can be a bad actor and it's perfectly appropriate.'

'What do you do?' I asked again.

'It depends on who I'm dealing with. Everyone's different, completely different, they've all had different experiences.

Sometimes it's an important and urgent interrogation, and sometimes it's routine. Sometimes the prisoner is a heavy character, and sometimes he's terrified. Or else he's calm and patient. There's a wide range.'

'What if they haven't done anything?'

'Most of them haven't done anything. But they usually have information my superiors want.'

'But what if they really don't know anything?'

'Then you get the small, trivial details out of them.'

'But what if they don't know anything, I mean anything important, and you think they do and really they don't?'

'In that case the interrogator can continue to torment the prisoner until he's bored or the prisoner makes something up or both.'

'You're confusing me. Tell me what you do.'

'I decide when I've reached the end. And I tell the person in charge I think it's the end. It's up to him to decide where to go from there.'

'And then what happens? I mean, where does the prisoner go from there?'

'Usually to court, not always. Sometimes he's released. Or else he just stays in detention.'

'So, I don't understand. Is it information you're after, or confessions?'

'They generally go together.'

'What if they resist?'

'What a strange question. Of course they resist. That's the whole point. Otherwise there wouldn't be any need to interrogate them. *Here I am, here's what I know.* You do get that sometimes, especially with kids, but that's just because they're scared.'

'So if they're not scared you have to scare them.'

'You have to find a way to get their defences down.'

'What's the worst thing you'd do, have done?'

'It doesn't work that way. There isn't a scale.'

'You have the job from hell.'

'It's just part of the scene here. It isn't cut off. It's part of living here, just a different part of it. It's hypocritical to set it apart.'

'You're at the heart of it, though.'

'That's true in a way. Well, I like being at the heart of it. If I have to be here, I may as well be where the action is, see what's really going on. There's the guy with drinks. Do you want lemonade?'

'Yes, please.'

'One laugh, one "please", things are picking up here.'

'It doesn't mean anything.' I switched to English. I said, in English, 'I still don't trust you. I'm not even sure I like you.'

༺ ❦ ༻

I switched to English because I didn't like the two Hebrew words I knew for 'trust'. One comes from the same root as the word *bitaḥon,* which means 'security' and is used to refer to the security of the State. The other comes from the same root as the word *emuna*, which means 'faith' and is used to refer to religious faith. I wanted something more personal.

There is a word for 'hell' in Hebrew, but it doesn't convey anything very specific, because hell is more of a Christian concept. The Hebrew word for 'hell', *gehenom*, comes from a biblical reference to the valley of the sons of Hinnom, where children were sacrificed by the heathen (and which for several centuries was associated with a sort of human rubbish dump where the bodies of people who didn't deserve a decent burial were thrown). You can still see that valley, if you go to Jerusalem. You can walk through the valley of Hinnom; you'll find it south of the Old City, west of the Kidron Valley. But, as many foreign students discover, rapists and muggers tend to hang out there waiting for prey, so it's best not to go alone.

The city of Yafo was originally Phoenician. Then it was taken over by the Egyptians, then by the Assyrians, then by the Hebrews, then by Alexander the Great, then by the Syrians, then by the Hebrews, then by the Syrians, then by the Hebrews, then by Vespasian, then by the Arabs, then by the Crusaders, then by Saladin, then by Richard I, then by the Arabs, then by Napoleon, then by the British, then by Israel.

The biblical name *yafo* became Joppa in the King James Bible, and it also appears as Joppe in the Apocrypha, but in English it's generally known as Jaffa, following the Arabic name *yaafa*. But Israeli censors get nervous about words like *yaafa*. The literary critic and poet Muhammad Al-Batrawi, for example, was forced by the censors to change *yaafa* to *yafo* in his writing if he wanted his books to circulate in the occupied territories. That ultimate vowel made the censors nervous. It made them think Al-Batrawi was inciting his readers, who would see his use of the word *yaafa* as meaning, 'Yaafa is ours, you know, and one day we're going to get it back, one way or another, even if it means killing you guys.' One can easily see that censors don't have much of a grasp of the way literature works.

∽——∾

We had supper at his place. We drove home from the beach and showered, and after sex we put together a meal of bread and dips and ready-made salads. I suggested an omelette, but Ami said one of the things I had to know about him was that he couldn't bear the sight or smell or thought of eggs. Even the word for eggs, *beytzim*, gave him the creeps. He couldn't use that word even when it referred to testicles. Especially when it referred to testicles. He liked his too much to refer to them by a word he detested so intensely.

He put on a cassette of Greek music and we ate sitting on the living-room floor, between the two speakers.

'I like sex with you,' he said. 'You're incredibly warm. You haven't got any inhibitions. How come?'

'It makes more sense to ask why people have inhibitions.'

'Maybe.'

'You don't seem very inhibited yourself.'

'I'm high most of the time,' he said.

'You haven't smoked this weekend.'

'No, because I have to go in to work on Sunday. I can't work stoned.'

'It's you too, it's the way you make me feel. You don't make me self-conscious. You do the opposite.'

'You trust me in bed.'

'Yes, come to think of it.'

'Well, it's a start. Here, I'll show you those brochures I told you about.'

'Brochures?'

He went over to one of the kitchen drawers and pulled out a whole pile of brochures and pamphlets and threw them down on the living-room floor.

They were from companies selling torture equipment. They were all in English. 'This can't be real,' I said.

'Someone has to manufacture these things, and then someone has to buy them, and there has to be a person handling the transaction. They keep sending us this stuff – this is only a small sample. I save my favourites.'

'"Safe, humane, clean",' I read. '"Effective". I can't believe this. What do they mean by "clean"?'

'The opposite of a mess. No marks, or not a lot. No messy side-effects.'

'What does "safe" mean? That it won't kill the person?'

'That's right.'

'And "effective" . . . This is beyond anything. Who buys these things? Do you?'

'No, we don't buy this stuff. Though, believe me, several people I work with would love to.'

'Most of this is electric-shock equipment. And chairs, beds . . . I feel sick.' I suddenly thought I was going to vomit. 'It's like Nazi paraphernalia. It's like the Nazis selling concentration-camp equipment.'

'Put your head between your knees.'

'No. No.'

'Well, lie down at least.'

I stretched out on the floor and covered my eyes with my arm. After a few minutes I felt better, but I didn't move.

'You're right,' he said. 'In actual practice, these things are used for sadistic purposes, not for getting information,' he said. 'Institutionalized sadism.'

'This equipment is "humane", though.'

'They have to put that in. It's a selling point.'

'How come you save these brochures?'

'To get inspiration.'

'How can you joke about something like this? Tell me the real reason.'

'I like to know what's going on in my field.'

'Is that the real reason?'

'No.'

'Do reps visit, or do you get these in the post?'

'I've never heard of anyone coming. These arrived by post.'

'How do they get your address?'

'I have no idea.'

I opened my eyes and looked at him. 'What if your department gets sucked into buying them? You know, what if after a while they think, Why not, we could try this out?'

'The way things are going, nothing would surprise me. But, right now, the preference seems to be for less imaginative methods. It makes it easier to pretend nothing's really happening.'

'It's funny how we met. Such a fluke. If I hadn't lent my roommate money. If I hadn't bought chocolate on the way to the bus. If I'd been there ten minutes earlier or later.'

'I thought about that too.'

'I suppose God had it all planned out.'

I didn't mean it literally, but Ami underwent a transformation when I said that. He became fierce. 'Don't bring God into it,' he said.

'I was just joking. What's the matter? You're scaring me.'

'I don't like religious people,' he said. I saw how intimidating he could be if he felt like it.

'Well, I'm not religious. I'm an atheist, I was born on a kibbutz, remember? The first time I heard that word, "God", was when we went back to Canada, and I went to Hebrew school. You can be scary.'

'Sorry.'

'Don't scare me like that again. The next time you scare me like that I'm leaving.'

'I didn't mean to scare you. You're very sensitive, Lily.'

'Why do you hate the religious?'

'It's psychotic to say this is what God wants, because that's what you want. This is what's written in the Torah, God said we should have this land, and the Arabs, who don't have a soul anyway, who are subhuman anyway, should just be demolished, because that's what God wants. Who can argue with *yehova*? I wish the ground would just open up and swallow them.'

'In my fantasy they don't die, they just all move to New York.'

He pulled me towards him and rolled me so that I was lying on top of him. He smiled at me. 'Yes, that's much more *humane*,' he said, in English.

'You have a nice accent in English. Different from most Israelis.'

'I went to acting school, remember?' he said, still in English.

'Yes, I remember. Anyway, not all religious people are the same. Some of them are really opposed to what's going on. And it's not just the religious. There are plenty of others who feel the same way, they're just less open about it.'

'Lily, I'm so in love with you.'

'You've only known me for a week.'

'A week is a long time, take it from me.'

I'll bet most Orthodox Jews don't know this, but in ancient times it was perfectly OK to say the word *yehova* or to write the four letters that spell out the word יהוה. For example, in some of the Lachish letters, which date back to 600 BCE, one finds that the convention was to begin a letter with the phrase, 'May *yehova* give you good news.'

But at some point, *yehova* became a forbidden word, and that's the way it's been for centuries. You mustn't say it and you mustn't write it and even when you read to yourself and you come across the word (which appears on every page of the Bible, about 6,630 times in total), you read *ha-shem* ('the name') or *adonai* (Lord) or *elohim* and not *yehova*.

If you use the word *yehova* casually in conversation you're showing contempt for your religion.

In Israel's early days, though, secular Israelis didn't really think of themselves as Jews. We thought of ourselves as Israelis. Hebrew was the language of Israelis, not of Jews, and the long history that came with being Israeli was to some degree incidental; it was about things that happened in the past, somewhere else, to people who spoke other languages, people who were for the most part wimps as well as backward and insular.

For a long time secular Israelis didn't even like to use the word Jewish, *yehudi*. It was an embarrassing word, full of unwanted associations. The word sounded strange and even ugly to them; they preferred the biblical word *ivri*, a Hebrew. They were part of the Hebrew nation, they went into the Hebrew army, they attended Hebrew schools, they enjoyed Hebrew culture. Tel Aviv was the first Hebrew city and its harbour was the first Hebrew harbour and it played an important role in Hebrew commerce. (The word 'Hebrew', by the way, seems to derive from a guy called Eber, a great-great-grandson of Noah, who appears in a genealogy in Genesis. Probably he had a significant role at one point, but his history has not survived.)

There's a traditional Purim song that originally opened with the words *ḥag purim, ḥag purim, ḥag gadol hu la-yehudim*. Which means, 'Purim, Purim, a great holiday for Jews'. But in Israel the words were eventually changed to *ḥag purim, ḥag purim, ḥag gadol hu la-yeladim*. 'Purim, Purim, a great holiday for kids'.

Since the word for 'kids', *yeladim*, is phonetically close to the word for 'Jews', *yehudim*, it was an easy switch.

But things have changed. Nowadays secular Israelis are very used to seeing/using the word *yehudi*, Jewish, because they're very used to seeing/using the word *p(h)alestini*, Palestinian, and in that discourse it's hard to avoid the word 'Jewish'.

The word 'Israeli' means everyone who is a citizen of Israel, including Arabs who stayed in Israel in 1948 and were given citizenship. But when people say 'Israeli' they aren't usually thinking of Arabs living in Israel. Arabs are in the word, but not in the word. They are there, but not there.

ᴖ‿ᴖ

I had trouble concentrating on my studies the following week. I kept thinking about Ami.

I wanted to tell someone about him but I didn't know who to turn to. I never spoke to my parents about my life, because when I tried to talk to my mother she went a little deaf on me, and when I tried to talk to my father he directed me to one of his favourite novelists: there, in Thomas Mann or William Faulkner or Jack Kerouac, I would surely find the answer I was looking for.

As for my best friend Sheila, who was also in Israel at the time, she was at Bar Ilan University and not accessible by phone. In any case, we had grown apart recently. I ended up confiding in one of my teachers, Dr Grubach. Dr Grubach liked me. She was the one I was writing my *Lear* essay for.

I saw her at the cafeteria on Wednesday of that week and I caught her eye. She waved to me and I went over to sit with her. She was in her thirties, and she looked a little like Virginia Woolf, except for her eyes, which were more ordinary. She lived with another woman, a violinist, in the Old City.

Everyone in the department seemed to have the same politics. I wondered whether they asked candidates who applied for teaching jobs what their politics were during the interview ('How do you feel about having Arab students?'), or whether teachers who turned out to have the wrong politics were sacked after the trial year.

'I'm finding it hard to concentrate today,' I told Dr Grubach.

'I'd noticed.'

'Can I ask you something? You know, advice?'

'Me? I don't know if I'm qualified, dear. I'm barely holding my own life together.' She was a dramatic person, which was why everyone loved her. Her classes were extremely entertaining. 'One day there will actually be a choice in this cafeteria,' she added, looking unhappily at her hard-boiled egg and bowl of grated carrots and raisins.

In other departments you called teachers by their first names, but in the English department you used last names. That didn't affect the level of formality, though. Which was not high.

'I met a guy, but he has a weird profession,' I said.

'Now you've aroused my curiosity,' she said.

'It's hard even to say what he does.'

'Undertaker? Taxidermist?'

'No, it's political.'

'Ah!'

'He interrogates people.'

Her mouth dropped open. 'Well!' she said.

'I don't know what to do. He wants to see me.'

She shook her head. 'Why would you want to associate with someone like that, dear?'

'That's what I thought.'

'You must get a lot of offers, with that hair of yours, my God.' She reached out and ran her fingers through my hair. 'Straight out of Botticelli.'

'I'm not as tall, though. As Venus, I mean. So it looks longer than it is.'

'Well, time to run, library closes in two hours. One is always rushing about in this country. When I visit my family it takes me several days to adjust to the quiet.' She was referring to Scotland, which she missed. 'Come and visit me one day when you're in the Old City.' She gave me her address. 'I'll introduce you to my flatmate.'

I went back to the halls but I felt too restless to do anything. I had two classes on Thursday, but I suddenly decided to skip both. I needed to see Ami.

I took the bus to Central Station and a shared taxi to Tel Aviv and then a regular taxi to Neve Avivim.

It was ten by the time I reached his house, but he wasn't at home. I sat on the doorstep and waited for him. It wasn't comfortable on the doorstep, though, so after a few minutes I walked round to the garden. I pulled two chairs together side by side and curled up on them, my knapsack under my head and my jacket over my shoulders. Somehow I fell asleep.

I woke up with a start. Ami was touching my cheek. He looked different in his uniform: taller and sadder. 'What time is it?' I asked him.

'Three in the morning.'

'Have you just got home?'

'Yes. Come on in.'

I followed him to the bedroom. He stripped off his uniform and underwear, threw them into a laundry basket on the landing, stepped into the shower. I couldn't tell if he was happy to see me. While he showered I used the other bathroom to brush my teeth and change into my nightgown. Then I poured myself a glass of iced tea. I poured a glass for him too, in case he was thirsty, and I brought it to the bedroom.

He was lying in bed, naked under the green and white quilt.

'Perfect, thank you,' he said, taking the glass from me. 'Come and lie beside me,' he said. 'I'm so glad to see you, Lily, you can't imagine.'

I lay down next to him. He seemed barely able to move. 'Now I know what David felt like,' he said. He took a cigarette from the packet on the bedside table and lit it.

I didn't say anything. He said, in English, 'Sixty-two fucking hours.'

He dropped the cigarette on to an ashtray, closed his eyes and fell asleep. I'd never met anyone who took one puff of a cigarette and let it burn out. I reached over, stubbed it out, and turned off the light. But I couldn't fall asleep for a long time. I was afraid, probably for the first time in my life, of the dark.

'Ami,' I whispered.

He drew me towards him and held me against his body. 'Be with me,' he said in his sleep.

⌒～⌒

The first Book of Kings begins with David's inability to warm up. We're told that David is old and can't get warm no matter how many clothes he's given. His servants come up with the suggestion that a young woman be brought in. This woman would have a two-fold job. She'd wait on the King and act as his nurse, and she'd lie down next to the King and be his human hot-water bottle. Only a very beautiful woman would do, so they hunted around the kingdom (a familiar motif) and finally found Abishag. She nursed David and waited on him, and presumably warmed him up, but they didn't have sex (we're told). Probably he was too old.

My daughter danced for me today. The Peter Handke show is in the last stages of rehearsal, and she showed me parts of her solo and tried to describe the concept as a whole. She was excited, and very beautiful.

Keys said, when she'd finished the small preview, 'It really is mind-blowing. You will hardly believe your eyes.'

My daughter said, 'Keys composed most of the music. He's brilliant.'

'What are you writing?' Keys asked me. 'Is it a secret?'

'No, it's not a secret. I'm writing about things that happened to me a long time ago, in Israel.'

'I have always wanted to go to Israel,' he said, 'but, these days, it's not very encouraging.'

'No, it's not very encouraging,' I agreed.

'So, you are Jewish?' he asked, surprising me. What do lovers talk about these days?

'Yes, didn't you know?'

'Ah, no, but I suspected.'

My daughter burst out laughing. 'You're so funny, Keys,' she said.

'My aunt is Jewish, married to my father's brother.'

'Guess how many cousins Keys has, Mum. Guess. Twenty-eight!'

'Yes, we have a complicated family, full of second marriages and third marriages and children from other liaisons. So, in fact, I have four Jewish cousins. I hope you will meet everybody one day.'

'I hope so too.'

'So, what are you writing about? Your memories?'

'Yes.'

'I would like to read it.'

'Me too,' my daughter said.

'I'll give it to you when I'm finished.'

'I won't read it if it's gloomy, though,' she said.

'I will read it first,' Keys offered gallantly. 'I can take out for you the gloomy parts.'

～⌒～

Ami slept until early afternoon the following day. I'd brought *The Turn of the Screw*, which I had to read for Sunday, and I finished it while he slept. I fried some frozen blintzes, which I found in the freezer, and after that I had bread and baba ghanoush and a large bowl of potato salad and four chocolate Danishes and a glass of milk.

Finally I heard the shower running. I made coffee and waited for him; he was in the shower for a long time. When he came out he was wearing a white bathrobe and holding a joint. He stood behind me and kissed my hair, placed one arm around my midriff, brought the joint to my mouth. I shook my head. 'Too early,' I said. I handed him a mug of coffee.

'Thanks,' he said, taking the coffee to the table. He sat down and pulled me on to his lap. 'How come you're here mid-week? Don't you have classes today?'

'I skipped them.'

87

'What happened?'

'I missed you.'

'I know an empty flat where you can stay in Jerusalem. That way when I have time off I can drive up and stay with you during the week.'

'OK.'

'They told me you were a star student.'

'I like university.'

'Don't skip.'

'Yes, Daddy.'

'What's this?'

'*The Turn of the Screw*. We have to read it for Sunday.'

'I think I read it once. A nanny, two kids, ghosts?'

'Yes.'

'Come to bed, my soul is consumed with desire,' he said playfully, as he slid his hands to my breasts.

'Don't you want breakfast first?'

'Breakfast can wait.'

All the Israeli men I'd slept with were matter-of-fact about sex and that suited me, because I was matter-of-fact too. But I'd never met anyone who talked the entire time. Usually you didn't say anything; for one thing, a lot of the time you were doing things with your mouth. And the rest of the time you were doing things that didn't seem to require discussion.

But for Ami sex was tied in to conversation. He never stopped making conversation, even when he was on the verge of coming, or when I was. Mostly the conversation was related to what was going on: a running commentary on what he was feeling, observing, noticing. For example: 'I love these fine white hairs on your legs. Were they that colour in Canada, or is it the sun? I wouldn't have expected you to tan so well. I can't believe how white you are where you aren't tanned, I didn't know skin could be so white. Even Ingrid's skin wasn't this white, and she was very fair. I would have thought you'd burn, but you really do tan. Look at these tiny freckles on your knee, so sweet. I think I have a foot fetish. I'm really into feet. I like to suck a woman's toes, if they're this cute, does that qualify? Toes are sexy. Toes and fingers. You've hardly got any hair down here at all, how come? Why are you getting defensive? Can't you see how nice it is? It turns me on, yes, it really turns me on, I get to see more. I get an excellent view here. You know, this is like a diagram in an anatomy book. Everything's so clearly defined. This is an amazing *kusi*. This little perfect dome here, adorable. Dome of the Kusi. Give me exact instructions about what you like. I don't like to guess . . . There's this lovely sweet smell coming from you, it isn't perfume, is it? No, it would be impossible for perfume to emulate a smell like that. Though if someone could they'd make a killing. I'm getting all squished here, move over a bit. No, I won't object, though it's going to make it more of a challenge not to come at once. When I was seventeen, this would have been it for me, but on the other hand I'd be ready to start all over again within a matter of minutes, those were the days . . . Are we ready for entry? The gates of Eden . . . I love that first moment, when I just go in. Is it the same for you? That moment when you just can't believe how good it is, you've forgotten. You're small inside, you know. There's a lot of variety. You're really narrow, it's bliss. Hold on, here, that's better. Can we manage it? It doesn't take you long to come, does it? How can men not know? You feel everything inside expand and move down, and your partner's face is suddenly several shades redder. Plus I can hear your heart beating. This one was better than the first one, I think, am I right? Last time it was the other way round. Do you want to come again? I'm not sure how much longer I can hold on. I'll do my best. Or we can go again a bit later, but it's already nearly three and I was thinking maybe we'd go out for a drive. I'll just go on for a bit longer, I think I can last, if I concentrate, though it's getting harder, especially if you . . . Here, if we move this way, yes, that's nice. Good idea. I think this is it for me. You have a knack, do you know? Your touch, it's a gift, you should give lessons, you should give lessons to other women how to touch men. If I hold on any longer I might explode. *Wallah* . . . Amazing.'

That sort of thing.

When it was over he shut his eyes and had a five-minute nap. Then he went to the kitchen and returned with a tray of cold chicken and potato salad and rolls and butter and he sat cross-legged on the quilt and ate. 'That was very good,' he said. 'I didn't think it could get better, but it did. Or maybe it only seems that way. And there's so much more I want to do with you. I have an insatiable appetite for you.'

'Is this all about sex, your feelings towards me?'

'Yes, and you'll find the money on the hall table as you leave. Don't be mad, Lily. Don't go mad on me. Do you want to see a film? We could go for a drive, then have dinner, then see a film. And then we can go to this tea-house in Yafo I think you'll like — maybe you know it. I have to get some groceries at some point, but I guess that can wait. What do you think?'

'Sounds good. Don't drive too stoned, though.'

'Yes, Mummy.'

'You look different in uniform.'

'Different how?'

'Sadder. How come your uniform is so plain?'

'Plain?'

'It doesn't look like other uniforms. You know, the soldiers you see on the street.'

'There are all sorts of uniforms.'

'What's yours?'

'It's just a work uniform.'

'Does it have a name?'

'B. As opposed to A.'

'I can't imagine you saluting.'

He smiled. 'Well, I don't salute much these days. I see you like this potato salad, it's almost all gone.'

'Sorry.'

'I'll get more next time. How can such a small person eat so much?'

'I don't know. I've been the same weight since I was twelve. The same height and the same weight.'

'Yes, your body is a complete surprise. It's a surprise to find a woman's body hiding there under your dress. Skimpy as it is. Lily, are you sure such skimpy dresses are a good idea?'

I laughed. 'You want me to dress like Nadya?'

'I just don't want you to get into a bad situation.'

'Nadya gets just as many hands on her arse as I do. I know, because she always gets so angry when it happens, and she complains to me about it. She's a bit disillusioned. She thought everyone in Israel would be like Abraham.' I used the term *avraham avinu*, 'our father Abraham', which is the way you refer to Abraham in Hebrew.

We both laughed. And we started making a lot of silly jokes about what it would be like at the bank, for example, or at restaurants, in an imaginary Israel peopled entirely by clones of our father Abraham and our teacher Moses and all our Sages of blessed memory.

~⌒—⌒~

'Stoned' in Arabic is *mastul,* and now that's the word in Hebrew too. *Wallah* is Arabic too: it's an exclamatory word and in Hebrew it means something like 'far out', but it can also be used merely for emphasis, the way you'd use 'I swear, man' or 'really' in English.

I wonder whether the Hebrew slang for reaching orgasm is also borrowed from another language. In English you come; in Hebrew you finish/end/complete. Like the word 'come', the word for 'finish' has a pleasant sound in Hebrew. The verb is *ligmor*; 'I came' is *gamarti*. I wonder what the equivalent colloquial term is in other languages. I wonder whether you finish or come or die. I wonder how many variations there are. I wonder which languages have a slang term for reaching orgasm and which ones don't. I wonder whether in some languages there's only a masculine form of the word.

I've tried finding out what the Arabic word is but I haven't had much success. Since my English–Arabic dictionary defines rather than translates 'orgasm', I sent an e-mail to a journalist friend who spent most of the eighties in Lebanon and the West Bank. I asked him whether he knew what the Arabic equivalent for 'come' was.

He wrote back a week later. He apologized for the delay:

he had just returned from Pakistan. He also apologized for not being able to answer my question. 'I once knew the word for "orgasm" in Arabic,' he wrote wistfully, 'but I have forgotten it.'

⌐~——~⌐

'What took sixty-two hours?' I asked him, in the car.

'The interrogation.'

'Not sixty-two hours straight!'

'No, of course not. I started on Sunday morning. Sixty-two hours adding it all up.'

'You slept there?'

'Yes. There's a room I sleep in. Luckily I can sleep through anything.'

'Do you always work in the same place?'

'Sometimes I get taken to different locations for specific cases. Otherwise it's the same place.'

'Do you work alone?'

'Yes, I always work alone, and I even have my own interrogation room that no one else uses.'

'You don't get any help?'

'Just some menial things. People bring in coffee and meals. But I'm in charge of my own prisoners, I give all the instructions.'

'Was this a hard case?'

'Yes. They give me all the hard cases.'

'What does that mean?'

'It means an aggressive or committed person with a lot of information.'

'Sixty-two hours in four days, that's over fifteen hours a day.'

'Well, in this case that seemed the best way. We had a two-hour break in the afternoon and eight hours at night, it wasn't too bad from that point of view. Actually, it was fourteen hours a day right until the end. We stayed up late at the end.'

'What did you do?'

'Talked to him.'

'You talked? That's all? You didn't hit him?'

'I don't hit prisoners.'

'I knew that. I knew you didn't.'

He didn't answer. I said, 'What about the others? What about the other interrogators? What are they like?'

'I wouldn't nominate them for the Nobel Peace Prize.'

'It's not that bad, though, is it?'

'As you can imagine, Lily, this job attracts a certain type of person, usually with the psychological acuity of a tree-trunk.'

'You mean it attracts violent people?'

'Yes. Maybe they weren't violent to begin with, but that's what the army brings out in people. There was this idea that you could have it both ways, put people through the army, train them to forget about their innate repulsion to killing and somehow, magically, have them come out writing poetry about birds. Most people can't handle power, even under the best circumstances. And with the situation in the territories, where nothing's really spelled out, it's even harder to control these things. When you combine that with a whole history of seeing the Arabs as some sort of inferior and malevolent species, you've got the perfect recipe for disturbed behaviour in people who might have had a chance otherwise.'

'I don't know how you can work in an environment like that.'

'I'm no different from the others. I just have a different style.'

'Well, was it successful? The interrogation?'

'Yes. I got everything out of him. I won't have to see him again.'

'How? How did you do it?'

'I have all sorts of strategies. It's complicated. I try to get into his mind.'

'Do you threaten him?'

'With what? If you don't tell us everything we'll take even more land away from you?'

'You know what I mean.'

'I don't use threats, it isn't necessary.'

'So all you do is have a conversation?'

'It's always hard on the prisoner, no matter what.'

'What's the physical part of it?'

'There's always loss of freedom and control. And that makes even ordinary things harder. When you're in combat you're not on your own: you're part of a larger plan, you have backing, you're armed, you get medals for courage. Your friends are there with you, you're all working together, and in theory you know what to expect, more or less. And that makes the whole situation of confronting the enemy a different experience. Not that combat is easy — it can be a voyage into the inferno, watching your friends explode next to you. But psychologically you've got resources a person being interrogated doesn't have.'

'Does he get to eat?'

'My prisoners eat what I eat and they sleep when I sleep. And we share the hummus and stuff, we eat from the same plate. I try to get into a rhythm with them. Unless it's someone I'm just seeing sporadically.'

'Why was he arrested, the prisoner you interrogated for sixty-two hours?'

'He's involved in all sorts of things.'

'How come he gave in? At the end, I mean.'

'There's no one answer to that question.'

'It's hard to believe just talking to someone could work.'

'Yes, it's hard to believe. I'm always surprised myself. That it's so easy, really, to get through, despite all the barriers the person tries to put up. Though the fact that most of these people haven't had any real military training is also a factor.'

'Military training?'

'Yes. In military training you are trained to resist questioning. You might even get to go through a mock capture, if you're in a special unit.'

'A mock capture! How does that work?'

'The idea is to get you used to shitting in your pants and not getting food or water and being called into an interrogation room. Even being beaten.'

'That's so weird. Would something like that really help?'

'I don't know. But being part of a military machine, being told in advance what to expect and how to deal with it, those things would help.'

'Do you think if someone's protecting someone they love they're less likely to give in?'

'It's always personal. It doesn't matter what you call it, love or ideology or commitment or confusion or rage or desperation. It's all about emotions.'

'My mother, you know, she wouldn't stand up to much to protect me. My father would, but not my mother.'

'That's a sad thing to say.'

'Yes, but it's true. And what about you? Would you protect your country?'

'I'd try, of course. I think I'd succeed.'

'Why am I talking about all this? I have no interest in these things. The whole subject makes me sick. Where are we going?'

'Lily, you understand that I'm not supposed to be talking to you about any of this?'

'You're not?'

'No, of course not.'

'I thought that's why you cleared me.'

'That was just to prevent certain hassles.'

'How come? How come you mustn't tell me anything?'

'It's against the law.'

'What could happen?'

'I'd be sent to prison.'

'I would never tell anyone,' I said. I was amazed at his trust.

'I know, I'm just reminding you. Is there anywhere special you'd like to go?'

'No, you decide.'

'Well, I thought I'd show you the house I grew up in.'

'OK. Is it far?'

'About an hour's drive. And then we'll see what's on tonight. There might be something at the Cinematheque.'

'My teacher, Dr Grubach, she said I shouldn't have anything to do with you.'

'Is that why you came down?'

'Yes.'

'To see whether I really had fangs?'

'No. Just to see you.'

❦

When Hebrew became a modern spoken language, words had to be
found for all the things that weren't around when Hebrew
developed.

At times the operating principle was semantic expansion. In
imitation of Indo-European languages, the word for 'pomegranate', *rimon*, was expanded to include (hand) grenade. Grenades
do look a little like pomegranates, I suppose, but to me it
seems incredibly perverse, almost sadistic, to take a word that
is connected not only to the actual (exquisite) pomegranate fruit
but to eros and sensuality (slice open a pomegranate and you
will see why) and attach it to something like a hand grenade.

Most semantic expansions are less arbitrary. For example,
eqdaḥ, gun, comes to us by way of the word *qdḥ*, which means
to make a hole in something and also to burn.

Obscurity can be exploited as well. The Septuagint, basing
itself on early Midrashic texts, translates the extremely obscure
word *ḥashmal* in Ezekiel's first mystical vision of God as gleaming fire. Hence the modern Hebrew word for electricity.

Similarly, *roveh*, rifle, is based on a poorly understood word
in Genesis 21:20, a word that appears in reference to Hagar's

son. Since Abraham's wife, Sarah, can't conceive, she suggests to Abraham that he do it with her Egyptian maid Hagar. Sarah regrets that suggestion later, because she ends up conceiving after all, and now her son has to compete with Abraham's son by Hagar. She tells Abraham to cast out Hagar and her son (Ishmael) and God assures Abraham He'll look after them. So Abraham (reluctantly) gives Hagar bread and water and throws her out of the house. The water runs out, and Ishmael is about to die of dehydration, but God sends some water his way and promises that he will father a great nation (the Arab nations, according to Muslim and Jewish tradition).

Then we're told that Ishmael grew up to be a *roveh* of bows. From the first no one had any idea what that word meant. Commentators just guessed. They thought it might mean someone who shoots from bows, or a youth with bows or someone who is skilled with bows.

Obviously it's the 'shoot' reading that inspired the adoption of the word *roveh* for rifle.

On the other hand, *tank* is the Hebrew for 'tank'. A *rimon roveh neged tankim* is an anti-tank grenade launcher.

❧

I'd seen impoverished neighbourhoods in Israel from a distance, through the windows of a bus or car, but I'd never been inside one.

The neighbourhood Ami grew up in was only one step up from a *ma'abara*, which is a shanty-town assortment of huts and shacks. The streets here were paved, but they were narrow and the pavement was cracked. Mud puddles filled the spaces between the cracks. The two or three-storey concrete blocks of flats also appeared to be in a state of disrepair. I liked the clothes-lines, though. They criss-crossed from one window to another and created a roof of sheets and socks and pyjamas above the narrow streets.

There were lots of children playing outside; they filled the street. That's the one advantage for children in poor (but safe) neighbourhoods: the culture of street play. The children become a sub-community; they create a world of their own. I knew that from my own past. When my parents returned to Canada from the kibbutz they were penniless; it took them two or three years to pull themselves out of poverty.

Ami parked his car and we stepped out. Several children strolled over and stared at us, but no one had the courage to say anything.

I followed Ami into one of the buildings. There was a heavy iron door on the landing. Ami pulled it open and switched on the light: a chaotic assortment of useless junk came into view and a childhood smell of old vinyl and dust filled the air. 'There it is,' he said. 'It's still here.'

'What?'

'The silver crown, there on the wall.' He pointed to the faded outline of a silver crown on the cement wall facing us.

'Did you paint that?'

'Yes. We had a club-house in here. Sons and Daughters of the Queen of Lapland.'

'Lapland?'

'I liked Elleh Kari.'

'*The Girl from Lapland*!'

Ami smiled, remembering. I smiled too. It was a childhood classic, a book of photographs of Elleh Kari, the sweet little blonde girl from Lapland.

'Remember the one where she's crying?' I asked.

'I'm not even going to bother answering that question.'

'What did you do? In the club.'

'Went for walks, mostly. We took sandwiches and went to the field at the back and played games. We wore cardboard crowns. I read them stories.'

'You read to the other kids?'

'Yes. *Hasamba*, or stories from *Mishmar Layiladim*.'

'My father hated *Hasamba*, he refused to read those books to me or my sister. He didn't like the idea of kids with guns, sneaking around, trying to kill the British and the Arabs.'

'Yes, *Hasamba* was far too blunt for a lot of adults. Why spell things out like that? Well, the children here loved it. They wanted to hear the same stories over and over again.'

'That's so adorable, that you read to them.'

'Well, I was the leader.'

'Why am I not surprised?'

'I started the club so I was the leader. I had all the ideas. We put on plays sometimes, usually about a damsel in distress that I had to rescue. I got to kiss her at the end, that was my reward for saving her.' He turned off the light.

Several curious children had followed us into the building. They huddled together at the bottom of the stairwell and watched us in silence. Finally one spoke up. 'Mister, did you live here?' a tall boy with curly black hair asked Ami.

'Yes, in flat two.'

'Gilda lives there now. She's mad.'

'She's not mad. You have to be extremely nice to her.'

'You know her?'

'Yes. She has secret powers, and if you aren't nice to her you'll be very sorry some day. I can't tell you why you'll be sorry, because it would upset you too much.'

The boy looked at him wide-eyed.

'You'd better tell all your friends the same thing,' Ami went on. 'It's a good thing I came today, to warn you. Now we have to go.'

'Where are you going?'

'We're going to the field, to look around, and then we're going home to Tel Aviv. We're on an important mission, children aren't allowed.'

'What's the lady's name?'

'It's a secret. I might tell you when we get back to our car. We'll see.'

'OK,' the boy said.

The field was a wasteground littered with empty cigarette cartons and broken glass, its borders lined with debris. A few limp patches of grass had somehow survived amid the rubble.

'Nothing's changed,' Ami said. 'I can hardly believe it. I was sure I'd see some changes.'

'How long is it since you've been here?'

'About fifteen years.'

'How come you lived in such a poor neighbourhood?'

'My father felt it was important for Ashkenazi and Sephardi Jews to mix. Plus he was a socialist, he didn't believe in upward mobility. Anyway, we really were poor.'

'"In 1492 Columbus sailed the ocean blue, and Spain got rid of every Jew".'

'Well, no one can accuse Israel of doing too much for the eastern immigrants. Why bother, as long as you have bodies for the census and the army?'

'How come you left?'

'My mother got fed up with all the social problems. We moved to Tel Aviv when I was thirteen.'

'What did your father do?'

'He taught, when he was well enough. He was a physicist before the war. In Russia. After the war he met my mother and they came here. He was a lot older than she was. He had a hard time with the climate here and with conditions in general.'

'What about during the war?'

'He wandered around, did odd jobs in villages.'

'And your mother?'

'She was taken in by a Catholic family in Lyon. They had a house in the country, they moved there and kept her safe. They were very good to her.'

'Did you learn French?'

'No, she never spoke French and my father never spoke Russian. They read books in those languages, but they didn't speak anything other than Hebrew. They wanted to fit in.'

We both saw the dead man at the same time. He was lying at the edge of the field, face down, his head surrounded by a pool of dark blood. He was wearing a suit and he was partly bald but he had a thin, youthful-looking body. There was a camera lying on the ground next to him.

My impulse was to go up to the man and turn him over, see whether he was still breathing.

But Ami grabbed me by the wrist and began running back

to the street. 'Everyone indoors!' he shouted. 'You too, Lily,' he said calmly. 'I'm going to the car.'

There were a few shrieks, and then, within seconds, the entire street was empty. A woman took my arm and pulled me with her into a ground-floor flat. I looked out of the window: Ami was in his car, speaking into a radio transmitter.

'Come, come away from the window!' said the woman who had pulled me in. Her fashionable short skirt contrasted oddly with the floppy print kerchief on her head. The kerchief was knotted on top, giving her two rabbit ears. She closed the shutters and with brisk, nervous movements ushered me into the kitchen. Twin boys and a girl were sitting at the table. The boys were four or five and had small, sweet faces. The girl, a few years older than her brothers, wore a pretty red and white checked dress with pearl buttons. The three stared at me as if I'd just descended from outer space.

A determined effort had been made to give the kitchen a polished look, but almost everything was either broken or falling apart: the chairs, the counter, the shelves, the tap. A bucket was collecting water from a leak under the sink and the plaster on the walls was blistered. The woman began crying. Huge tears ran down her cheeks. 'Now this, now this, what next?' she said, with a sob. The children ignored her.

'Lord, oh, Lord, why me?' she wailed.

I was becoming increasingly aware of a pleasurable sensation.

It took me a few seconds to identify the source of pleasure: there was a delicious smell in the room. And the source of the smell was a baking dish just out of the oven, crammed with roasted potatoes and onions. The potatoes had been sprinkled with herbs and spices. Suddenly all I could think about was the potatoes. I wanted them. I had an overwhelming craving for them; I was like an addict who had to have a fix.

'What a wonderful smell,' I said, looking at the potatoes.

But the woman was too occupied with her grief to hear me.

'Can I have a taste, please?' I asked. 'They look so good.'

'We're all going to be murdered in our own houses!' the woman moaned.

I got up and, with my fingers, I scooped up a potato. The children continued to stare at me. 'Delicious!' I said. 'These are the best roasted potatoes I've ever had.'

'Slaughtered in our own houses!'

The girl got up from the table and handed me a plate and fork. Even the plate was chipped.

'Thank you, sweetheart,' I said.

She smiled.

I piled potatoes on to the plate. 'Who else wants some?' I asked. All three children raised their hands, as though they were at school. They were sure that I was in charge now. In the distance I heard sirens. I found four more forks and brought the baking dish to the table. 'Please join us,' I said to the woman. 'Your children would be so happy if you had some potatoes.'

'She's not our mother, she's our aunt,' the girl corrected me politely.

The woman nodded. She sat down at the table and I handed her a fork. We all dug in.

There was a knock on the door and I heard Ami's voice. 'It's OK,' he said. 'Everything's safe, false alarm.'

I opened the door for him. 'We've been having potatoes,' I said.

He looked at me. Then he said, 'He had a heart-attack. He just cut his head when he fell. You can come out now.'

'Goodbye, children,' I said.

'Wait, wait,' the woman said. She opened her handbag, fished around inside it, and pulled out an amulet against the evil eye, a delicate silver hand embedded with an oval turquoise stone. 'This is for you, my angel.'

I took the amulet and hugged her. 'I'll keep this for ever,' I said.

I left the woman and the children and followed Ami to the field. An ambulance and several police cars were parked near the body. A few soldiers had arrived on the scene as well.

The man had been turned over. I crouched down next to him. His face was covered with earth and streaks of blood. 'So he's dead?' I asked them.

'Yes, he's dead,' a police officer said. 'Natural causes. A tourist, he was taking photographs from the looks of it.'

I bent down and touched the man's hand. It was cool and stiff and I tried to warm it up a little by holding it between my palms.

'What are you doing?' Ami asked.

'Just touching him. Poor guy, dying all alone like that. How long has he been dead?'

'At least a couple of hours,' one of the medics said.

'We couldn't have saved him, then,' I said.

'Let's go,' Ami said, taking my arm and helping me up.

We returned to the car. The street was still deserted.

'You're not bothered by dead bodies,' Ami said.

'No. That sort of thing doesn't bother me. Is something wrong with me?'

'It's just a bit unusual.'

'I was always the person who did things no one else wanted to do,' I said. 'I got rid of a dead mouse once, at school. It was in one of the lockers. No one could believe I didn't mind, but why would I? It was dead, it wasn't going to bite me, and I used a glove, I didn't actually touch it. And I was always the person they called when someone vomited. I would have made a good nurse.'

'Yes.'

'Maybe some part of me is cold.'

'You're just brave.'

'I'm not brave because those things don't bother me. It's not like I'm making an effort. I don't like caves, though. I'd die if I had to go into a cave.'

We drove for a while in silence. Suddenly he pulled up at the side of the road. 'I have an overwhelming and irresistible urge to kiss you,' he said.

'OK.'

We kissed for a while. We were both sorry we couldn't do more, right there in the car.

'We'd better stop before it's too late,' Ami said. He started up the car.

'How come you never brought Ingrid to where you grew up?'

'You know, I loved that woman, but there were things she couldn't understand. It wasn't her fault, she just came from a different world. I know you're seeing what I'm seeing.'

'What language did the two of you speak?'

'English.'

'It's weird, a relationship in which both people speak a second language.'

'It's common here. Look at my parents.'

'I know. Four years ago, on the plane coming here, I met a woman who had just married an Israeli. Her husband was sitting next to her. They'd met in Holland and they got married, just like that. Her husband only knew about three words in English. Apparently he had to look up his marriage proposal in a Hebrew–English dictionary. He said, "Will you to marry me?" And she burst out laughing because he couldn't even get his proposal right, and he thought she was laughing at him. Will you to marry me! Anyhow, she said yes. And she wasn't even Jewish, and here she was following him to Israel, and they'd never even had a conversation! I wonder how long that marriage lasted.'

'Maybe some people prefer it that way. You don't have to face anything about each other if you can barely communicate. You can just pretend things are perfect.'

'I'm the opposite. I like to know things.'

'I've noticed. What was that about potatoes?'

I described the scene to him. 'I just had to have them,' I said. 'I couldn't resist. Nothing could have stopped me. Why didn't you come inside to use the phone?'

'That neighbourhood isn't connected yet.'

'How come you have a transmitter in your car?'

'Well, as you see, it came in handy.'

'Did you really think we were in danger?'

'Yes. It looked as though the man had been shot, and no one had taken his expensive camera, it was lying next to him. So there was a good possibility that he was killed by terrorists and that they were still around. And, well, as you know, I have inside information.'

'Do you think your job increases your paranoia?'

'My job decreases my paranoia.'

'Really?'

'Yes.'

'Is that why you weren't scared to get into the car instead of going indoors?'

'I was scared. I was very scared. And very happy to have a gun on me.'

'You have a gun?'

'Yes, haven't you noticed? It's in the glove compartment.'

'And you would have used it?'

'Yes, Lily, of course I would. I don't want to die.'

'How come you have a gun?'

'I need it for my job. We're not permitted to work without a weapon.'

'You know that explosion in Jerusalem last February? I was on that bus only an hour before.'

'I hope you didn't tell your parents that.'

'It wouldn't have made any difference if I had or hadn't.'

'How is that possible?'

'They don't think like that. I'm not saying they don't care what happens to me. But I'm not on their minds.'

'Why?'

'I don't know.'

'Just you, or your sister too?'

'Both of us. But my sister doesn't care. She's exactly like them. That's how she coped. She imitated them.'

'Maybe you're on their minds more than you think.'

I was furious when he said that. 'What do you know about it? I hate that, I hate it when people say mindless, stupid things like that, just because they want it to be true. You think I don't know my own parents? You think I'm making it all up? How dare you? How dare you comment on something you know nothing, absolutely nothing about, and never will. I don't need to prove anything to you. I don't want to talk to you right now.'

He didn't say anything.

'Well, say something,' I said.

'I'm sorry. I didn't mean to hurt you.'

'It's OK.'

'People have places inside them that are minefields. You never know when you're going to step on one of the mines.'

'You make it sound like there's no rhyme or reason to it. There is.'

'Yes, there's a reason, there's always a reason, but it isn't always easy to see that reason from the outside. That's why it's like a landmine. Because you can't see it. I understand why you got angry.'

'I'll tell you a story. Once I was at my friend Sheila's house and I decided to test my mother. I got Sheila to phone and say she was me. She called and said, "I'm at Sheila's and I've been invited for supper, is that OK?" And my mother said yes, that was fine. She didn't even notice that it wasn't my voice. I didn't expect her to.'

'That's an amazing story, all right.'

'There were some advantages. I used to miss school a lot, especially during the last year. And later, I found out that the head had called my parents and told them I'd been absent for weeks. They never said anything. That was the good side.'

'Where were you when you missed school?'

'In town, seeing films, hanging out. I was with Sheila, we bummed around.'

'Did the head call her parents, too?'

'Yes, and they confronted her right away, but she told them we went to the library and worked together and they believed her.'

'They must have been very gullible.'

'Not really, because we were good kids, you know. And a lot of the time we did work together, they saw us doing that. They knew we both wanted to end up with good results. Sheila gave me the idea of coming to Israel to study. It didn't occur to me. I'd spent so many years fantasizing about coming back that I assumed that's what it was, a fantasy, it couldn't actually happen. I'm such a moron.'

'She's in Jerusalem?'

'No. Don't be angry — she's at Bar Ilan. Her parents made her go to a religious university. They wanted her to be chaperoned.'

He laughed.

'Sorry I got so upset,' I said.

'I'm finding out more about you all the time. When you're angry your lips turn white. And when you see dead bodies you reach over and touch them.'

'Were you sad seeing that crown in the storage room?'

'Yes, in a way. It brought back a lot of memories.'

We didn't speak again until we reached Tel Aviv. We parked on Gordon Street and began strolling aimlessly through the city. Ami told me all sorts of stories about things that had happened to him at different spots. At a kiosk on Hertzl Street a man had grabbed his testicles when he was fourteen. There was a big crowd at the kiosk, and the man took advantage of it. At first Ami thought (optimistically) that a woman had been responsible. Then he saw who the culprit was, and he told him, 'Try that again and you'll lose yours altogether.'

On Rabbi Meir Street a young prostitute propositioned him when he was seventeen. 'But that's a story for another time,' he said.

On Jabotinsky Street he bumped into the poet and playwright Natan Alterman and ended up having tea with him at a café.

We wandered around until nine. There weren't any films we wanted to see, and we were just starting to think about getting something to eat when someone called Ami's name. A tanned, robust man and a pretty woman were waving at us. They were both in their forties, and they were both laughing, amused by life, amused by each other. They insisted we join them for supper, followed by a satirical revue that was playing nearby. Ami looked at me to see what I wanted. 'Sure,' I said. I enjoyed meeting new people.

We ate at a pavement café. While we waited for the food the man found a telephone and reserved two more tickets for the show. 'Got the last two,' he reported, when he came back to the table. 'I had to offer my grandmother, but they relented in the end.'

'Where do you know Ami from?' I asked.

The man laughed. 'Ami's a great guy,' he said. 'One in a million. A genius, and with a heart of gold. You don't meet too many people like him.'

The woman, who was a lawyer, began telling us stories about her cases, about the corrupt people she was trying to help, the corrupt people who were prosecuting her corrupt clients, and the corrupt people being called to the witness stand on both sides. Her laughter was infectious, and Ami and I joined in, even though the stories were appalling. The man put his arm round his wife's waist and said, 'Isn't she something? Tell me, isn't she something? What doesn't she have going for her?'

The woman said, '*Nu*, in public, Emil?' and they both smiled happily and kissed.

They insisted on treating us. While the lawyer was in the lavatory and her husband was paying at the cashdesk, I asked Ami where he knew them from. 'I've never met her before,' Ami said. 'I just know her husband.' That was all he said.

We walked to the theatre. It was packed, and there were

extra chairs on the stage. I didn't get all the jokes in the show, because some of them had to do with internal government politics. I always skipped that part of the newspaper: I found it too confusing.

In one sketch the stage darkened and an actor dressed as an Orthodox Jew with a skullcap and prayer shawl and that little black box strapped on to his forehead began crawling in the dark on all fours. He had a prayer book and a naked doll strapped to his back. Another actor shone a torch on the religious guy, picked up a phone and called a third actor, who was playing Rabin. 'Mr Prime Minister, an illegal settler is making his way to Hebron,' he said on the phone.

'Give him some biscuits!' the Rabin character said, and they handed the Orthodox man a packet of biscuits.

Then another Orthodox guy came crawling on all fours. This one had the packet tied to the back of his head. The telephone man got on the line again. 'Mr Prime Minister, another illegal settler is making his way to Hebron!'

'We've run out of biscuits, give him some shares!' the Rabin guy said.

This went on for a while. At one point the Rabin guy ordered the phone guy to give the settler a photo of Jabotinsky. 'We're out of those,' a voice off-stage yelled.

'Then give him a photo of Mussolini,' the Rabin guy said, and someone in the audience burst into cheers and applause.

Finally Rabin ran out of things to give the settlers, who by this time were all piled on top of each other at one end of the stage. From their midst they pushed up a banner that said, 'Arab-free zone: cheap housing for young couples.'

I don't remember the end of the sketch. Or maybe that was the end. Ami explained the things I didn't understand in a whisper, and between sketches he slid his hand under my hair and tickled my neck. I giggled. I was very happy.

❧ ❧

Surprisingly, the Hebrew word for terrorist (*mehabel*) has innocuous origins. In fact, the word appears in one of the most beautiful and poetic passages in the Bible, in the erotic love poem Song of Songs: 'Oh, my dove, in the clefts of the rock, in the covert of the cliff, let me see your face, let me hear your voice, for your voice is sweet, and your face is comely. Catch us the foxes, the little foxes, that spoil [*mehablim*] the vineyards, for our vineyards are in blossom.'

If the images strike us as suggestive, we may be sure it's intentional. The poem was meant to be recited during sex, as you explored your lover's body, with all its clefts and cliffs and foxes. (Or maybe the fingers are the foxes.)

It is even possible that the root *hbl* merged with the Arabic *habal*, pregnancy, to create the Hebrew word for labour pains, which appears in the Song of Songs as well: 'Who is that coming up from the wilderness, leaning upon her beloved? Under the apple tree I awakened you. There your mother was in travail with you [ḥiblatkha], there she who bore you was in travail [ḥibla].' (Here the lovers are turned on not only by the woman's genitals, but by the thought of conception and birth, the whole cycle of wonderful things that happen in that place.)

The word 'terrorist' was well entrenched in the Hebrew language by the time of the British Mandate. But, for some reason, a new word was created for Arab terrorists. At first (in the fifties and early sixties) Israelis used the word '*mistanenim*', which means infiltrators. But there were all sorts of infiltrators, including people who were merely trying to sneak back to their homes or pick up a few chickens. So a new word was coined for terrorists. The word was *meḥabel*, from the root *ḥbl*. Literally it means 'one who sabotages' but in actual usage it means 'terrorist'.

The plural form, *meḥablim*, has at times been used to refer to the entire PLO. Israel invaded Lebanon in order to destroy the *meḥablim*.

Palestinian prisoners who have been convicted of an illegal act, from failure to have a proper permit to deploying a mortar that either kills or does not manage to kill civilians, are referred to by the prison staff as *meḥablim*. A soldier who was assigned to search visitors at a military prison said she checked the vaginas (all women) and anuses (random women) of wives and mothers and sisters coming to visit the *meḥablim*. The most common forbidden articles she came up with were notes hidden in plastic capsules, though she once found a phone inside a woman's pants.

⌒～⌒

The Jerusalem flat Ami said we could use on his days off could have been a replica of Freud's house in Vienna.

'Who lives here?' I asked, following Ami into the living room. 'It's incredible. It's like I've travelled through time.'

'Friends of mine from my theatre days. They're set designers – they've gone off to Europe and the Far East to get new ideas. They'll be gone for eight months.' He plugged in the fridge and began putting away the groceries we'd brought with us.

'Are they old?'

'No, they're my age. They just like this style, I suppose.'

'Look at this roll-top desk! And the bottle of ink, and these paintings . . . The only thing here that was invented in this century is the fridge.'

'I have two weeks off now, I can stay here with you. Maybe I'll even sit in on some classes with you. I'd get a kick out of being in a classroom again.'

'I don't even know what you studied, or where.'

'I was at Tel Aviv University, in the drama department.

My subsidiary subjects were literature and philosophy. I didn't graduate, though, because I broke rules about not being in other shows.'

'Were you also working?'

'Yes, I had several jobs. Lab assistant, copy-editor, radio technician – I even worked with Kishon for a while, as a stage hand.'

'There's so much I still don't know about you.' I sat down in a massive armchair with curved wooden arms. 'So, my good friend,' I said in English, with a German accent, 'what childhood traumas have ruined your life? Tell all to the Herr Professor.'

'I caught my parents reading Jung,' Ami said.

I looked at him and sighed. 'I've fallen for you,' I said, still in English.

'As in fallen in love, or fallen into a trap?' he asked, also in English.

'As in fallen in love.'

'And?'

I switched back to Hebrew. 'And I'm getting used to the whole idea of your job. It doesn't shock me any more. I don't even think about it. It's strange, how that happens.'

'I told you we start forgetting in this country.'

'But how can you be horrible at work and not horrible outside work? It isn't like being in a play, like being Lenny. It's real.'

'Yes, it's real.'

'And not only that, but horrible to people whose cause you

seem to support. It doesn't make sense. The more I know you the less I understand any of this. How did Ingrid feel about your job?'

'She didn't know about it.'

'She didn't know!'

'She thought I had an administrative job.'

'I can't believe you didn't tell her.'

'I told her, but she didn't seem to register it. And she never brought it up again. She wasn't interested in politics. She didn't even know who our neighbours were. She thought we had borders with Turkey and Iraq.'

'That's so weird.'

'Not everyone thinks our problems here in Israel are at the centre of the universe.'

'But she was Jewish?'

'Yes, but very assimilated. She wasn't even familiar with the holidays — it was really like being with a non-Jew. The only reason she came to Israel was because she had a boyfriend at the time who came here to volunteer on a kibbutz. She thought it would be an adventure.'

'Turkey and Iraq . . .'

'Well, geography wasn't her strong point.'

'But you felt close to her.'

'Yes, we were close.'

'Was she a student too?'

'For a while she was enrolled in the music department at Tel Aviv University. She wanted to be a classical singer. She got accepted right away, but then she started having her asthma problems.'

'I guess I'm a bit jealous. Though I'm not really the jealous type.'

'What I felt for her pales beside what I feel for you, and I'm not just saying that. I shouldn't be saying it because it's a betrayal, but it's true. Because I feel you're part of me. I never felt that with her or any other woman. I'd like to see your kibbutz, where you were born.'

'I haven't been back.'

'You haven't been back to see it?'

'No, I haven't had the courage.'

'Meaning?'

'Too many emotions tied up with that place.'

'You remember it?'

'Yes, I remember it as if it all happened yesterday. I remember the shape of the tiles in the Children's House. I remember the red spots on Miri's feet. I can recall entire conversations word for word.'

'Maybe we'll drive up there together.'

'Yes, I could go with you, I think. I haven't done a lot of travelling, you know. If I'd grown up in Israel I would have seen the country on school trips and if I'd come here as a tourist I'd have seen the country on tours but I didn't do either, so I haven't even been to Masada. I haven't been to Latrun or Caesarea or even all the sites here in Jerusalem. Bracha thinks it's a disgrace.'

'What about the Dead Sea?'

'Yes, I've been there, and even to Sinai. I fucked on the sands of Nuweiba.'

'That's one of my landmines you've just stepped on.'

'Oh! Oh God, I'm so sorry.'

'Just don't do it again. It isn't jealousy, it's a feeling I'm being taunted. It makes me angry.' He really was angry, though he was controlling himself.

'Say you forgive me. Please say you forgive me.'

He looked shocked when I said that.

I got up from the armchair because I felt myself blushing, and I was suddenly confused. I opened the door to one of the bedrooms. 'Oh, look at this bed!' I shrieked. In the centre of the room stood an antique four-poster bed with white gauze curtains on all sides. 'I'm Marie Antoinette!' I said, and I jumped on to the bed, stretched out on it. 'Is it OK for us to do it here?' I asked. 'Would your friends mind?'

'They'd be pleased. Anyway, this bed could use some heterosexual activity.'

'My period started this morning, though.'

'And?'

'Well, just warning you.'

'I stand warned.'

'The diaphragm will keep it from getting too messy.'

'Periods are sexy.'

'Really?'

'Yes, really. I'll go and switch on the hot water.'

We'd brought linen and pillows, and together we made up the bed. When it was ready I went to the bathroom and put in my diaphragm. Then I came into the bedroom and we lay down together, the gauze curtains flowing all around us, hiding us from the world.

'You're my equal,' Ami said, as he pulled off my pants. 'I don't have any power over you, I'm not someone you need to ask forgiveness from.'

'OK.'

'Let's try some new things.'

'New for us or new for you?'

'Both.'

❧

My daughter and Keys are having sex. The sound is faint, because we're all doing our best to solve the delicate problem of this sound-sensitive flat: they play Indian music on my CD player, and I keep the radio on. Army Radio from Israel, reaching me via the Net. Right now I am listening to a public-service announcement, which is directed, I assume, mostly at the younger soldiers, at the teenagers who have only recently been conscripted. 'This is a game [sound of Nintendo]. This is a game [sound of tennis]. This is not a game [sound of a rifle being cocked]. Your weapon: NOT for the playground.'

I am looking at the photo of Ami that hangs on the wall, next to my desk.

Maybe the time has come to give Ibrahim a call, ask him to come and visit. Every year at Christmas Mary Jo sends me a card and a short letter. At first she included news about Ibrahim, but she must have lost touch with him because eventually his name vanished from her annual updates. She's a teacher now, in Africa. A real teacher, not a missionary: she's no longer religious.

It would not be difficult to find Ibrahim. There's a good chance he's still living in Tel Aviv, maybe even in the apartment on Edelson Street, though David and Michel have probably married and moved out by now.

I think I am ready; not because I am less vulnerable to memory than I was, but because I am ready to see that I am not alone in my vulnerability.

☙ ❧

Our first week in Freud's flat seemed removed from ordinary life, because of the flat and because it rained, and because we had showers together and listened to late-night radio and slept in the four-poster bed and Ami came with me to my poetry and Shakespeare classes. I introduced him to Dr Grubach; luckily she'd either forgotten our conversation, or assumed that I'd taken her advice and that Ami was someone else, not the interrogator I'd mentioned. At one point Ami disappeared for a few hours; when he came back he told me he'd been to see his mother.

On Thursday morning Ami went home to look after his plants and laundry and groceries and bills, and I wouldn't let him pick me up on Friday: I insisted on getting down to Tel Aviv by myself.

The first thing he told me when he picked me up at Central Station was that Ibrahim had been arrested on Wednesday for getting into a scuffle with someone at the garage. He had been released the next day but he was in a bad mood, very gloomy and angry. It wasn't clear whether he was angry with the prison guard and the judge, or about being arrested in the first place, or whether he was still fuming about the car owner who had accused him of cheating and ruining his car and lying and replacing good parts with second-hand parts when, in fact, he had taken extra time over this man's piece of junk and performed a small miracle.

Because of Ibrahim's bad mood, the Friday-night party was cancelled, but Ami suggested we take him and Mary Jo out to eat and then for a drive, maybe to the Nitzanim beach.

So that was what we did.

We went to an expensive restaurant near the Yarkon River and sat on the patio. A weeping willow sprawled over the patio and its delicate leafy branches draped our chairs. Fearless birds swooped down towards the empty tables looking for pitta crumbs; one landed on Mary Jo's shoe and refused to fly away even when she shook her foot. Mary Jo was amazed. 'This is either the stupidest bird I have ever come across or the bravest,' she said, and we both laughed. 'Hey, Hercules! Shoo!'

Our high spirits didn't penetrate Ibrahim's gloom. He sat fuming in silence, his arms folded and his feet stretched out on an adjoining chair. Ami didn't say anything either, so Mary Jo and I did all the talking. We gossiped about all the people we knew at the university. She was as placid as ever, and I envied her a little. I wondered what it was like to be so placid all the time.

After the meal Ibrahim began to feel a little better. We drove down to Nitzanim, and I could hear him and Mary Jo kissing in the back seat.

It was dark by the time we reached the beach and there was no one around. Ami and Ibrahim stripped and ran into the water. Ibrahim gave a loud shout as he threw himself on to the cold waves. Mary Jo and I had brought swim suits, but Mary Jo said we should give Ami and Ibrahim a chance to talk. So we only removed our shoes and dug our toes into the sand. We were both trying to keep an eye on our lovers. Every time we lost sight of one of them we panicked a little, because at night the sea seemed even more like a living entity with a mind of its own than in daytime.

'He seems to be cheering up,' I said.

'Oh, he's fine,' Mary Jo said. 'He'll get over it.'

'Do you think you'll stay in Israel when you've finished your studies?'

'Yes. Ibrahim can't leave his family. He doesn't want to. I don't mind staying here. I'm happy in Israel. Anyway, it's simpler if we stay here, especially if we get married. I wouldn't be allowed to marry him in the States unless he divorced first.'

Her answer took me by surprise. I had not realized that Mary Jo was in love, that she saw herself as staying with Ibrahim for ever. But now I saw that she would not have broken the sexual taboos of her faith without a strong incentive and I wondered how I could have been so blind.

'I'm in love too,' I said. I hadn't told anyone I loved Ami, and I felt I was revealing a thrilling secret. 'I've never felt like this before.'

'Ami's a great guy.'

'Some things about him are confusing. His job . . .'

'He's brave to do that job, it's something no one wants to do. Can I ask you something?'

'Sure.'

'It's a bit personal.'

'OK.'

'I wonder, do you think I should go on the pill? I mean, I don't really know where to go, who to call?'

'The pill has all sorts of side-effects. Maybe you're better off with a diaphragm, that's what I use. I can give you the name of a doctor, if you like, but you'll have to pay. Or you can just go to the clinic on campus – it's free.'

'If you could give me a name, that would be great.'

'What have you been using until now?'

'Nothing, really. Just, you know, counting days.'

'That's really unreliable. Use condoms at least.'

'I'm too embarrassed – you know, to buy them. And, anyway, I don't think Ibrahim would want to . . .'

'Well, I'll ring you tomorrow with the phone number.'

'Thanks.'

I could tell there was something else she wanted to ask.

'You can ask me anything you want,' I said.

'Well, there is one other thing . . .'

'Uh-huh?'

'I don't know exactly how to put it. It's just, Ibrahim, he goes on for a really long time. And it starts, you know, hurting eventually, but I don't want to tell him. I don't know what to do.'

'Maybe you just get a bit dry after a while. Try buying some almond oil or something like that.'

'I didn't think of that. Thanks. I never knew it took so long. I thought it was like three minutes and that was it.'

'Sometimes it is three minutes, depends on the man!'

'I thought that was the norm.'

'Three minutes is definitely on the short side.'

'I didn't think it would be an hour, though.'

'Lucky you.'

'Actually, it's a bit too long for me.'

'Do other things. He can come other ways.'

'I'm shy. I'm shy about these things.'

'Just give it time.'

'If my parents knew, they'd have a heart-attack.'

'Are you sure they don't know?'

'Are you joking? Every time we talk on the phone they read me verses and sermons about chastity for about half an hour.'

'Really?'

'Yes.'

'They don't know that you've moved in with Ibrahim?'

'They think I live next door.'

'They must suspect, Mary Jo. Otherwise why would they read you those sermons?'

'They've been doing it for years. But you know, Ibrahim and I are married in the eyes of God. I asked God if it was OK, given the circumstances, and I felt that He said it was all right.'

I nodded. 'I haven't spoken to my parents once since I've been here,' I said. 'I visited them one summer, that was it.

I was there when you met Ibrahim . . . I'm glad we've had a chance to talk. We should get together more often, the four of us.'

'How come you're so . . . you know?'

'Not shy?'

'Yes.'

'The way I was raised, I suppose.'

'I remember once in the halls you were giving this girl detailed advice, in the kitchen, on how to have an orgasm. I was so shocked. I thought you were like a prostitute or something.'

I laughed. 'Sorry. Maybe the kitchen wasn't an appropriate place.'

'Now I know I've been having them all my life. I just didn't know that's what they were.'

'You've really made Ibrahim happy. He's been even more cheerful than usual since he met you. Except tonight, that is. I hate so much of what's going on in this country.'

'You have to look at the good that's out there. There's a lot of hope.'

'Do you think so? Do you think there's hope?'

'Of course. We're all just people.'

'What made you come here?'

'What could be more exciting than being where Jesus lived? There are so many places that even look the same – you can imagine you're living two thousand years ago.'

Ibrahim and Ami came back from their swim and we handed them their towels, like two biblical servant girls.

'Freezing!' Ibrahim said, hopping as he pulled on his jeans.

'Is the water cold?' Mary Jo asked.

'The water's fine. It's coming out that's cold.'

We warmed up in a smoky tea-house in Yafo. Gold nargilla pipes and the carved gold discs of low Oriental tables gleamed in the dim light. We reclined on embroidered cushions on the floor. I stretched out next to Ami and Mary Jo curled up with Ibrahim. We didn't get home until nearly three in the morning.

'That was fun,' I said. 'That was a fun evening.'

'I was tense the entire time,' Ami said.

'Really? I didn't notice.'

'I'm good at hiding it.'

'Are you still tense?'

'Yes.'

'Why?'

'Because Ibrahim felt totally humiliated by what happened. He still feels humiliated.'

'What happened?'

'As you can imagine, the man at the garage basically called him an Arab thief. That's what made him lose his temper. He has to put up with enough shit without this sort of thing being thrown in his face. It was probably the last straw. Then in jail he got into another big argument with his Arab cellmate, who called him a traitor. Ibrahim told him to go to hell and they finally had to be separated, and the guard made a comment about how Arabs can't get on even with one another. Then the judge who let him go was patronizing. Actually, he was on Ibrahim's side. He told the other man, a German no less, that his behaviour was a disgrace to the State and his language was entirely out of place and he should apologize and pay his bill without further ado. But then he told Ibrahim to be a good boy. Really, that judge would have said the same thing to anyone — he's a hundred years old himself so everyone under fifty is a boy to him. But, understandably, Ibrahim was in no mood to see it that way.'

'You were in court?'

'Yes, I went to pick him up. Also in case he needed a character reference, because the owner of the garage was down in Eilat for the week. But it never got that far, the judge dismissed the case when he saw who he was dealing with.'

'I talked to Mary Jo. She and Ibrahim don't talk the way we do about things. They're both shy, I think.'

'Ibrahim? He's not shy.'

'Maybe you'd be surprised.'

'I would. I would be surprised.'

'They haven't even discussed contraception.'

'That's because he wants to have a child with Mary Jo.'

'Would she have to convert to marry him?'

'No, although if she did all she'd have to do is tell two

witnesses that she accepted God and Muhammad. It's not like converting to Judaism.'

'That's it? You just say you're ready to be a Muslim and you become one?'

'Yes.'

'No wonder there are more Muslims than Jews.'

'There may be other factors . . .'

'Mary Jo's parents read her sermons about chastity on the phone.'

'I think they're in for a rude awakening.' He used two words I didn't know and I had to ask for an explanation.

'My Hebrew's really improving with you. I'm learning all sorts of words I never knew . . . We've known each other for only three weeks, it's hard to believe.'

'I want to marry you too, you know.'

I laughed. 'You're planning a double wedding with Ibrahim?'

'No, I want one of my own. Not a wedding, just the marriage ceremony.'

'How can you be so sure after such a short time? You don't know enough about me.'

'I'm very sure. I suspected within the first ten minutes of talking to you, and I knew by the end of that first meal at Mandy's. I had a particularly hard time restraining myself when you started examining the meat for "a vein, or blood, or fat, or something gross".'

'Maybe it's just that I remind you of Ronny.'

I hurt him when I said that. He reached out for a cigarette, lit it, took his one puff.

'I'm sorry,' I said.

'That's OK. I can see it from your point of view.'

'How are we the same, me and Ronny?'

'You just are. There's no way to explain it.'

'I'm sorry. I really didn't mean it the way it came out.'

'You must have had some really bad experiences with guys to be so distrustful. I'm not surprised. Most men are incapable of establishing a normal relationship with a woman.'

'You're right, it's hard for me to believe men now,' I said. 'I'm always looking for the catch,' I added, in English. I didn't know how to say that in Hebrew.

'The catch!' he exclaimed.

'Is there a way to say it in Hebrew?'

'I don't know, I'll think about it. Is it hard for you to believe someone could love you?'

'Maybe.'

'You haven't had enough practice, maybe.'

'I think, with those other guys, I was starving. I was starving for some attention. I wanted someone to give me attention because I never had any from my parents. And it made me a poor judge of character, because in retrospect it was pretty obvious those guys weren't going to deliver. Then I decided I wasn't going to do that any more. No one nice ever paid me any attention. So you're right. This is a first for me.'

'You've decided I'm nice?' he said.

'I have to go by what I see. I can't reconcile it with your work, but I can't not notice how you are outside work.'

'So, *will you to marry me?*'

I laughed again. 'Maybe,' I said. 'I have to think about it.'

⌒‿⌒

Sometimes uncanny things happen to words.

If you want to say 'go to hell' in Hebrew, you say *lekh le'azazel*, or 'go to Azazel'.

That phrase comes from an obscure ancient ritual described in Leviticus. You take two goats and you have a lottery to see which goat gets God and which goat gets Azazel (whatever that is: Muslims think it refers to the angel of death, Christians think it's some sort of desert demon, Jews think it's probably the name of a hill but they aren't sure). The goat that gets God is sacrificed to God as a sin offering, while the goat that gets Azazel goes through the Azazel ritual. This consists of the priest laying his hands on the head of the (live) goat and confessing all the sins of all the people (it's very inclusive: 'all their iniquities, all their transgressions, all their wrongs') then sending that goat off into the wilderness, 'to Azazel'.

The goat carries away all those sins with it, and everyone feels better.

It's a good plan. Except when the scapegoat is human, of course.

Anyway, at some point Israelis started shortening *lekh le'azazel* to *lekh le'aza*. Go to Aza.

On the one hand, Aza was merely a shorter form of Azazel. A bit like saying 'a pain' when what you mean is 'a pain in the arse'. But at the same time, Aza is Gaza. Aza is a real place. So what you were saying was 'go to Gaza'.

What came first, the abbreviation or the new meaning? I suspect they came into being simultaneously. The shortened form, 'go to Aza', was tempting because it had an additional meaning. It was a pun.

And the pun made sense. As anyone who had been to Gaza knew.

Our second week in Freud's flat wasn't as perfect as the first. I caught a cold; Ami slept in the other bedroom because he thought I wanted to be alone; I got angry with him for deserting me but didn't tell him; instead I burnt the rice I was cooking and ruined one of Freud's heavy iron pots.

Ami suggested I come with him to visit his mother. He said I needed a change of pace.

The psychiatric hospital was new and very clean. Morning

sunlight poured into the open rooms through large windows, and the inmates, wearing pyjamas or casual day clothes, wandered freely up and down the halls. 'You're beautiful!' one called out to me.

'Thank you,' I said. 'Why do I feel so at home here?' I asked Ami.

He smiled and knocked on a half-open door. 'Rachel? It's me, Ami, and I brought my friend Lily.'

Ami's mother was sitting primly on her bed, dressed in a navy blue nightgown and yellow cardigan. She was a tiny woman, and it was hard to believe she'd given birth to Ami, as well as three other people. Her skin was as smooth as the skin of a young woman, and her eyes were the colour of pebbles on a rainy spring day. She seemed vibrant and alert, despite her frailty. 'Come in, come in,' she said. 'I knew the Messiah was coming.'

Ami kissed her and handed her a box of chocolates. She took the box and hid it under her bed.

'I haven't filled in the Messiah application forms yet,' Ami said, sitting down in one of the two chairs in the room. 'This is Lily, my new friend. My very good friend. We're staying in Jon and Pietro's apartment here in Jerusalem.'

'Don't neglect your teeth,' Ami's mother told us. I hadn't expected her to be that far gone. 'I had an excellent bowel movement this morning,' she announced.

'I'm glad to hear that, Rachel,' Ami said. 'Do you need anything?'

'I wouldn't mind a *husband*,' she whispered nervously, looking around to see whether anyone was listening.

'Anything else? Anything I can bring you?'

'I wouldn't mind a *husband*,' she repeated.

I started laughing. I tried not to laugh, but I couldn't stop myself.

Ami joined in, and his mother began to laugh too.

'We're having a party!' She clapped her hands happily.

'Poor Rachel,' Ami said, when we left.

'I had no idea she was that bad,' I said.

'She likes it when I visit her, though.'

'I can't imagine what it's like to be in that sort of state. Was she OK before, you know . . . ?'

'Yes, she was perfectly fine. She worked at a bakery, there wasn't anything wrong with her. Of course, she had her eccentricities. Her own parents and grandparents vanished from her life when she was fourteen and she never saw them again. I guess it made her a worrier. She was a great worrier, she was always afraid of losing us. She wanted to leave Israel so we wouldn't have to go into the army, but my father wouldn't hear of it. She really doted on us.'

'So sad! Such a sad family!'

'There aren't any happy families, you know. That's why they're all alike, because they only exist in our fantasies. Besides, there are a lot of families like ours in this country. This is a land that devours its inhabitants,' he said.

We were still in the grounds of the institution, walking down the lawn towards the car. Several inmates sat on benches, enjoying the sunshine after days of rain. I stopped walking and turned to look at Ami. 'Yes,' I said.

'Yes what?'

'Yes, *I will to marry you.*'

He lifted me off the ground and slung me over his shoulders. Two inmates began to clap.

'What are you doing?' I shrieked.

He ran towards the car and threw me on to the back seat. Then he joined me, shut the car door and began kissing me. The inmates left their benches and surrounded the car. They watched us kiss through the car windows and seemed pleased with what they were seeing.

⌒‿⌒

The story of the spies in Canaan appears in Numbers. When Moses and all the other ex-slaves reach the outskirts of Canaan, God advises Moses to send some tribal leaders to check out the land, look around, see what's what.

They come back with oversized fruit and a mixed report. On the one hand, the land flows with milk and honey, but on the other, the land is full of large people and large fortified cities. The Amalekites are in the Negev, and the Hittites and

Jebusites and Amorites are in the hills, and the Canaanites are along the coast and the Jordan River.

Caleb, the chief spy, isn't too worried. 'Let us go up at once, and take possession of it, for we are well able to do so,' he says. But the others are less confident. They feel the inhabitants are stronger than they are. 'The land through which we have gone, to check it out, is a land that devours its inhabitants,' they say.

Mass hysteria ensues. Caleb gives it another shot: 'Do not fear the people of the land,' he says. 'For they are bread for us; their protection is removed from them, and the Lord is with us.'

But the people refuse to calm down. They decide to stone Moses and Aaron for bringing them to this pass – which makes God so angry that He's ready to do away with them all, and Moses has to talk Him out of it. Think how bad it's going to look, he tells God. 'The Lord is slow to anger,' Moses reminds God.

So God agrees to a compromise. He'll just kill the spies (excluding Caleb, of course) and postpone entry to the land for another forty years. 'Your little ones shall know the land which you have despised,' he tells the people. 'But as for you, your dead bodies shall fall in this wilderness.' He means of old age, because forty years is a long time.

It's when God says 'the land which you have despised' that the whole story seems to take on a different tone. Suddenly the land becomes something else: something involving kindness rather than gratitude. Kindness towards God. You hurt God's feelings if you despise His land.

∽——∾

The next weekend we drove up to the kibbutz where I was born.

It was a beautiful autumn day, the sky a deep clear blue, the sun lazy and warm on our backs. We set off at nine in the morning and made several stops along the way, to look at the scenery and have lunch.

We reached the kibbutz in mid-afternoon, siesta time. No one was around; the place looked deserted.

'Maybe it's been captured and everyone's been shot,' I said. 'Or maybe there was a plague, and everyone died.'

'You really have a lot of love for this place, I see.'

'Actually I do, for some things. For the landscape. You can see why.'

'Yes, it's striking.'

'My mother said they were fools, taking this site. She said several groups had already rejected it. But maybe the view won them over.'

We parked the car by the side of the road and got out. For a few moments we stood and looked at the green and grey mountains in the distance. Then I shut my eyes and breathed in the pure, sweet air. I remembered the smell: wet wood and grapes.

'We used to think we were really safe here, when we were kids. The adults let us wander around by ourselves, even when we were only seven – can you imagine? They never once told us to stay close to the kibbutz. The fact that we were three kilometres from the border and that there were incidents all the time didn't seem to bother them. They were in denial, I guess. This was their country, that was it.'

'I'm sure they were keeping an eye on you, Lily. I'm sure there was *shmira* going on.'

'You'd think so, but one time Michael and I were naughty. We ran away during nap time, and I remember we came across this Arab in a *keffiyeh*. He was sitting on a box peeling potatoes, so we must have been pretty far from the kibbutz. We asked him why his teeth were so small. They looked as though they'd been ground away.'

'Probably he was just an extra hand . . . These houses are unusual, Jerusalem stone, you don't often see that.'

'I don't know if I can do this,' I said. 'I can see the roof of my parents' room from here – it's the third from the end. Imagine just living in a room. You didn't need more than a room because the entire kibbutz was your one big happy house.'

'Does it look different?'

'No, everything looks exactly the same, so far. Maybe once we go in I'll see changes.'

I began walking towards the path that ran through the kibbutz. Well-tended bushes and gardens lined the path, but they somehow drew attention not to themselves but to the obsessive pruning and hard work that had brought them to life; the effect was stifling and faintly frightening.

Two people passed us, but they didn't say anything. 'They must assume we're here visiting someone,' Ami said. 'I guess it's not like in the old days. Everyone would know we weren't expected.'

'Technically I'm still a member,' I said. 'I don't need to ask anyone's permission,' I added childishly.

'Uh-oh,' Ami said.

'What?'

'Kibbutz attitudes are filtering in from the air.'

'No, I'm just regressing. Soon I'll be asking to go peepee.'

'Well, are things the same?'

'Yes, exactly. Isn't that strange? You'd think at least the proportions would seem different now, but they don't. There's the Children's House. Oh God, there it is.' I started crying.

A woman wearing a straw hat came up to us. I dug around in my bag for a tissue and I blew my nose and tried to disguise the fact that I was crying. 'Who are you?' she asked, in a friendly tone, smiling at us. She had a wide toothy smile. Suddenly I remembered her.

'Edna?' I said.

'Yes.'

'I'm Lily. Ilana.'

'Ilana!' she exclaimed. 'I can't believe it!'

'Lily now. This is Ami.'

Edna and Ami shook hands. 'I heard you were in Israel,' Edna said, still smiling at me. 'We were wondering when you'd come up to see us. You're feeling emotional?'

'No, no, it's nothing, really. It looks so deserted. Are the children having a nap?'

'No, they aren't here — they've gone on an all-day hike. You can go in and have a look round. You'll stay for supper?'

'Yes, thank you.'

The three of us walked to the Children's House, a simple, square structure with rectangular windows. I couldn't decide whether the ascetic architecture was reassuring or spooky. The mauve tiles of the porch floor were still there, each one a different shape, like drops of oil in water. They were smooth and cool in summer and on hot days I used to press my cheek against them; I remembered wishing they were edible. Our hair was washed with petrol several times on that porch; we weren't told why. We weren't told anything about anything.

I opened the door and entered the main room and stood there in a trance. Bars of light fell on the kitchen sink, the small tables and chairs and the box of toys in the corner. The doors to the two bedrooms were open but the shutters were down and the rooms were dark.

'Everything's the same,' I said.

'We put in new wash-basins,' Edna said, 'but you wouldn't notice that.'

I entered one of the two bedrooms. 'I slept on this side. The beds were arranged a little differently. Mine was in the corner. Gila there, Dalia on the left, Michael at the opposite corner, poor Boaz here. Whatever happened to Boaz?'

She didn't want to say. Her entire body seemed to fill with dismay. 'He isn't with us any more,' she said sadly.

'Oh! I didn't know. My parents never told me.'

'I'm surprised. Well, he killed himself.'

I walked into the bathroom area. Everything was as I remembered it: three showers, two toilets, four tiny wash-basins.

'I have to run,' Edna said suddenly. 'I'll see you at supper. I'll tell everyone you're here. You're very welcome.'

'Thank you.'

Ami put his arm around my waist. 'Are you OK?'

'I remember something funny. Once we were showering and Michael came up to me and said, "Do you know how you make babies?" Well, of course this was a progressive kibbutz – we all knew. I said yes, I did. And he said, "Do you want to try?" And I said sure. We were standing there in the shower with all the other kids, and he touched me with the tip of his penis. It was so sweet.'

'Are you OK?' Ami asked me again.

'Why?'

'You look weird. You look and sound weird.'

I said, 'Well, you know, sad things happened in this room. Everyone was supposed to be so enlightened, they supposedly gave us total freedom, and we were supposedly the most important people in the kibbutz, the children. And no one was allowed to hurt us, they all had this shared responsibility to look after us. It's really ironic, it doesn't make sense, you know?'

'Let's go for a walk.'

'No, I need a few more minutes here. Look how small the basins are! They were just my height. Our careworker, Miri, was sadistic. She was selectively sadistic, she didn't dare touch me because she was scared of my parents. She went after Boaz – Boaz and Dalia, because they had no protection for some reason. She'd force us all to watch, too. And no one did anything – the adults, I mean. I still don't understand that. It went entirely against kibbutz rules. They didn't even believe in shouting at children, and hitting was unthinkable. I told my father, I even demonstrated what was going on, but somehow she kept getting away with it. She had these fits when she beat Dalia and Boaz, she humiliated them, she threw them on the floor and kicked them and pulled their hair. She tied Boaz to the bed, always in a fit of rage. And we all had to watch. Watching was always part of it, to humiliate the victim, and I guess to scare us too. Did you have to take cod-liver oil when you were a kid?'

'God preserve us.'

'But you've tasted it?'

'Yes, once, my mother gave it a try. I didn't actually swallow it. I spat it out and started running around the room clutching my throat and yelling that I'd been poisoned. I was preparing for my acting career, I guess.'

'Well, we had no choice. We had to line up and have a teaspoon each. It's impossible to describe what it was like, the helplessness of it. But Boaz, he was probably so nervous or just so sensitive that he always vomited. He'd swallow that stuff and then he'd vomit. We all wanted to vomit, but the rest of us managed to keep it down. We were given a sweet to help us. But he couldn't do it. And she'd just keep giving it to him over and over again, even though that stuff was expensive, probably, and she was wasting it . . . OK, let's go.'

'We don't have to stay for supper if you don't want to,' Ami said, as we headed down the path.

'I want to find this one place, this really nice place just on the outskirts of the kibbutz. It has berry trees, it's right next to this cave where some famous sage is buried.'

We asked someone where the burial site was. I didn't remember how to get there: I only remembered what it looked like near the cave.

The burial cave was on a small, isolated hill. The view from the hill was thrilling: one thousand shades of green, mountains that looked at you knowingly across time. The voice of my lover, here he comes: leaping upon mountains, skipping over hills.

We sat down under one of the berry trees and I touched the ground with the palm of my hand. Then I lay flat on the ground on my stomach, with my arms stretched out. 'I love this earth. I love these barley stalks.' I kissed the earth, then rolled on to my back, pulled a handful of wild barley stalks out of the ground, scattered them over my face. I continued to pull at the stalks and to scatter them over my body until they covered me like a blanket. 'There was a mosque right in the middle of the kibbutz when they took it over,' I said. 'I didn't know about this when I was a kid, of course, I only found out recently. There was a mosque and they didn't know what to do with it. Leave it? Blow it up? Turn it into a storage room?

'They put it to a vote and they argued and argued. The Trotskyites in particular were against destroying it. In the end the army came and said it wasn't up to them, and the soldiers put all this ammunition in it and tried to blow it up, but it refused to fall. They kept trying and trying, they had no idea it was built so well. It had iron bars or something, inside the walls, and they just couldn't demolish it. They had to come back the next day, and that night there was a big fight about whether to stop the army. Because the soldiers didn't really care, the kibbutz could have talked them out of it. But in the end the army went ahead. My mother said the top suddenly rose to the sky like a parachute – she said it was really spooky.'

'How did your parents vote?'

'Both my parents were in favour of blowing it up. Otherwise, they said, the Arabs who used to live here would never lose their attachment to the place, they'd keep thinking about their mosque.'

'Brilliant,' Ami said.

'They were in a quandary, they didn't know how to get out of it. They didn't know how to think about things. Before forty-eight they were in favour of one state, you know, Arabs and Jews together. But after forty-eight the policy changed. *"Ki lanu lanu eretz zot,"*' I sang. *Because it's ours, it's ours, this land.* 'They were so elated, you know? There was such elation about having this little piece of land with a mosque in the middle of it. My father kept saying, "Finally, a place that's ours, a Jewish government, Jewish police, the end of being a despised minority, finally a place where you don't have to worry about Nazis getting into power or not being allowed to attend university." That's what happened to him, you know. He couldn't go to university because of the quota. Well, no one could keep us out of the universities now because we had our own universities. We were the ones who decided. Now we had our own small corner of the world. He kept saying it was a dream come true.

'You should have seen on holidays, especially agricultural holidays like Bikkurim, what went on, the ecstasy of it. And how hard they worked. They killed themselves working, they never stopped. You have to be really convinced about what you're doing to work that hard of your own free will. Of course, some of them, like my parents, had been through the Depression back in Canada and the States so they were used to deprivation. But life was even harder here. They really believed they were doing something good. Something glorious and new and important. Such a sense of mission! First they had nothing, just some leaky buildings the Arabs left behind and twenty acres of Arab vineyards, and I think some olive groves. But they kept getting stuff. For a while they had to walk to the nearest city just to get bread, fifty kilometres there and back. But then they got a van. And then they got another van. And then they got cows, then chickens, then a mule, and then an expert to figure out how water could be diverted to the kibbutz. And they hired Arabs to help them pick the crops and put up the new buildings – can you imagine? The government allowed thirty Arabs to come back to gather the tobacco they'd left behind in their houses. That must have been so weird. Well, you've lost the war and you've lost your homes, but you can have your tobacco. I guess the kibbutz didn't have any use for tobacco – smoking was against Hashomer Hatza'ir policy . . . But what about me? What about what I feel now? I'm exactly the same!'

'It isn't attachment to the land that's the problem. It's what you do with your attachment.'

'We'd come across these fields full of deep red anemones – it was like nothing else existed, nothing else could be bad. Even these wild barley stalks, they made me high. I thought wild barley stalks were the most beautiful thing in the world. I still think that. And there were other good things too. I liked being close to the other children, especially Dalia. I liked the way everything was so clean and orderly, and the way we were encouraged to have our own opinion about everything. I thought kibbutz life was cool, I felt really cool being part of that, even as a young child. I liked all those clean, ironed clothes and going out at night in our pyjamas as a treat. I liked seeing my parents in the afternoon. And there was this amazing chocolate yogurt that I've never been able to find anywhere else.'

Suddenly I wanted to leave. 'I think I'd rather die than eat supper in the communal dining hall and smile at everyone,' I said. 'I think if I see those pale green and flesh-coloured plastic dishes I'll faint. Let's escape.'

'Good idea. But we have to let someone know.'

'You tell them, please, Ami. Find someone and make up an excuse. I'll wait in the car.'

I sat in the car and waited for Ami. I remembered the day we left the kibbutz. My mother had told me only the night before that we were leaving, and Michael gave me a shiny white belt that he found who-knew-where as a going-away present. I wasn't allowed to take the belt, though. My mother told me to leave it on my pillow.

Ami reappeared, striding towards me in his jeans and denim jacket, and I smiled at the way he walked, at the unmistakable walk of Israeli men: determined and assertive and at the same time completely casual. 'They were disappointed,' he said. 'Disappointed and apologetic.'

'What did you tell them?'

'The truth.'

'That I hate their crockery?'

'That you felt overwhelmed.'

As we drove away I said, 'Can you imagine moving from this setting to a Canadian city? Canada seemed so endlessly grey, nothing but concrete and grey skies and snow and more snow. Even the summers seemed grey to me. I can't describe how much I missed the beauty of this place. That and the songs. Such beautiful songs — do you remember them? "Be-pundak katan . . ."'

Ami and I started singing together. We sang for a long time, song after song. It was amazing how we both remembered the words to all those songs, or how if one of us forgot one part the other could fill it in. Some of the songs were charming and some were haunting and some were pure Zionist kitsch. The kitschy ones we sang at the top of our lungs, emphasizing the pioneering message or the melodrama, even though it seemed cruel at times, especially if the song was about fallen soldiers and weeping mothers. I'd never felt so close to anyone before.

'Let's go walking up here another time,' I said. 'I just had to get this bit over. We'll come north another time and have fun. Fun will be the only thing on the agenda.'

'How come your parents left?'

'Oh, I don't know. My father got into a dispute with some people and my mother wanted an easier life.'

'Are you hungry?'

'You know the answer.'

'There's a fantastic restaurant near the Kinneret.'

'I love travelling with you.'

'We can go to some of the places you haven't been to yet.'

'I'd like that. Though not Masada, I don't know why. I don't like doing things everyone else does. Masada, Masada, who cares?'

'OK, Lily, not Masada. We can fly to Paris too, if you like, or London. We can go for a few days when you're on your break, it's not a long flight.'

'I keep forgetting I'm going out with a millionaire.'

'Not exactly.'

'I have to spend some time preparing for exams, though.'

'I don't ever want to lose you. I can't imagine not having met you,' he said.

'You say things men don't say usually.'

'Are you such an expert?'

'Israeli men certainly don't say things like that.'

'We're too tough and macho?'
'Yes.'
'I'll try to remember that.'

⌁

In Hebrew the verb 'to have' does not exist. Instead of saying 'I have' you say 'there is to me' (*yesh li*). Or 'this is mine' (*zeh sheli*).

One wonders how the Bible manages with this deficiency, because it seems at first that the Bible is all about having and not having. Right from the start Adam and Eve have that garden to stroll around in. And then they don't have it any longer.

But when you look at the text itself you find, amazingly, that there are not all that many references to having. In fact, the actual words *yesh li* (I have) or *yesh lanu* (we have) appear only seven or eight times in the entire Bible. The most famous occurrence of *yesh li* is found in Genesis, in the story of Jacob's reconciliation with his brother Esau. Jacob has tricked Esau out of his inheritance but now, twenty years later, he's in a repentant mood. He decides to offer Esau two hundred female goats and twenty male goats and two hundred ewes and twenty rams and thirty camels and their colts and forty cows and ten bulls and thirty asses. He hopes this gift will pacify his brother and prevent Esau killing him for what he's done.

Esau responds by appearing with four hundred men. Either he doesn't trust Jacob and brings the men just to be on the safe side, or else he really wants revenge. More likely it's the first reason, because as soon as he sees Jacob (who quickly bows seven times to the ground) he embraces him and they both cry. Jacob offers all the stuff he's brought with him.

But Esau says, movingly, 'I have enough, my brother. Let what is yours be yours.' *Yesh li rav, aḥi, yeheyeh le-kha asher le-kha.*

Kinneret is the Hebrew name for the Sea of Galilee, where Jesus walked on water, and also Peter until he lost his nerve and started to sink. When you stand on the shore of the Sea of Galilee, you can see why it came to be associated with miracles and faith in the unseen.

You can also see what inspired the famous Hebrew poem by the poet Rachel (1890–1931), which includes the lines, 'Oh, my Kinneret, were you real, or only a dream?' (The possessive pronoun is not always about possession.)

The word *shmira* means 'keeping guard' or 'guard duty'. It's a word you hear a lot in Israel, because everywhere you go there's *shmira* (guarding) being done by a *shomer* (guard). Hashomer Hatza'ir, the Marxist-Zionist youth movement my parents belonged to, means 'the young guard'.

The word also means 'to keep' and that's the way it's mostly used in the Bible: keeping God's laws, keeping justice, keeping order, keeping things in place. 'The Lord will keep you from all evil. He will keep your life. He will keep your going out and your coming in. From this time forth. And for ever.'

My daughter and Keys have left. They went back to Belgium, to dance and play music and enjoy their young love.

❧

Ami couldn't stay with me in Jerusalem the following week: he had to go to work. I moved back to the halls of residence because all my things were there and because I didn't really want to be alone in Freud's flat, even though it was closer to my classes than the halls.

I was disoriented at first: now that I was involved with Ami I felt removed from student life. The Americans were too cheerful and the Russians were too gloomy and the Israelis were too serious. Only my three European friends, from Germany and from Sweden, still seemed to belong to the life I was drifting into. I wondered whether my life had really changed, or whether my sense of alienation was merely an extension of missing Ami.

In those days the Hebrew University was on a campus in West Jerusalem, while the halls of residence and a few older university buildings were on Mount Scopus in East Jerusalem. From my window I had a panoramic view of East Jerusalem, with the golden Dome of the Rock gleaming in the distance.

The Mount Scopus halls of residence were new and quite pleasant, but they were cut off from the city and it was lonely there, especially in the evening. There was nowhere to go, even if you only wanted a walk, and unless a film was on everyone was pretty much stuck indoors. The same films ran over and over again because of a shortage of stock, but we were all so desperate that most of us had seen *Il Conformista* and *A Clockwork Orange* several times. I was glad that at least my classes were in West Jerusalem. The campus there was large and inviting, and seemed designed for socializing and hanging out with friends.

I had not been in touch with Nadya for over two weeks, and when I entered the room she jumped out of her chair, looked at me with fear in her eyes, then quickly returned to her books.

'It's just me. Did I startle you?'

'No, it's fine,' she said.

'No bad news from home?' Nadya's family in the Soviet

Union was waiting for permission to join her in Israel.

'No, no, all is good.'

But at bedtime, after we'd turned out the lights, she suddenly said, 'I have something to tell to you.'

I turned the light back on. 'Sure, what is it?'

'I have done something very wrong.'

'I'm sure it can't be that bad.'

'Yes. Some men were here to ask questions about you.'

'I know. I'm sorry, did that upset you? It was just routine, you know. My boyfriend works for the army, they were doing a security check. It happens here all the time.'

Instead of being reassured, Nadya rushed to my bed and knelt on the floor, wide-eyed and pale. Had I not read Russian novels I would have been frightened. 'I told them about the demonstration you attended,' she said, trembling. 'Can you forgive me?'

I burst out laughing. 'Nadya, get up. This isn't the Soviet Union, silly. We're all on the same side here. No one cares whether I went to a demonstration or not. They just want to know whether I can keep secrets. You didn't do anything bad. Come on, let's go have tea in the kitchen.'

The kitchen was brightly lit and smelt of cold mashed potatoes. We sat on stools and waited for the water in the *finjan* to boil. Nadya, looking like a misplaced Gothic heroine in her long flannel nightgown, was still uneasy. 'This isn't the Soviet Union,' I repeated. 'You did the right thing. The absolute worst that could have happened is that they would have decided I'm not reliable. That's all. I wasn't in any danger, neither were you, we're all safe here. It's our army, you know. Protecting us.'

'All the same, I should not have said. They looked so serious when I told them – they wrote it down and looked at each other. I was sure you would be in trouble.'

'I should have told you they were coming, but I didn't know myself.'

'So we are still friends?'

'Of course.'

'I wrote to everyone at home about you. You're my best friend, always so kind to me. That's why it was unforgivable to betray you. But they kept asking and asking. And I was scared. They made me feel it was right to tell them, but afterwards it seemed to me wrong.'

'Well, it was right. My boyfriend has a job that's full of secrets. Things no one is allowed to know, not even me. And they wanted to make sure I'm reliable, that's all.'

'He is in the Foreign Office?'

'No, he's an interrogator. And he hears a lot of secrets from his prisoners.'

She looked horrified, and I knew immediately that it had been a mistake to tell her. 'You cannot be friends with such a man! You must not!' she said.

'Well, you're right. Interrogators are not the best sort of

people. But he actually only works with children,' I said. 'And he's gentle with them.'

She seemed relieved. 'Yes, I knew you would not see such a man.'

'I hope they all get out, Nadya. Your family.'

She sighed. 'No one is happy where they are,' she said, and I didn't know whether she missed Russia, or whether she was worried that her relatives would be disappointed with Israel, if ever they were permitted to leave their home.

～⌒～

I have written Mary Jo the following letter: 'Dear Mary Jo, please excuse this rushed note. I am writing to ask whether you have a recent address for Ibrahim. I would like to see him. Hoping you are well, Lily.'

～⌒～

Early on Friday morning I went to Tel Aviv, weighed down with books and notes; I was falling behind with my work.

I was sitting at Ami's kitchen table, jotting down ideas for a linguistic analysis of a passage in *Alice in Wonderland*, when Ami stormed into the house. He was so angry I thought he'd pick up a chair and throw it against the wall. Instead he took his tools, went out into the garden and started ripping out weeds.

When someone around you is in a rage you have to tread carefully, and treading carefully makes you vulnerable, and your vulnerability makes you angry. But it's not like that when you're in love. When you're in love you don't get angry. You just feel bad for your lover, and you wonder what it's all about.

Ami was in the garden for an hour. Then he came in, made himself coffee, rolled a joint, and smoked it with his coffee.

'What happened?'

'Let's go for a drive,' he said.

'OK.'

He filled a metal canteen with water and we set out, driving south towards the desert. The landscape changed as we drove, from soft, unassuming dunes to a lunarscape of craters and furrows, all glowing softly as though an invisible fire lay just beneath their surface.

I lost track of time, and didn't notice that Ami had left the main highway until I saw that the road we were on had ended. It ended without warning, in the midst of copper red mounds that rose from the ground like bizarre modern sculptures competing for attention.

We stepped out of the car and drank from the canteen. It was a lot warmer here than in Tel Aviv. 'A road to nowhere,' I said. 'Literally.'

'Oh, this road leads somewhere, all right,' Ami said.

'An invisible city?'

'Invisible from here, anyway.'

'I guess you have to get there on foot.'

'No, a jeep is the usual mode of transport. Let's sit down.'
He lifted himself on to one of the mounds, gave me his hand
and pulled me up. We sat down side by side like the king and
queen of the castle. Or desert.

'We could be on Jupiter,' I said. 'We could be in another
galaxy.'

'Yes, these vast deserts make you feel how small you are.'

'Where are we exactly?'

'Somewhere between Egypt and Jordan.'

'"My name is Ozymandias, king of kings. Look on my works,
ye Mighty, and despair!"'

'I like that poem.'

'It certainly fits this landscape. So, you've been here before?'

'When I did my service we were stationed around here.'

'Nice view.'

'Yes, it suited the experience. Sorry, Lily. Sorry to drag
you into all this.'

'What are you sorry about dragging me into? Your mood?
Your work? The desert?'

'Not the desert.'

'I like knowing about things.'

'Well, you're the exception in this country.'

'What happened?'

'Oh, nothing really, Lily. Nothing new, nothing unusual, it's just that now and then it gets to me.'

'Why were you so angry?' I asked.

'I'm still angry.'

'I can't tell now.'

'Because now I feel other things too. Before there was only anger.'

'What other things?'

'You. Being here with you.'

'What happened?'

'It's too complicated to explain.'

'Tell me. I want to know. Unless you can't . . .'

'No, it isn't that.'

'Tell me, then.'

He didn't answer. His face closed, and he looked like an entirely different person: cold and immovable. He might have been made of stone.

I was afraid to speak, afraid of him.

He saw me staring at him, and he broke into a smile.

'You scared me again,' I said.

'Yes, I can see. Sorry, Lily. Sorry.' He laughed.

'What are you laughing about?'

'Just remembering something. Our first day in training, and this guy gets yelled at and he says, "Sorry." And the guy training us says, "What am I, your aunt?" And we all had a fit of hysterics.

We just couldn't stop. The angrier our officer got, the harder we laughed. I don't know why I just thought of that.'

'Did you get into trouble for laughing?'

'I don't remember,' he lied.

'What happened at work today?'

'The only way I survive in my job is having some control over the situation. When that control is jeopardized I get angry.'

'Control, how?'

'It's complicated,' he repeated.

'I want to know.'

'OK. All right.' He paused. 'I'm on the army payroll,' he said. 'I'm technically in the army, but that's not where I work, really.'

'I thought you worked in a prison.'

'Yes, but it's not an army prison. I started off working for the army, doing interrogations for them. But the Shin Bet does the main interrogating, and they wanted me to work for them. They tried to recruit me, but I refused – I didn't want to work for them. Well, in the end they moved me there anyway. So now I work in one of their detention centres, even though I don't in fact work for them. And that gives me some advantages. Somehow, in the midst of it all, I've managed to take some control. Because they need me. The other interrogators have only sporadic success, and the information is unreliable or incomplete. So they need me for the important and hard cases. And because they need me, and because of my success rate, I've managed to get some things. Like having my own interrogation room. And usually the prisoner stays in that room the whole time. There's a bed for him to sleep in during the night, so instead of going back to his cell he stays in the room, and I stay on the premises. I sleep there too. I'm the only one who does that, of course. The others come and do their job and leave. They have lots of different prisoners. They can't tell one from another, it's like an assembly line. You can't imagine the things that go on down there, Lily. Sometimes you wonder if they even remember what they're there for. The interrogators, I mean.

'Anyway, by the time I get a prisoner he's already in bad shape, usually, from the arrest and the detention . . . I don't know, maybe I shouldn't be telling you all this.'

'No, I want to know.'

'Well, the arrests are usually accompanied by violence. Sometimes more violence, sometimes less, it's unpredictable. So the prisoner's already been through a lot, usually. But if he's been interrogated on top of it, it's really hopeless. I told them I couldn't work with other interrogators on the same person. I had to be the first interrogator and the only one. And they agreed. So prisoners are marked out for me and I get them and I keep them until I'm through.

'Everyone knows that no one's allowed to touch my prisoners. Everyone knows that about me. I put up with everything else, with all the insanity. But that's the one rule I have.

Sometimes I get called away for big, urgent cases, even though the people calling me have their own interrogators. It isn't supposed to work that way, but I have a reputation so they call me. The first time they did that I found it hard to believe they wanted me, given who my friends are and how I live. But it didn't matter to them, they didn't care what I did in my spare time.

'It was the same thing there. I told them right from the start that I refused to be a last resort. I refused to be the last thing you try after everything else fails. I had to have first access to the prisoner. They were after me at first to take some cases they'd started and bungled, but I wouldn't do it. I'd make up some excuse. I'd get out of it. So finally they got the idea.

'But you get compulsive characters in this job. You get very fucked-up and very compulsive people. And then there are bureaucratic mess-ups. The usual red tape, things getting lost or misplaced. I was working with someone easy this week, polite, thoughtful, interesting to talk to. They considered him a hard case because he's active, but in fact he was easy. I didn't have to spend more than a few hours here and there with him. He had the choice of staying in the room or going back to his cell for the rest of the time. He chose to go back to his cell, he had friends there, he didn't want to be alone. And I was making good progress. I was right at the end – I could tell. I could tell I was reaching the end. I last saw him on Thursday morning and then I came home. There wasn't any need to hang around. I went in today expecting to have one last meeting with him.'

He paused. 'Things are deteriorating very fast now. I've watched them deteriorate over the years. They were very bad to begin with, but they've got even worse. The people on top are getting more desperate, there are more and more prisoners coming in, ridiculous numbers of prisoners, and there's more pressure to get information faster, growing paranoia, growing panic. I see where it's headed. It can't stay like this, the dam's going to burst one of these days. But they think they can shore up that dam. They think the solution is to get more and more frantic, step up everything, hire more guards, more interrogators, set up more detention centres, get increasingly brutal with the prisoners, make their stay in prison even more unbearable, if that's possible. It's straight out of a Russian surrealist play, except that it's real. And no one in this country seems to be aware of what's going on. They don't want to know, or they know but they pretend they don't, and the people who make all the decisions seem to be sleepwalking too. Or else this is what they want, this is what turns them on. Power, aggression, winning. Maybe they really think this is what's going to get them what they want, whatever that is. Though often it feels like no one's in charge. Sometimes it feels like there's total anarchy, with everyone issuing different orders, one hand doesn't know what the other is doing, contradictory directives coming in all the time, don't do this, don't do that, avoid the head, avoid the genitals. Each one gets swallowed up by the others, like voices in a dark cave. If you knew the things that go on, if you knew, Lily, you wouldn't believe it. No one could invent such farce, even if they tried.

'As a result there's less control over what happens. With more people in charge, more people taking and giving orders, there's more confusion, every day another *fashla*. Two new guys took my prisoner and pressed his face into shit. They made him drink some concoction – who knows what? – so he'd vomit and have diarrhoea. Then they pressed his face into the vomit and the shit. Laughing, I'm sure, the entire time.'

When he stopped talking I became aware of how silent it was around us. A vacuum of sound, like being in space. Usually you hear something, even if it's distant; you don't usually come across perfect silence.

'It's so quiet here,' I said.

'Yes.'

'You think there are snakes?'

'Yes, here and there, but I don't think we'll run into them.'

'How can you bear it, Ami? I mean, even if it isn't your prisoner, how can you bear to be in that environment?'

'Not seeing things doesn't make them not happen.'

'You could be fighting this instead.'

'It won't help. This is what we've decided. We've decided

torture is OK, detention is OK, war justifies everything. We're doing this to survive, to avoid repeating our history.'

'What will you do? About your prisoner?'

'There's nothing I can do.'

'Did you see him again?'

'Yes, I spent the morning with him. We played *shesh-besh*. We ate breakfast and drank coffee and played *shesh-besh*. Neither of us spoke.'

'Will they release him?'

'No, he's got at least ten years coming, probably more.'

'What did he do?'

'He was involved in some things.'

'Will you see him again?'

'Probably, but I'm not interrogating him any more. They'll try to get me to continue, and I'm not going to refuse to see him if that's what they want to pay me for. If they want to pay me to play *shesh-besh* it's fine with me.'

'But if you don't succeed, will they send him to someone else?'

'He already told me a lot. I think they'll be satisfied. I'll tell them it's the end, in my view. They usually believe me.'

'How come they keep you, with your sort of attitude?'

'I'm the best interrogator they have, Lily. They're terrified of losing me. They need me. And it isn't as if they can imitate me. It isn't as if I've got this one method that I can pass on to other interrogators. They keep wanting me to train the others but I can't. Because I improvise. Because everyone's different and I never do the same thing twice. They don't know how I do it and I don't know either.'

'Who won at *shesh-besh*?'

'It was pretty even.'

'What happens to the information you get?'

'I don't deal with that part of it.'

'But is it useful? Do you think lives are saved because of information you get?'

'Yes, now and then, but that isn't the point. The point is to get to the root of the problem. No one seems to see that. It's pointless, what they're doing, it's completely pointless. It's like the Wise Men of Chelm going to sea with a sieve to collect water. The Wise Men of Chelm are geniuses next to the people coming up with the strategies we're using to deal with a problem we don't even believe exists. How do you get people to hate you less, be less aggressive with you? Kick them around some more, make them really miserable, turn their lives into a nightmare, yes, that should work. What do they think? What goes on in their minds? Do they really believe that you can just bully people out of existence? That you can demoralize them into giving up? That isn't going to happen. All you do is create more anger, more hatred. What could be easier to understand? You know, Lily, in all the years I've been interrogating I've never once had a prisoner attack me. Never. I can't work with prisoners who are restrained, and we're always alone, the two of us, though there's an emergency button just in case. I'm armed, but the prisoners don't know that. And in all the time I've been doing this, even with really aggressive prisoners who are at the end of their rope, who are really at the edge, not once has anyone tried to attack me. The worst that ever happened was I got spat on, and that was always at the beginning, never after we'd spent time together. And sometimes they even apologized later.

'Anyway, I don't even want to think about that part of it. It's an entirely different department, sorting out all the intelligence. It hasn't got anything to do with me. I'm way down at the bottom of the heap.'

'You don't sound way down to me.'

'They need me, but I'm at the bottom, which is where I want to be. I don't make any decisions about anything, I just do the interrogation and my job ends there.'

'Why do you do it then, if you're so uncommitted?'

'I told you, Lily, questions starting with why don't have simple answers.'

'Are you doing it so they won't do worse things?'

'I'm just as bad as the others, Lily. Don't deceive yourself, don't make me into a hero. The whole situation has a built-in perversity that you can't escape. I take advantage of people's vulnerabilities and I manipulate them into telling me things they don't want to tell me. I manipulate them into betraying a cause they believe in, people who are their friends. I'm against violence, it's wrong, and it won't get them what they want. It will only make things worse for everyone. But you can't imagine how desperate they are. And I'm part of what's making them desperate, no matter how you look at it.'

'It isn't exactly the same. Some things are bad but they're not as bad as other things.'

'That's the worst trap you can possibly fall into. I see it happening with the others all the time. Even the ones who don't seem to have an iota of conscience start falling into that trap. They go around saying, "Well, at least I don't do this, at least I don't do that. I would never go that far. I'd never do what they do in Syria, this is nothing compared to what our guys went through in Egypt. I'm a good person. I'm nice to my children, I give money to beggars, and that proves I'm a good person at work too. So what if I break a few bones? So what if I lock people up in box-cells and squeeze their testicles and piss on their food and hit them over the head and humiliate them in any way I can? At least I don't pull out their fingernails . . ." It totally destroys people, thinking that way. It's the worst thing anyone could possibly do.'

'But you are a good person.'

'People aren't good or bad. They just do good and bad things. Your only hope is to know which is which.'

'So stop, Ami.'

He didn't answer. He didn't say any more. We stayed there for a long time, and then an open jeep came down the road, the kind we had on the kibbutz, the kind I used to love to ride in, sitting on my father's knees. There were two officers in it and they jumped out when they saw us: they were tense and alert and suspicious. Ami went over to talk to them, and he must have reassured them because they didn't ask for our ID. They only told us to leave. We got into Ami's car, turned round and drove away.

We drove to Arad and filled the tank just before the service station closed for the weekend. The wild cliffs and rifts and chasms that surrounded us seemed to be heaving, as though preparing to take over the world. It was impossible in the midst of this geological drama to maintain the illusion of a reasonable existence. The dizzying angles evoked essential questions: what are we doing here, and where have we come from, and why. I wondered whether the people who lived here became accustomed to living without answers.

'My father always wanted to live here,' I said.

'Yes, it's breathtaking.'

'That wasn't why, though. He didn't care about that. He was happy wherever he was, as long as it was Israel. But he liked the air here. He liked its purity.'

'Why didn't he move to Arad instead of leaving for Canada?'

'I think he was angry with Israel.'

'Angry with Israel?'

'Well, I just pieced this together. He never talked about it, but I think he applied for a job with El Al and they gave it to someone else, someone he thought was less qualified but who was a relative of the person hiring. And he was insulted. So he left.'

'So much for Zionism.'

'He was always sorry he left. He always regretted it, he wanted to come back. But for some reason he never did. Let's eat, I'm starving.'

We ate supper at a falafel stand, and then we drove to the Dead Sea and crawled into a thermal sleeping-bag that Ami kept in the boot of his car. But neither of us slept. I stayed up because I couldn't fall asleep and Ami stayed up to keep me company. Just before dawn we rolled up the sleeping bag and walked barefoot along the shore of the Dead Sea. When the sun rose, we sat on the wet sand and watched veils of crimson and pink and purple spread across the sky. Then we drove home.

⌒──⌒

Fashila **is an Arabic word meaning to fail, lose courage, despair, be** disappointed, act in a cowardly way.

In Hebrew slang *fashla* means mess-up, snafu, an embarrassing or disastrous or humiliating mistake. You can use it for small things, like forgetting you had to meet someone, or you can use it for big things like the Yom Kippur War.

A box-cell is a cell that is five feet by five feet by two and a half feet. The person inside can't stand up or stretch out. You find box-cells in most Israeli prisons: they're punishment cells, and nobody lasts very long in them – people start going mad fast and they don't want to go back in once they've been let out.

The word for box-cell is *tzinok*, from the verse in Jeremiah: 'The Lord has made you priest instead of Jehoiada the priest, to have charge in the house of the Lord over every madman who prophesies, to put him in the *mehapekhet* and *tzinok* [ancient torture devices].'

Shesh-besh is the Farsi/Turkish/Arabic and now Hebrew word for backgammon.

Chelm is a real town in Poland, south of Lublin. In Jewish folklore, however, Chelm is a town of fools. The Wise Men of Chelm do things like carry the town-crier on their shoulders when there's been a snowfall so that his footsteps won't ruin the pretty landscape.

Nuclear reactor is *kur gar'ini*, from *kur*, furnace, and *gar'in*, seed.

❧——❧

Ami reminded me that I was neglecting Bracha, and when I phoned her she invited us both for dinner. 'I thought you'd forgotten all about us,' she said.

We set a date for the following week. Ami went back to work, I assumed in order to sort things out with the *shesh-besh* prisoner, and I returned to Jerusalem. At the end of the week, on Friday night, we went over to Bracha's for dinner.

As soon as we arrived we heard loud sobs coming from Noga's room.

'Ai, ai,' Bracha said. 'Come in, children, come in. Maybe you can help me, I can't do anything with her. She's been locked in there for two hours.'

Bracha led us to the kitchen and told us the whole story in a low voice. 'I can tell you,' she said to Ami. 'You're in the army yourself. And Lily is family.'

It turned out that Noga had a boyfriend who lived in Haifa. He'd just completed his service, and he was at Haifa University studying engineering, which was what Noga planned to study too. He always came to pick her up when she was on leave. She'd get a ride or take a bus to an intersection near her base, and he'd pick her up from there. But this one time, for some unknown reason, he decided to pick her up at the base. He seemed to think that because he'd just finished his own service, it was OK for him to know where her base was, even though she was on a base that was considered out of bounds. And probably they wouldn't have minded, maybe she'd have got off with a warning, but the inexplicable part was that her boyfriend had a hitchhiker with him, an Australian hippie he'd picked up on the road. And he had driven right up to the base, with this sweetly smiling hippie in the car, and said he was there to pick up Noga.

Noga's superiors had had a fit. First, they spent an hour lecturing and humiliating her. Then they put her on dishwashing duty for three days. But, worst of all, they told her she could forget about her application. She had applied for an army job that would be related to her field when she came out of the army, and which she was desperate to get into.

They told her that now it was out of the question. Even though it was her boyfriend's fault that there had been someone in the car with him, it was her responsibility, because she had revealed the location of the base.

So now she'd lost her chance to move into the area she wanted to be in, she'd been publicly humiliated with her dishwashing punishment, and on top of that she had a huge fight with her boyfriend and they weren't speaking to each other.

'I'll see what I can do,' Ami said, when Bracha had finished.

Bracha stared at him in disbelief. 'You can do something?' she asked.

'I can't promise, but I'll try. I just need some information from her.'

Bracha looked as if she was ready to throw herself at Ami's feet. Instead she gave him a huge hug. Then she wobbled over to Noga's door. 'Noga'le, Noga'le, I have something important to tell you. Open the door, I beg you, open the door.'

At first Noga didn't answer, but her mother finally persuaded her that she really did have some good news.

'I can't promise,' Ami repeated, when he told Noga he'd try to help her, 'but I'll do my best. Give me all the details. Maybe I know someone.'

Noga didn't look too excited, but that was because she wasn't ready to switch from misery to happy mode yet. And she was still furious with her boyfriend and at the same time terrified that she might lose him for ever. I noticed how red and chapped her hands were, I assumed from the dishwashing.

Before we sat down to eat Bracha turned on the television for the news. 'Let's see whether we still exist,' she said. Israelis never tired of saying that before they tuned in to the news.

We watched the first twenty minutes and then we all squeezed round the table in Bracha's tiny kitchen. Ami and I had starved ourselves all day because we knew what would be waiting for us, and I had to concentrate on avoiding his eyes when Bracha began apologizing profusely for not having had time to prepare more. As it was, there was barely room on the table for all the dishes, which could have fed us several times over.

'You shouldn't have gone to so much trouble, Bracha,' Ami said.

'Who else if not me?' Bracha said. 'I'm her only relative here and I have a responsibility to her parents to look after her. What do your parents say about your nice new boyfriend, Lily?'

'I haven't told them yet.'

Bracha was baffled. 'It's not a secret, is it?' she asked, looking a little worried.

'No, I just haven't written recently. I'll tell them in my next letter.'

'I've already informed them of everything!' she said, with satisfaction, as though she'd arranged the match herself. 'They'll be so pleased. Such a nice boy!'

'He's not a boy,' Noga said. There was something strange about the way she was looking at Ami. 'You must be very high up in the army,' she said.

'I'm very low down in the army. But I know a lot of people. I probably know someone who knows someone who can pull some strings for you.'

'I deserve that job! I had the highest marks on the test.'

'What do you do in the army, if I'm allowed to know?' Bracha asked Ami.

'I do interrogations. I interrogate Palestinian prisoners.'

'Really! Palestinians . . .' She looked confused. She wasn't accustomed to the word. 'So you work in the territories?'

'Yes.'

'Ah, they're lucky they're in Israel, where we treat them so well. You wouldn't find that anywhere else.'

'We don't treat them well. Their conditions in prison are terrible and the interrogations are increasingly out of control.'

Bracha waved her arm dismissively. 'What you consider out of control, in other places they'd be laughing.'

'No one would laugh, believe me. No one would laugh and no one's laughing, least of all our prisoners.'

'Well, what do they expect? They shouldn't be planting bombs. Then no one would be asking any questions.'

'You know, a lot of them get arrested for things like having newspapers that are perfectly legal outside the territories.'

'I'm sure there's more to it than that,' Bracha said, with conviction.

'Can't we talk about something else?' Noga said. 'At least in the tiny bit of time I get on leave can't I have a break from all this bullshit?'

'Such language at the table,' Bracha said indulgently. 'I don't know where you pick it up.'

'In the army, *eema*,' Noga teased, but she didn't take her eyes off Ami. She continued to stare at him until we left.

On the way home I said, 'How come people don't know about what's going on?'

'They don't want to know. They really don't want to know, and whatever information filters in they manage to block it out. Besides, even the police aren't allowed into the interrogation wings. Even the prison authorities aren't allowed in. It's off-limits to everyone, soldiers included, and it's more or less soundproof. And people who do work there aren't allowed to say anything – it's against the law.'

'But the prisoners . . . when they come out . . .'

'Yes, Israeli journalists are just lining up to hear their stories. The whole nation is waiting with bated breath. They get the spotlight in the evening news. And now,' he began imitating a television news announcer, 'live from our studios, Marwan Hassan will describe in detail the torture sessions he endured in the special Shabak wing of one of our newest detention centres in the occupied territories.'

I couldn't help smiling at his imitation of Israeli broadcasting style, with its odd mixture of sensitivity and dramatic intensity. 'Why do they talk like that, all the news announcers? It's like they're being heroically calm in the face of disaster. It only makes you even more anxious about what's going on.'

'Heroism is part of the culture here. How else do you get people to be enthusiastic about joining an army?'

'Were you? Were you enthusiastic?'

'Questions about the army aren't allowed in this car.'

'What about outside this car?'

'And also outside this car.'

'I suppose newsreaders always try to sound serious, in Canada too. But somehow it sounds different here. Maybe it has to do with the language. It's so formal. You can just tell they've got a vocalization expert in the wings, going over every word, and it would be like a national catastrophe if they made even one little mistake.'

'Everyone spoke like that not too long ago. All the adults, anyway.'

'Yeah, Hebrew jumped from Henry James to Allen Ginsberg in one generation . . . But there must be some journalists who are interested in all this. I mean we have a free press. What about *Ha'olam Hazeh*?' I asked, referring to a popular anti-establishment tabloid. Its real agenda was political (a Palestinian state, an end to land expropriation, equality) but it lured readers with stories about prostitutes and strippers. The Shin Bet (referred to as 'the instrument of darkness') was one of its favourite targets.

'Yes, there are articles now and then, but no one pays any attention. Torture is not something anyone's ready to deal with. People are barely aware of the arrests. How they're done, how many of them take place.'

'How come Noga was staring at you like that?' I asked.

'Was she staring at me? I didn't notice,' he said.

'How could you not notice?'

'She's just grateful that I offered to help her.'

'No, it's you. You're charismatic.' I think it was the first time I realized that Ami wasn't ordinary. There was nothing ordinary about his appearance or his presence or the way he spoke.

'I'm sure you imagined it,' he said, and I let it go because he wanted me to.

～ ～

Hebrew had a hard time with the word Palestinian. At first, before 1948, the English word 'Palestinian' referred to Jews living in Palestine. After 1948, when 'Palestine' became 'Israel' and 'Jordan' and 'Egypt', that usage, both in English and in Hebrew, became obsolete.

Looking through my bookshelves I find that the 1975 Langenscheidt Hebrew-German dictionary, the 1976 and 1988 Larousse Hebrew-French dictionaries, the 1989 Yale University Press Hebrew-English dictionary and the 1963 Alcalai Hebrew-English dictionary have no entry at all for 'Palestinian'. The Even-Shoshan Hebrew dictionary, which was published between 1966 and 1970, has no entry for 'Palestinian', but the 1983 addendum includes the word *palestinai*:

'Thus the nation of Arabs who were born in the Land of

Israel or who immigrated to it in the last centuries call themselves, and they claim to have rights to independence in the state of the Land of Israel.'

Nowadays, of course, you can't open a Hebrew newspaper without seeing the Hebrew word for 'Palestinian' on every page, though none of the papers agree on the spelling. One paper uses the foreign spelling without the *aleph*, another uses Hebrew spelling without the *aleph*, a third uses the Hebrew spelling but keeps the *aleph*. And the newspaper of the religious right in Israel jumbles everything together, deploying several forms of the word on the same page, along with a refusal to use the word at all, and references instead to 'Arabs' or (in order to draw a link between present-day Palestinians and various biblical enemies) 'Ishmaelites' or, when in a more genocidal mood, 'sons of Amalek' (the tribe God asks Saul to wipe out, both man and woman, infant and suckling, and even ox and sheep).

Radio broadcasters are also a little inconsistent. When I listen to Israeli radio on the Internet, what I usually hear is *palestini*, with the initial consonant following Hebrew pronunciation, but every now and then someone says *phalestini*, following Arabic pronunciation.

Another word that presents difficulties in Hebrew is the word for 'occupation'. Occupation is a relatively recent military concept. You wouldn't say that the Romans occupied most of the lands we now know as Europe: they simply conquered them, collected tribute, and that was that.

The word 'occupation' implies that you're taking into account the indigenous population of the conquered land. It suggests that there's such a thing as a nation-state, and that if you occupy a territory, that territory basically belongs to someone else. Hebrew has no word for 'occupy'. Either you are somewhere or you aren't there. Either you enter a place or you leave it.

The only way to refer to (military) occupation in Hebrew is to use the word for 'conquered'.

Several other adjectives emerged in Israel when the territories were first occupied: 'held', 'liberated', 'administered'. For a short while after 1967, 'liberated' enjoyed wide popularity (though a few prophetic voices, like that of the philosopher Yeshayahu Leibowitz, warned against this breezy attitude right from the start). But eventually that word migrated to the auspices of the Greater Land of Israel movement, and became solely theirs. No one else wanted it. 'Held' had its day but was probably too vague and awkward to stick. Or maybe euphemisms can go only so far. 'Administered' enjoyed some success, mostly among the administrators. The word 'administration' suggests, however, something tame and helpful, and grew increasingly ragged under a barrage of bullets, tear gas, clubs, etc.

So what you're left with is 'conquered territories' and that's what you say if you're trying to make a point, but in general people in Israel just say 'the territories' (*ha-shtaḥim*). It's less of a strain if you omit the adjective altogether, and anyway, everyone knows what you mean. The word *ha-shtaḥim*, the territories, doesn't have any other meaning in Hebrew. It means the territories occupied by Israel since 1967. It's remarkable how much weight and meaning and resonance a single word, 'territories', can have.

～ ～

In December Ami had to go away for three weeks. He said he'd been called for a big job; he didn't know where it was, but they were flying him there and he wouldn't be back until the interrogation was over. He would be staying in a hotel and the interrogation would take place in a villa somewhere.

It rained in Jerusalem almost the entire time Ami was away. It was also windy and cold. I moved back into Freud's flat because my sense of not fitting in at the halls of residence was becoming more acute, and also because the flat reminded me of Ami. And I found that I was sleeping a lot. I started feeling sleepy at eleven in the morning, and I felt sleepy all day. I sat in class daydreaming about beds, and as soon as I came back to the flat I lay down on Jon and Pietro's four-poster bed, my hair still wet from the rain, and I drifted off almost immediately. I'd wake up at midnight, make myself supper, and go back to sleep.

It may have been my drowsiness that made me feel I'd stepped into a slanted world, a world in which supernatural events were possibly taking place around the corner. One morning at the Mahaneh Yehuda market I bent down to stuff olives and cheese into my knapsack, and I lost my balance when I tried to stand up. A man caught me and helped me carry the rest of my groceries through the crowds and then to the flat. As we walked he tried to convince me to marry him. He offered my father a camel; or maybe he said he'd marry me if my father bought him a camel, I can't remember. He said I'd have excellent conditions, I'd have my own radio. I imagined myself sitting in a tent listening to the radio and feeling lucky, and it seemed to me that it really was an option, that I could get used to that sort of life, sitting cross-legged in a tent, wrapped up in oyster-coloured fabric, listening to music on my transistor radio, and I thought vaguely that if not for Ami I'd consider his offer.

The next day I boarded the number nine bus on my way to class, and as soon as I sat down a man on the seat facing me gasped. He gasped and started as though he'd seen a ghost. He was a survivor, and clearly he was witnessing a resurrection. We looked at each other and I wanted to go over to him and be the person he wanted me to be, but I didn't move. I let him stare at me in anguished disbelief and when the bus reached my stop, unforgivably, I got off.

At the cafeteria, between classes, everyone wanted to know about my new boyfriend.

'No one sees you any more,' my American friend Ellen said. 'You used to be the life and soul of the party. Now you've vanished.'

'It's my boyfriend.'

'I know, the one who came to Dr Grubach's class with you?'

'Yes.'

'God, is he a hunk! Where did you find him?'

'Hitchhiking.'

'He's gorgeous.'

'I'm used to him, I don't really notice.'

'Someone said he was famous. A writer or something?'

'He used to be an actor, but that was ages ago. Now he works for the army.'

'He looks old to be in the army?'

'He's not doing his service. He's employed by the army.'

'Oh! I didn't know they did that.'

'Every army has salaried soldiers,' Eric, my friend from Frankfurt, said contemptuously. 'The IDF especially needs them, with Israel's tiny population. Though, of course, what really keeps this fascist occupation going is the billions that come pouring in from the US, in return for those nice Jaffa oranges.'

Eric never missed a chance to air his views on Zionism in general and Israel in particular, and I often wondered why he'd come to study at Hebrew University in the first place. His parents, who were both survivors, must have pushed him into it.

'How come he doesn't act any more?' Ellen asked.

'His brother died.'

Suddenly the room swirled and I slid off my chair. Eric caught me.

Everyone was concerned. 'Just dizzy,' I said.

I went to the cloakroom to splash water on my face and when I opened the door an old man was standing there, looking frightened and apologetic. 'I'm Avram. Avram Beiner,' he said, trying to hold on to the one thing he remembered.

I found a chair for him in the hall and told him to wait while I went to look for help, but by the time I returned with one of the campus guards, he'd vanished.

A few days later I was reading *Paradise Lost* when I, too, forgot where I was. In fact, I was in the library in the Lauterman building on campus. I'd been reading for a while, and I forgot I was in the library. I thought I was at home and I started reading aloud, which was something I often did when I was alone. 'Thoughts, whither have ye led me? With what sweet/Compulsion thus transported to forget/What hither brought us?' I said. Everyone stared at me, and fortunately thought I'd done it on purpose, smiled and shushed me.

In this absent-minded state I left my tape-recorder in the

cafeteria. I always took a tape-recorder to my linguistics class, because the class was in Hebrew and I couldn't take notes quickly enough. I kept it in a plastic bag, and I left the bag on a chair in the cafeteria. When I returned an hour later to look for it, I was greeted with icy glares. The entire cafeteria had been evacuated because of me; the bomb squad had been called; the tape-recorder had had to be lowered into a security pit. Before I could get it back, I had to go to the security office and receive a lecture on irresponsible behaviour.

I went to the security office in a daze. The man behind the desk was furious, and he'd been gearing up for the lecture. But I must have looked pitiful, because when he saw me he lost heart. He tried to yell at me, but he couldn't do it. I apologized tearfully, and left with my tape-recorder. I was amazed that it had survived the bomb squad's attempts to detonate it. Even the cassette was intact.

Although I'd moved into Freud's flat, I was officially still living in the halls of residence, and I had to do guard duty when my turn came. Nadya ran into me on campus and reminded me that I was on guard that night.

My instructions were to sit at a table next to the door of Building One from midnight until four in the morning and ask everyone coming in for their ID. And if the person wasn't an Israeli and didn't have a student ID, I couldn't let them in. I had to tell them to come back during the day. At four o'clock I'd be replaced.

Since I wasn't armed and I didn't have a walkie-talkie I couldn't protect the building from armed terrorists on a killing spree. If they came while I was on duty, it would be my bad luck. But (the idea was) I could prevent a terrorist coming in with an explosive. He'd have to leave the explosive somewhere else. So I huddled up in sweaters and a warm coat and I sat at the table and guarded the building.

An hour after I started, at around one a.m., a man walked through the door. I looked at his ID and I wasn't surprised to see that he was neither a student nor an Israeli: I had known when they were giving me my instructions that this was going to happen. I had had a premonition. The man's clothes were shabby, he was unshaven, he appeared to be in his forties. He looked utterly defeated.

I was never so confused in my life. I forgot what I was supposed to do, or why. I stared at the tattered ID and then I looked up at him helplessly.

He was very understanding. It's OK, he seemed to be saying. He seemed to be speaking telepathically to me. It's OK, I'm used to this and it doesn't humiliate me any more, because it's become part of me now, this humiliation. I'm used to being asked for my ID by twenty-year-olds who are part of the regime. Don't feel bad and don't be scared, it's OK that I'm here.

I handed him back his ID and watched him disappear up the

stairs. One thing was certain: he wasn't carrying explosives. He wasn't carrying anything.

I never found out who he was or what he was doing in the building. Someone's relative, maybe, or just a friend, stranded illegally in Jerusalem, looking for a safe place to stay.

I missed my classes the next day; I was too sleepy after being up half the night. I spent the day in bed and when I woke up I decided I was spending too much time alone and too much time sleeping. I decided to visit Ellen at Shikunei Elef, the halls of residence on the West Jerusalem campus.

The Shikunei Elef halls had been built as temporary accommodation and were supposed to be torn down as soon as new ones could be built in their place. But the new ones had been built on Mount Scopus instead, so the temporary halls remained as they were. They looked more like barracks than university halls. The rooms were tiny and had to be heated with paraffin stoves. The rent was a lot lower than on Mount Scopus, though, and you had the advantage of being able to walk to class.

I made my way to the bus stop, but it was pouring outside and when I saw a taxi coming my way I began to wave my arms wildly. In my excitement I forgot to check the colour of the numberplate. West Bank drivers weren't allowed to drive into campus. They could only take me to the gate, and it was another two or three kilometres from the gate to the halls.

The taxi screeched to a stop and I got in. 'Shikunei Elef, please', I said.

'That's not for me,' the driver said.

I felt myself blushing. 'Just take me to the gate.'

When we reached the gate the driver tried to get through. He knew it was hopeless but he tried anyway. The guard said no. I was mortified.

I paid, adding a large tip that I knew didn't change anything but which the driver seemed exceedingly happy to receive. I got out and asked the guard if I could wait inside his booth until I got a lift.

'It's against regulations, but for you I'll make an exception,' he said.

I entered the small glass booth and shivered in my wet jacket.

'Don't you know blue numberplates aren't allowed in?' the guard asked me. He was very annoyed.

'I forgot. I forgot to check. Why, anyway?'

He shrugged. 'Security.'

'I hate this country.'

'No one's forcing you to stay,' he said. 'No one asked you to come and no one's forcing you to stay, and if you don't like it you're welcome to leave.'

'Thank you,' I said. He was a young guy, with mischievous eyes and a smile that said he'd triumphed over adversity by being clever and resourceful. I knew I seemed foreign to him, and very lucky. A rich American, attending university, an undreamt-of life.

'By the way, I was born here just like you,' I said.

'So how come you talk like an American?'

'I grew up in Canada.'

'If Moses hadn't had a stutter that's where we'd all be now, Canada,' he said.

'I've heard that one.'

'He meant to say Canada but he said Caaa . . . Caaan, and God thought what he wanted was Canaan.'

'I already know that joke.'

'So, who asked you to come back?'

'No one.'

'So don't complain.'

'Think of that man's feelings. He's old enough to be your father.'

'No one asked him to stay either.'

'He was *born* here!'

'Oh, you're one of *those* . . .'

'I just feel bad for that driver. If you had a heart you would too.'

'I have a very big heart. Go out with me and I'll show you.'

'I already have a boyfriend.'

'Yeah? Does he agree with your politics?'

'You'll have to ask him.'

'So tell me, every time a terrorist gets killed while planting a bomb, do you burst into tears?'

'You think I support terrorism because I want a taxi driver to be allowed on campus?'

'He could be hiding something in the boot of his car.'

'Everyone's paranoid.'

'Yeah, well, if we weren't paranoid we'd all be dead by now.'

'If we had peace we wouldn't have to be paranoid.'

'Keep dreaming. Nice necklace.' I was wearing a necklace of tiny gold and silver coins. 'Where'd you get it?'

'The Old City.'

'How much?'

'Twenty lirot.'

'You were ripped off.'

'Good to know.'

'Open your jacket, I want to see what kind of jeans you're wearing.'

'No, thanks.'

'Come on, don't be a child. I work in jeans.'

'Oh, all right.' I unzipped my jacket and he inspected my hip-huggers.

'Lee.'

'Yes.'

'Very good make. I can sell you a pair of jeans, highest quality, any make you want, half the price you'd have to pay anywhere else. A third the price.'

'I have all the jeans I need.'

'There's no such thing. Maybe your boyfriend wants a pair. What's he do?'

'He's in the army,' I said.

'Hey, he must go away for months. You can go out with me in the meantime.'

'That's really tempting – but, look, here's a car.' I ran out to see whether I could get a lift. It was a Morris Minor and there were already four passengers inside, one in front and three crowded into the back. But they told me to get in anyway and sit on someone's lap, because it was only a short ride. So I climbed inside and sat on the lap of one of the passengers. All four passengers were blind, and I could feel the one I was sitting on becoming aroused. I tried to shift forward, but he held me back and pressed me down towards him. I thought, Oh, what does it matter? He's blind, after all.

When the car finally stopped I pulled myself from the blind man's grip and ran out.

I no longer wanted to see Ellen. I sat down under the prickly branches of a pine tree and hugged my legs. I didn't care about the rain. I shut my eyes and rested my forehead on my knees.

A voice near me said 'Hey.' I looked up. A young man with a machine-gun was pointing his torch at me. 'Hello there,' he said. He had a kind voice. 'What's going on?'

I got up. 'Nothing. Nothing. Everything's fine.'

'Why are you sitting in the rain?'

'No reason.'

'American?'

'Israeli.'

'There's a psychologist on duty at Health Services.'

'I'm fine. I'm fine.'

'Boyfriend trouble?' he asked.

I looked at him. He had a sad, intelligent face. 'No.'

'Where do you live?'

'Resnik.'

'Visiting someone here?'

'I was, but I changed my mind. I'll just go home. I'll take a taxi back.'

'Come, I'll make you tea first.'

I followed him to the kitchen of one of the barracks. A student dressed in full hippie gear – headband, peace chains, embroidered jeans – was sitting in the kitchen smoking. He dropped his cigarette ash on to a half-finished plate of spaghetti.

'Who's this? Looks like something the cat dragged in,' he said to the man with the machine-gun. He had an Australian accent.

'Are you Australian?' I asked. I wondered whether, by some odd coincidence, he was the hitchhiker Noga's boyfriend had taken to the army base.

'Yeah.'

'I don't believe this.'

'What?'

'Did you ever get a lift with an engineering student from Haifa?'

'Engineering . . . yeah, come to think of it. You know him?'

'Did you stop to pick up his girlfriend?'

'Yeah, we tried, but she wasn't available, and the guy was upset for some reason. He must have thought she was dumping him.'

'Where was he picking her up?'

'Just some farm she was volunteering at,' he said.

I burst into hysterical laughter. I couldn't stop laughing, and the two of them stared at me, the man with the machine-gun sadly, and the hippie in confusion.

Eventually I calmed down, obediently drank tea, and took a taxi home.

∽——∾

About twice a year I have a recurring dream that dates back to this period of my life, and maybe even to the night I went to visit Ellen in Shikunei Elef. In this dream Ami's left for work, but he's forgotten his blue numberplate. And it's extremely important for him to have it, because on the plate there are three Hebrew letters that only he can understand. He's the only one who knows what they mean and it's crucial that he interpret them. I begin running frantically after him, running past the crowds and the stalls at Mahaneh Yehuda and through the Old City and down the streets of Yafo, but every time I think I see him, he turns a corner.

This dream always fills me with anguish. I'm anguished in the dream and I'm anguished when I wake up.

There are several variations to the dream; the details keep changing. I don't always run through the same streets, and I don't always see Ami turning corners. Sometimes he gets on a bus, and sometimes he's in a car and doesn't see me.

But the letters on the numberplate are always the same, and they always mystify me, not only in the dream but also when I wake up. The letters on the numberplate are *aleph*, *lamed*, *nun*. Vowel-sound, L-sound, N-sound.

Ellen? A truncated form of my own abandoned Hebrew name, Ilana? Or simply *ilan*, tree?

Or maybe it's the Arabic word, now also a Hebrew word, for hello, *ahlan*.

Lately a new possibility has occurred to me. Maybe the letters are transposed, and what they spell is *le'an*.

Where?

Where do we go from here? Or maybe the question is more personal. Where do I go from here?

⌒──⌒

Ami returned from the three-week interrogation in a state of complete exhaustion. He came up to Jerusalem, collapsed on the four-poster bed, and slept for three days straight. He only woke up to shower, eat, smile at me. Then he went back to sleep.

After three days he finally recovered. He sat up in bed and apologized for being so out of it. 'I think I'm ready to rejoin the human race,' he said.

'I missed you so much,' I told him. 'I had the weirdest three weeks, it was like something out of Agnon.'

'I can't wait to hear. But first I need to see whether my equipment is still in working order. If you're available to verify it, that is.'

'I'm available.' I started unbuttoning my shirt.

'No, let me undress you. I'm in a romantic mood.'

Later he said, 'Isn't the end of term coming up?'

'Yes, in January.'

'Let's go to London.'

'Really?'

'Really. And since I've just got a huge bonus, we'll go in high style. What do you say?'

'How high?'

'Very high. We'll stay at the Savoy.'

'The Savoy? Is that a real place?'

'So I've heard.'

'I've never been to London. I've never been anywhere. I had a stop-over at Heathrow once, but that was it. Four hours at Heathrow airport. Even that was exciting, hearing all the accents.'

'You'll like London.'

'I feel like I'm dreaming. I'm nervous about all this good luck. I'm nervous about being so happy.'

'Don't worry, it won't last.'

I was shocked when he said that. 'What do you mean?' I asked.

He laughed. 'Don't look so frightened. I didn't mean me. I didn't mean us. I want to make you happy, of course. Let's hope the good angels co-operate.'

'Are you happy?'

'Right at this moment, yes.'

I told him about everything that had happened while he was away. He wasn't too pleased about the horny blind man in the Morris Minor. 'Arsehole,' he said.

I asked him how the interrogation went. He said it went as well as could be expected. He said he couldn't perform miracles, but he had done an OK job, under the circumstances. A heavy character, extremely smart, extremely committed, and with military training ('though he wasn't trained for me,' Ami said); but he had done his best. A battle of wits, which on occasion he won. And he didn't want to think about it any more. He wanted to go dancing.

'Dancing?'

'Yes. Let's head back to Tel Aviv and go to Bar-Minan.'

'*Barminan*! Doesn't that mean corpse, or something?'

'It's a pun.'

'I've never been there.'

'It's a disco, right on campus. We can walk there from my place. But first we'll go and eat somewhere. Somewhere really nice.'

'I'm living off you,' I said. 'It sort of goes against my principles. To live off a man.'

'Don't think of it as my money. I don't. I think of it as a hand-out from the defence budget.'

'That's what this person I know at the university said. Eric. He said you were getting paid by the United States.'

'Yes, war is big business.'

Ami's attitude to money was even more careless than mine. He hated banks and kept huge amounts of cash in a kitchen drawer. He told me his bank manager was constantly after him to invest or at least open a deposit account, but he couldn't be bothered. Every now and then, when the manager couldn't bear it any longer, he simply went ahead and put some of the money away, and Ami signed on the dotted line.

'You're such a liar,' I told him, when we were back in Tel Aviv. He was cramming bills from the drawer into his wallet.

'You said you kept going back to your job because of the money. You don't seem to care about money at all.'

'I like having this house. I like having my car. I like helping my sister.'

'You know, Ami, some parts of you will always be a mystery to me.'

'I'm a mystery to myself, too. *Yalla*, let's go.'

Ami drove us to a small Polish restaurant and we ate a lot of heavy food, then went dancing at Bar-Minan and we danced almost non-stop for three hours. Ami was a good dancer, and we really got into it. I remember the dress I wore that night, and the sandals. A wine-coloured backless dress with spaghetti straps and high platform sandals. Ami wore jeans and a T-shirt that had the words 'Here for the long haul' printed on it in English.

The next day he made a few phone calls, booked a flight to Heathrow and made a reservation at the Savoy Hotel. He couldn't get a suite on the river side, he said, but the travel agent had promised him the next best thing.

～──◯

A postcard from Ibrahim today. The sun rising over the sea, or maybe setting. On the other side, in Hebrew: 'MJ says you're looking for me. Call me. Call. Ibrahim.' Followed by his old phone number in Tel Aviv. I was right, he hasn't moved, he's still there, in the same flat on Edelson Street.

~~~~~

On the first day of my break Ibrahim called and asked Ami for a lift up north. He wanted to see his family and he suggested that the four of us go together, make a day of it.

We drove to Ibrahim's apartment on a Monday morning in late January. It was drizzling and overcast, pissy weather, Ami said. Ibrahim was already downstairs, wearing a long-sleeved white shirt and his favourite waistcoat, black felt with elaborate green embroidery. He was surrounded by cardboard boxes, which were filled with the things he was taking to his family: a rolled-up carpet, dishes, a kettle, jeans of all sizes, shoes, notebooks, clothes pegs, food. Also tools and some building supplies. We began loading the car. The box I was carrying contained about a dozen packets of Osem soup bits, a pair of corduroy trousers, and (for some reason this broke my heart) a colouring book and crayons. 'I have one who's crazy about these Osem bits,' Ibrahim told me, when he handed me the box. 'He's an Osem bits addict.'

There wasn't much room left in the car after everything had been loaded, and I offered to sit in the back with Mary Jo, since I was almost exactly half Ibrahim's size.

Ibrahim wanted to go to his village alone, so the plan was to give him the car in Nazareth and wait for him there. It was nearly ten by the time we reached Nazareth, and Ibrahim said he'd be back by two at the latest. We decided to meet at a café on Paulus VI Street.

We saw Ibrahim off and began walking somewhat aimlessly through Nazareth. It was still grey and chilly, but at least it had stopped raining. Mary Jo was delighted to be in Nazareth, and we were impressed by how well she knew the city. She led us through the narrow, ancient streets with breezy indifference to the open sewers that ran through some of the streets and the dank alleys that smelt of refuse. She'd brought her camera, and when we passed a docile donkey standing alone at the entrance to a small courtyard, she insisted on taking a photo of me and Ami standing next to it. I still have the photo, with the black wet spikes of the courtyard gate in the background, the donkey staring vacantly into space, and Ami with his arm around me in the foreground. Ami is smiling: he was amused by Mary Jo's enthusiasm.

'Sorry I couldn't get on the donkey,' I said, then regretted my words immediately, thinking I might have offended Mary Jo.

But she only laughed. 'Yes, too bad we don't have a pillow to stuff under your shirt.'

We had lunch at the café on Paulus VI Street. Then we waited for Ibrahim, but he didn't turn up. Mary Jo suggested we visit the Salesian Church of Jesus the Adolescent, and return in an hour. 'It's an amazing place,' Mary Jo said. 'You wouldn't want to miss it.' We gave the waiter a message for Ibrahim in case he arrived while we were gone.

We set out on foot, but the uphill walk was too much for me, and we took a taxi for the last stretch.

The church really was impressive, with angled stairways on either side leading to a massive arched door and more arches alternating with circles all the way to the spire. It stood on a hill that overlooked the entire city. The three of us stopped to look out at Nazareth, at the tiny faded houses, still and silent in the misty haze. We all felt the same thing: the impossible weight of history, the beauty and sadness of it.

'Can we go in?' I wondered.

'I don't know whether it's open,' Mary Jo said.

We climbed the stairs. The door was unlocked, but the church was empty. I led the way down the aisle, and sat in one of the pews. Ami and Mary Jo sat down beside me. The distant ceiling, a dizzying display of intersecting arches, was somehow both delicate and assertive, and made me feel magically protected. I was exhausted by the day's excursion and I lay on the pew with my knees up and my head on Ami's lap. Mary Jo shut her eyes and appeared to be praying.

We stayed there for a long time. Ami stroked my hair while Mary Jo prayed. A nun appeared out of nowhere and walked up the aisle. Her small, determined steps woke us from our trance and we rose self-consciously from our seat and left the church. We returned to the restaurant but there was still no sign of

Ibrahim. We had coffee and cake, and then we waited. We waited another two hours. I was bored and restless and Mary Jo began to fret. 'He's never this late,' she said. 'Something must have happened.' Ami decided to enquire at the police station. He offered to go alone, but I could tell Mary Jo wanted us to stay together. We walked to the police station and Ami asked whether there had been any problems in the area, but the police officer said everything was fine. 'Arabs have a different sense of time,' he said pleasantly. 'Relax. He'll be back.'

We had no choice but to go back to the restaurant and order supper. We weren't very hungry, but the food was excellent and we enjoyed it. The waiter was amused by our despondent appearance. 'Still waiting for your friend?' he chuckled.

At eleven Ibrahim finally returned. We were on our fourth round of coffee and pistachio nuts. 'Sorry,' he said cheerfully. 'I got caught up in a huge dispute, unbelievable. I couldn't leave, I had to help settle it. It's a good thing I showed up today.'

'We may as well stay here for the night,' Mary Jo said. 'What do you think?'

Ami and I didn't answer. We had no idea how much money Ibrahim had on him.

But the waiter overheard Mary Jo and, like an angel sent from heaven, he came to our rescue. 'Yes, yes! Stay! I know a good place, cheap. Come, I'll take you myself, a real bargain, twelve lirot for the night.'

We all got into Ami's car; the waiter in front, Ibrahim driving, Ami, Mary Jo and me in the back. 'Nice car,' the waiter said. 'Very nice. Your car?'

'No. His car,' Ibrahim said.

'Your car?' The waiter turned round to look at Ami.

'It was a present,' Ami said.

'Why doesn't God send me such presents?' the waiter said. 'Here, here!' he exclaimed. We pulled up in front of a monastery. 'Wait,' the waiter instructed us. He left the car, walked through the gates of the monastery, knocked on the heavy door. After a few minutes two elderly monks in grey habits opened the door and the waiter spoke to them in a low voice. Then he turned towards the car and waved us in.

The monks were welcoming, despite the late hour. The one in charge of the guest rooms wrote down our names in an account book. He asked for our IDs so he could record the numbers next to our names. Ami, Ibrahim and I produced ours, but Mary Jo didn't have anything on her. Since she wasn't a citizen she didn't have an ID, and she'd left both her student card and her passport in Tel Aviv.

The monk puzzled over the situation for a moment, then decided to cross out her name. The price was even better than we'd expected, because although it was twelve lirot for a room, it turned out we'd be sharing one room. Ami paid and told Ibrahim they'd settle it later; Ibrahim slapped him on the back and said something in Arabic; something slightly lewd, I think, judging by the guilty look on Ami's face as he smiled.

The monk shut his account book and showed us to a large high-ceilinged dormitory room that held eight or nine beds. There was no lock on the door.

Ibrahim and Mary Jo pushed together two beds at one end of the room and Ami and I pushed together two beds at the other end. Ibrahim pulled a joint out of his shirt pocket and lit up. Ami and I joined him and the four of us sat together on the improvised double bed and passed round the joint.

'What a day!' Ibrahim said. 'First this huge dispute. My great-uncle spent six years waiting for a permit to build a house for his son and daughter-in-law. Meanwhile his son died and now the widow's father thinks he should be allowed to use the permit for his daughter and her kids, but my great-uncle thinks the permit is his, because he's the one who applied. The whole village was split – you can't imagine the level of tension. I finally managed to settle it. I got them to come to an arrangement, though I almost had a nervous breakdown in the process. And then there's my eldest, Tufiq. I don't know what I'm going to do about him. He's stuck, he's completely stuck. I keep suggesting he come to live with me, help out at the garage, but he says he'd rather die than work for Jews.'

'How old is he?' I asked, surprised that Ibrahim had a son old enough to help out at a garage.

'Seventeen.'

'That's impossible!' I said.

'I started young. I was his age when he was born.'

'Is he the Osem soup bits addict?'

Ibrahim laughed. 'Yeah, he won't work for Jews but he can't get enough of their food.'

Ami said, 'Why doesn't he continue his studies?'

'That's exactly the problem. He won't work for Jews and he won't study with them either. I'm telling you, he's out of his mind. Meanwhile his closest friend is a volunteer from the kibbutz next door to us, a Jew from Birmingham. They've been in trouble, the two of them. Driving without a licence, trespassing, I don't know exactly, my wife was a bit vague. I need to spend more time at home.'

'Teenagers go through all sorts of things,' Ami said.

'I don't know.' He took a last drag on the joint and stubbed it out on the iron bedframe. 'I need to give him something, but I don't know what. It eludes me.'

'Why doesn't he come to stay with you without working?'

'He has to do something. He can't sit at home all day sulking. He takes after his grandfather, my wife's father, possibly the most stubborn man ever born to the human race. Of course, it's thanks to our grandparents' stubbornness that we still have our village. One day I'll show you around, when I have more time. It's so beautiful up there, it takes your breath away.'

'What's your wife like?' Mary Jo asked suddenly. She spoke to Ibrahim in English, which he understood but didn't like to speak, and he spoke to her in Hebrew, which she understood but didn't like to speak. 'Does she know about me?'

'My wife is brilliant,' Ibrahim said. 'She's working on trying to get money for a library for our village. She writes, she sings, she's amazing, that woman.'

'Do you miss her?'

Ibrahim put his arm around Mary Jo. 'Of course I miss her, what do you think?'

'Does she know about me?'

'You know, sweetheart, some things belong in our hearts, not in our conversations.'

'Sorry.'

'Life's a mess, Mary Jo.' He used the word *balagan*.

'I just wouldn't want to think I was hurting her.'

'She's very independent. She wants to integrate the women's liberation movement into Muslim culture. There's a challenge . . .' He drew Mary Jo down on the bed and stretched out on top of her, pressing his forehead against hers. Ami and I retreated to our own beds. Ami turned off the light, and the four of us undressed.

Ami and I settled into our usual sleeping positions, his legs twined around my legs, his arm around my waist. Suddenly we heard a small bird-like fluttering, tiny little breaths, followed by uninhibited masculine groans and the unmistakable sound of a mattress bearing rhythmical activity.

Ami and I had no idea what to do: it was impossible to

stay in the room, impossible to leave. We were also afraid
that we would start laughing, and that Ibrahim and Mary Jo
would be offended. The only solution, it seemed, was to be
polite and follow suit. I remembered the conversation I'd
had with Mary Jo about Ibrahim's powers of endurance and
I wondered how we'd manage for an entire hour. At some
point we'd finish and they'd still be at it, and we'd be back
where we started.

Luckily, though, Ibrahim was either unusually turned on by
all the activity in the room, or else it was his second time that
day and he was tired; in any case, he and Mary Jo finished
before we did. We knew it was over because Ibrahim's orgasm
was accompanied by a loud roar. I hoped the monks wouldn't
be alarmed.

Ami lost his erection at that point. Unlike Ibrahim, he
couldn't quite ignore the fact that he had an audience.

'God be praised,' Ibrahim said, to no one in particular. He
said it in Hebrew and then he said it in Arabic.

Ami and I burst out laughing.

Ibrahim laughed too. 'What else were we put on this planet
for, I ask you?' he said.

'I'm sure you're right,' Ami said.

The conversation between the two men continued along
those lines until Mary Jo, who seemed to feel that things had
gone far enough, interrupted them: 'I need the bathroom,' she
said firmly. 'Ibrahim, turn on the light.'

The two of us dressed and left the room, and by the time we returned our men were snoring.

$\sim\!\!-\!\!\circ$

A man and a woman can meet near the well or at the marketplace, they can marry or not marry; but knowing one another, as in 'Cain knew his wife and she conceived and bore Enoch,' is a different thing entirely. To know the men and women we love and desire is to know the bodies under their clothes. You can't know what you can't see or touch or feel. Until then you're only guessing.

The Hebrew word *balagan* comes from the Farsi word for the improvised stage on which plays are performed on market days in Iran. The word came to refer to improvisation in general, then expanded semantically to mean, in Hebrew, mess or disorder, whether during a battle or after a birthday party or because of a divorce. The word is usually used indulgently, in a resigned way; sometimes it is applied to the entire political situation, the entire conflict, the entire Middle East.

༄ — ༄

Two days later Ami and I flew to London.

Even though I was excited about the trip, I slept from the minute the plane took off until we landed at Heathrow. We took the underground and then a cab to the Savoy. Hundreds of English novels were coming to life around me, and every detail was a delight: the antique-looking black cab, the white-haired driver in uniform, his astounding courtesy.

'I can't believe I'm here, it's like someone said "Open, Sesame" and the door of a magic cave slid back to let me in,' I said. 'That's how I felt when I got to Israel.'

'How long did it last, that feeling?'

'I still have it, in a way. And I think if I lived here I'd have it permanently too. It's something basic, some sort of connection you feel with certain places.'

The driver let us out at the hotel. 'Not bad,' I said, as we entered the lobby at the Savoy. 'I could get used to this.'

I noticed people staring at us surreptitiously. They were sure Ami was famous, and they were trying to place him. We did not look very glamorous: we had one knapsack between us; Ami was wearing his jeans and denim jacket; my brown corduroy jacket had lost some of its pile. But this only made us more interesting: we were not only stars, apparently, but stars who were too cool to care.

As soon as we were in our room I announced theatrically, 'I am entering the WC.' I was pleased with my English vocabulary.

I was wearing a black dancer's leotard with my jeans, which made going to the bathroom a bit of a hassle because I had to strip just to pee. Ami was amused by my difficulty.

When I was finished, I stretched out on the bed. 'Have you ever been here before?' I asked.

'Not to this hotel. I've been to London once before.'

'With Ingrid?'

'Yes.'

'Where did you stay?'

'A small bed-and-breakfast.'

'So you know London.'

'No, not at all. We got lost several times.'

'What did you do here?'

'Well, as you know, Ingrid was into music, and she wanted to go to concerts and recitals. So we spent the entire time doing just that. In fact, that was the main reason we came here.'

'What about what you wanted?'

'I was perfectly happy going to concerts, Lily. We heard Janet Baker. It was an unforgettable experience.'

'Imagine living your whole life in places like this. You'd have to become decadent, you'd have no choice.'

'While our faculties are still intact, let's decide what we want to do.'

'I want to walk. I want to go to the National Gallery and walk around and see plays. I want to see *Bathers at Asnières* in real life. I want to see Trafalgar Square.'

So that was what we did on the first day. We walked and window-shopped and people-watched. Ami said he could no longer bear my ratty shoulder-bag, once bright-striped linen but now rather grey, and he bought me a hand-made leather one. The sun made a brave effort to warm us until early afternoon, then gave up. Ami didn't mind the cold, but I was shivering, so we took a cab to the National Gallery and wandered happily through the rooms until dinner-time. We ate at a basement restaurant on St. Martin's Lane. Its brick walls were decorated with artistic black-and-white photos of naked people, some of whom appeared to be our waiters. In the evening we went to the Royal Court theatre to see *Sizwe Bansi is Dead*.

We were in the foyer, waiting for the doors to open, when Ami said, 'Use all your intuition, Lily. Right now. Focus.' I'd just returned from the cloakroom and I was watching the urgent line-up at the bar with interest. One thing I liked about Israel was that no one drank. I didn't have to feel left out.

'Focus on what?'

'Something's happening, right now in this place. Try to feel it.'

'I don't know what you mean.'

'Concentrate.'

'Is it something I can see?'

'No, just something you can feel.'

'We're not about to be taken hostage?'

'No, nothing like that.'

Then it came to me. 'We're being followed!' I exclaimed.

'Very good.'

'Uh-oh, maybe I shouldn't have said that so loudly. Are we in trouble?'

'No, we're perfectly safe. In fact, it's like having our own personal bodyguard.'

'I don't get it. Who's following us?'

'Israeli intelligence, who else?'

'Why?'

'They don't trust me,' he said.

'But you work for them, why would they follow you?'

'They use me. But they know how I feel about everything, I never make a secret of it. So they figure I'm doing it for the money, and that if I can be bought by them I can be bought by anyone. They think I might be here in London to make some contacts.'

'That's almost impossible to believe.'

'They like to think of themselves as being on top of things.'

'Are they listening in to this conversation?'

'You tell me.'

I looked around discreetly. 'No,' I said.

'That's right. They're keeping their distance, and it's too crowded and noisy.'

'You know who it is?'

'I have an idea.'

'When did you notice?'

'I had a feeling at Heathrow, but I wasn't sure until we got to the gallery. I think I was half expecting it.'

'What about the last time you were here? Were you followed then, too?'

'I don't think so. We were living like hermits in those days, they weren't that worried about me.'

'Oh, God, this is my fault!'

'Of course not.'

'It is. I should have lied at that interview, I should have pretended to be an entirely different person, I should have said that Salim broke up with me because of my politics!'

'Who's Salim?'

'They knew I'd gone out with this guy I met on a film set. I was an extra in this film, I was an Israelite coming out of Egypt, and I met him there. It wasn't anything, we only went out for a short time, and then suddenly, just like that, he wouldn't see me. He never said why. I never knew why. I don't know what happened, he seemed to really like me.'

'They asked you about that at the interview?'

'Yes, I have no idea how they knew, he never came

to the halls, I never had a chance to introduce him to anyone. But that's probably why they're on your case now. Because of me.'

Ami stared at me, and for once I couldn't tell what he was thinking.

Then he said, 'It has nothing to do with you, Lily. It has to do with me. I'm sorry about the interview. If I'd known I would never have arranged it.'

'I didn't mind. It didn't bother me.'

'I'm really sorry,' he repeated.

The lights flashed and we entered the theatre and took our seats. The play was short but full of wonderful twists and turns, and the production was excellent. I hoped whoever was following us was enjoying it as much as we were.

When we returned to the hotel we found ourselves alone in the lift. Ami pressed a red button and it came to an abrupt stop between two floors. He slid his hand inside my pants.

'Ami! What are you doing?'

He didn't answer. He was too busy.

'You've gone crazy,' I said, but I didn't stop him.

Finally he released me. 'I've always wanted to do that,' he said, pressing the button to our floor. 'Since I was sixteen.'

'Jesus.'

'Yes. And now I've done it. And at the Savoy Hotel.'

'You're such a boy! Well, did it live up to your expectations? Or, shall I say, fantasies?'

'In this case I'd say reality surpassed fantasy.'

As he unlocked the door to our room he motioned to me not to say anything. We stepped inside and he shut the door and began looking for a bug. He found it almost immediately, on the inside of a lampshade.

He decided to have some fun.

'I've made arrangements to meet my contact at Hyde Park, tomorrow at three in the afternoon,' he said. 'Will you be OK on your own, Lily?'

'Uh-huh,' I said.

'I'm a little concerned about the Mossad,' he said. 'I have to admit I'm worried about their competence. How can I sleep safely at night knowing my protectors are not ever-vigilant? "For he shall not sleep, he shall not slumber."'

'Who?'

'The enemy, Lily. And I put my faith in the Mossad. I trust them to protect us from the insomniac enemy. And now all my confidence is shaken. That ad I put in the London *Times*, "Israeli state secrets for sale", they didn't even notice it.'

It was hard not to giggle.

'I wonder what I'll do with the twenty-five dollars the Palestinians gave me for revealing their own secrets to them.'

'Oh, no, Ami,' I said. 'It's Monopoly money!'

'Never mind, there are plenty of others lining up in response to my ad. Already the Albanian secret service has contacted me.'

'Let's have sex,' I said, in English. 'My lips are hot for you.'

'Yes, but we'd better take some security precautions first. In case this room is *bugged*.'

He removed the bug from the lampshade. Then he checked the phone receiver but he couldn't find anything. He used my nail file to unscrew the bottom and he took it apart. In the end the recording device was in the receiver after all, he just hadn't identified it at first.

'How do you know about bugs?' I asked.

'You call this knowing?' he said, looking at the demolished telephone, its various parts scattered hopelessly on the bed.

We both burst out laughing.

'The hotel's going to charge you for ripping their phone apart,' I said.

'I'll tell them to send the bill to the Mossad.'

'What will they think?'

'That we're Israeli spies. Or rich eccentrics with a phone fetish.'

He wrapped the bugs in a towel and stuffed them into the wardrobe.

'A part of me wants to throw them down the lavatory,' he sighed, 'but I know how expensive they are, and I just can't. We'll take them home with us.'

'I feel nervous now. Isn't this like contempt of court, or

something? I feel like I've done something really illegal, making fun of our secret service.'

'I'll visit you in prison.'

'I'm serious.'

'I wouldn't worry too much about it.'

'But you probably weren't supposed to tell me about the bugs. And I made those cracks!'

'They shouldn't have put them there in the first place.'

'How did they do it?'

'Just like in espionage films.'

'They really don't trust you.'

'Think how much I know. I know much more than someone like me is supposed to know. They're in a fix.'

'Is your house bugged too?'

'Of course not. Think how illegal that would be. That's not our style.'

'Will they keep on following us?'

'Yes, but we'll ignore them. We'll make them jealous by showing them how much we love each other and what a great time we're having.'

'Sounds good.'

He lay down beside me on the bed.

'Am I entitled to all this?' I asked.

'Let's discuss that after sex.'

'Thank you for bringing me here. Today was a perfect day.'

'Yes, it was.'

As usual he began pursuing various topics of conversation in bed, but when he reached my breasts he suddenly stopped talking. It was as though he'd suddenly noticed something strange about me. He went on stroking me, but now his touch felt inquisitive. Then he slid his hand down to my belly and looked at me.

I looked back at him in confusion. 'What's going on?'

'When did you have your last period?'

'I don't know, I'm not regular.'

'You don't keep track?'

'I've never been regular. It's always been erratic.'

'The last period I remember was in Freud's flat, our first day there. Unless you had one while I was away for my three-week stint?'

'No . . . no, I think that was the last time, probably. But it doesn't mean anything. I often go for a long time without having a period, and then suddenly it comes.'

'You're pregnant, Lily.'

'I'm not. I've been using a diaphragm.' I bit my lips. In fact, I'd run out of spermicide at one point and I hadn't bought a new tube right away.

'What aren't you telling me?' he said, and for a split second I imagined what it might be like for his prisoners to hear that hypnotic question, asked in what I can only describe as an irresistible tone of voice.

'I ran out of spermicide. But that was just once or twice . . .'

He beamed at me. His face really seemed to be glowing.

'I can't have a baby!' I shrieked.

'Calm down,' he said.

'I can't have a baby,' I repeated.

'Because?'

'Because I'm too young and I want to do a Master's and a Ph.D and I don't want to experience labour and it's entirely out of the question. It's the furthest thing from my mind.'

He smiled happily. 'I was afraid you'd say it was because of something to do with us, with me.'

'No, that doesn't come into it. I feel I've known you for ever.'

'Let's think how far gone you are.'

'How can you be sure I'm pregnant?'

'I'm not sure. But I think there's a good chance, Lily. What do you think?'

'If my last period was when we first tried out that bed, that was . . . the beginning of November? And now it's January . . . I don't know how you count this sort of thing.'

'I think from your last period. You know, this would explain why you've been sleeping so much, and why you had those dizzy spells when I was away. And why you've been going to the lavatory even more than usual.'

'I can't believe it. It's impossible.'

'I don't know how it took me so long to notice.'

'I can't have a baby, Ami. I'm scared. I'm *terrified*.'

'Let's not talk about it now. Why don't we just give it time to sink in?' But he couldn't stop grinning.

'Why do you look so happy? This is a disaster!'

'I want a child,' he said simply. 'I want a daughter. And I want her with you.' He began stroking my belly, then kissing it. Then he lay his cheek on it.

'You're making it impossible for me to refuse,' I said. 'This is so unfair. What about my exams?'

'You wouldn't be due until . . . August? You'd make it. Or you could take your exams later, they're flexible about things like that.'

'I'm not having a baby. I'm only twenty.'

'We'd get help, you could go on with your studies.'

'If you think I'd leave my baby with anyone after what I went through on the kibbutz, you're crazy. I wouldn't leave my baby with a stranger for five minutes, let alone days at a time. I don't know how anyone can.'

'I'd look after her when you went to your classes.'

'How could you go on with your job if you had a baby? You'd have to split yourself into two.'

'I've been living that way for years.'

'I can't do it. I'm scared of labour.'

'We'd take Lamaze lessons, and I'd stay with you the whole time. We could even go to Sweden if you want – they have all sorts of things they do there to make it easier.'

'Sweden . . .'

'Yes. If you want.'

'I'm scared. This is so out of the blue.' But suddenly the idea of a tiny child growing inside me was thrilling.

'Take time to think about it.'

'You really want this?'

'Yes.'

'I suppose we'll have to find a way to get married now.' We hadn't made any marriage plans because Ami was disgusted by the idea of a religious ceremony, which was the only way to get married in Israel. And so we put it off, thinking only that we'd do it some time before August, when I was due to be drafted.

'We can go to Cyprus,' Ami said. 'Or we can get Shulamit Aloni to marry us – she performs civil marriages.'

'I don't think Shulamit Aloni is a good idea – her marriages aren't really valid. Think of the bureaucratic hassle. We'd be better off with Cyprus.'

'Or else we can find one of those kibbutz rabbis who cheat.'

'Kibbutz rabbis?'

'Rabbis who aren't that strict. They do all the kibbutz weddings – I can get a name.'

I realized that he looked completely happy for the first time since I'd met him.

'Now that I know you have our baby inside you I'm even more turned on by you, if that's possible.'

'I'll have to call you *ba'ali*!'

'We're stuck with a five-thousand-year-old language.'

'I'm confused. I'm scared. I'm sort of dazed.'

'I'll help you through everything.'

'Is there really a human being growing inside me?'

'It *does* seem improbable — like something out of a science-fiction novel. I'm sorry, I can't wait any longer, I'm plunging in, is that OK? You seem pretty wet.'

'Plunge ahead.'

~—~

Ba'al was the Zeus of the Canaanites. He was a very alluring god, the sort of god who kept drawing people in, much to the biblical God's rage and dismay.

There were some lesser or more localized Canaanite gods as well, such as Ba'al Zvuv (Lord of the Flies; the inspiration behind Beelzebub), but they didn't have the same mass appeal as Ba'al.

The Hebrew word *ba'al*, not surprisingly, means 'lord', 'master' or 'owner'. It also means 'husband'. In biblical and rabbinic times the verbal form meant 'to have intercourse with' (or, oddly, 'to have adulterous intercourse with a lover'), but that usage didn't penetrate colloquial Hebrew, although it appears in formal contexts.

The inflection *nu*, added at the end of a noun, means 'our'. For example, casualty is *ḥalal*; 'our casualties' is *ḥalaleynu*. That inflection (first person plural) used to be very widespread in Israel. On the news, the announcer would say; 'Our forces [*koḥotaynu*] sustained one dead and two wounded. The families have been notified.' (You don't hear that any more, they no longer say 'our forces' in the media, they say 'IDF forces': they've become more sophisticated.) There was even a safe-driving advertisement on the radio that asked people not to drive recklessly because when people died on the roads it depleted our (human) resources.

It gives you a safe family feeling to use that inflection: you're not alone in the world. There's something reassuring about saying 'our language' and 'our presence' and 'our secret service'. You get swept into these things. And you never really get them out of your system. Deep down you always think, 'our forces'. Deep down you always think, 'our country'. Deep down you always think, 'our failure'.

✺

At breakfast the next morning an American woman approached us. She was wearing a jacket made of turquoise and scarlet patches stitched together with leather thongs. Her hair was stylishly wild, and she wore a wide belt with a metal buckle in the shape of a crocodile. 'Please excuse me, I couldn't control myself another minute,' she said, careful to smile warmly at me but really addressing Ami. 'I'm Marilyn Rose. I know I shouldn't be interrupting you like this but if I don't find out where I've seen you, I'll burst.'

'I'm sure you haven't seen us anywhere,' Ami said. 'Unless it was yesterday when we were out walking.'

'I can't place your accent. Where are you from?'

'Israel.'

'I thought I recognized a word of Hebrew here and there. I've been to Israel twice now. Beautiful. We climbed Masada, my husband and I, an amazing experience.'

'I'm glad you enjoyed it,' Ami said.

Her eyes narrowed slightly and she smiled reproachfully: she was no fool. 'So, Israeli . . . But I've seen you in a movie. I just know it.'

'No, I've never been in one. You can sit down, you know, if you like.'

'Oh, thank you! So you're not an actor?'

'I was once, but that was long ago.'

'I knew it! I knew it, I knew it, I knew it. In Israel?'

'Yes, years ago.'

'Listen, there are some people I want you to meet. Join us for dinner tonight. I think I have something that will interest you.'

'I don't act any more, Marilyn. I've retired.'

'Don't be ridiculous, there's no such thing. I think I have something very, very exciting for you,' she repeated. 'How about tonight at eight? In the Grill? May I ask you your names?' She looked at me and gave me a conspiratorial smile. She didn't want me to feel left out, especially if I might have some influence over Ami.

'I'm Lily,' I said. 'This is Ami. Ami Sarig.'

'Lily and Ami. That's so sweet. Will you persuade him to come, Lily?'

'We're seeing a play tonight,' I said. '*Dusa, Fish, Stas & Vi.*'

'Great, great! Come after the play, then, join us for drinks. We'll be at the bar, waiting for the ghosts of Hemingway and F. Scott to show up. And for you. Here's my room number. Well, I'll leave you two now, sorry for interrupting.'

When she left I said, 'She wants to turn you into a Hollywood star.'

'Who knows what she wants?'

'It's obvious. She must be some sort of agent or producer or something. Would you go if you were offered a part in a film?'

'I don't think it works like that.'

'Would you?'

'No, of course not.'

'Even just once, for the hell of it?'

'Even just once, for the hell of it.'

'Because you don't want to act?'

'Because I don't want to act.'

'Can we meet her just for fun?'

'If you want, Lily.'

But a few minutes later a waiter brought Ami a message on a slip of paper. Someone had phoned, he had to return the call immediately – it was urgent.

Ami swore. '*Kusukhtak*,' he said. 'Shit.'

'What is it?'

'I have no idea,' he said, tearing up the note and dropping the pieces into an ashtray.

'What's it all about?'

He didn't answer. His misery seemed to fill the lift as we rode up to our room, and I could tell that the four or five people who were with us sensed it as well. The phone in our room had been discreetly repaired while we were at breakfast; it was ringing when we walked in. At first Ami tried to ignore it, but finally he picked it up.

He listened to the person at the other end and then he said, again, '*Kusukhtak.*'

There was a long response and finally Ami slammed down the phone, without saying goodbye. His only contribution to the conversation had been that one word, *kusukhtak.*

'What is it?'

'I'm sorry, Lily, I have to leave. You can stay, of course. I don't know how long I'll be, though.'

'I don't want to stay without you. It's OK, Ami, it doesn't matter. We can come back any time, London will still be here. When do we have to leave?'

'Now. They're picking me up in ten minutes and driving me to the airport. They've already checked us out, we just have to return the key. But you can stay. I can tell them at the desk.'

'I'm coming with you.'

He was in a very bad mood. We packed our things, returned the room key and got into a car that was waiting for us in front of the hotel. The driver didn't speak to us and we didn't say anything either. We drove to an airfield somewhere, boarded a small aeroplane and flew back to Israel.

∽——∾

Is any other country in the world called, simply, 'the Land'? In Hebrew 'the State of Israel' and 'the Land' (*ha-aretz*) are perfect synonyms.

Things happen 'in the Land' (*ba-aretz*) and people go 'to the Land' (*la-aretz*) and anyone who isn't in Israel is 'outside the Land' (*ḥutz la-aretz*).

I would even say that 'the Land' is more common in everyday usage than 'Israel'.

After 1967, though, the word 'Israel' became more problematic. Before 1967 it meant 'the State of Israel'. But 'the State of Israel' did not include the territories, with its one million Palestinians.

When Begin became Prime Minister in 1977, he solved this problem by reintroducing the concept of the 'Land of Israel' (*eretz yisrael*). 'Israel' would refer to the land within the 1967 borders, and 'Land of Israel' (which before 1948 referred to Mandated Palestine) would refer to the whole shebang. Territories and all.

From now on 'the West Bank' would be known as Judea and Samaria, which is what some of those places were called in ancient times (and from now on we'd also be using the biblical unit *shekel* instead of pounds, as in 'Ephron answered Abraham and said, "My lord, listen to me, a piece of land worth four hundred *shekel* of silver, what is that between you and me?"')

The religious settlers, the ones who settled in the occupied territories because they felt the territories were a God-given inheritance, liked the phrase 'Land of Israel', *eretz yisrael*, because *eretz* is an important biblical concept. In the Bible, the word *eretz* means 'land' and 'earth' and 'nation'. It's one of the Bible's central preoccupations. For the religious settlers, 'inheritance' and 'salvation' and 'redemption' are all tied up with the idea of *eretz yisrael*. 'Expulsion of the Arab population' is also tied up with the idea of *eretz yisrael*.

Before the first *intifada*, 'Israel' (*yisrael*) and 'Land of Israel' (*eretz yisrael*) got muddled a lot of the time. People forgot about the distinction between the two.

But for a long time now, everyone in Israel has been acutely aware of the difference between 'Israel', which is the place within the 1967 borders, and 'Land of Israel' (or, alternatively, 'Greater Israel'), which includes the occupied territories.

But 'the Land' (*ha-aretz*) still means the place now known as Israel. With or without the territories. With or without Sinai. With or without the Golan Heights. Before or after the British Mandate. Before or after the creation of a state. That word doesn't deal with borders or governments. It's a free-floating word, flexible and accommodating.

◦—◦

The plane landed in a military airfield at dusk. In the silvery gold light the helicopters and oddly shaped planes looked hazy and small, like toys on a window-sill. Two cars were waiting for us: a taxi for me and a black Mercedes for Ami.

I held on to Ami. Until that moment I had accepted the change of plan, the uncomfortable flight back, the rushed return to Israel. But suddenly I could not bear him to leave. 'Don't go,' I said. 'Don't go, I have a terrible feeling I'll never see you again if you leave now. Please. Please, please.'

Ami smiled. 'I promise to be back, Lily. I'm not going anywhere dangerous, just to Jenin. It's a short drive away.'

'Don't go,' I begged him.

'I promise to phone you. I'll phone you as soon as I get there.'

'Why is it so urgent?'

'You know why.'

'*Nu*, Ami,' the driver of the Mercedes called out.

Ami pulled three hundred lirot out of his pocket. 'Good thing I didn't change all our money,' he said. 'Here, buy some groceries, we're all out. I'll take the knapsack. And I'll be back as soon as I can.' Then he kissed me. 'Take care of our baby.'

I didn't answer. I watched him leave, I watched the black Mercedes speed away. Then I climbed into the back seat of the taxi. 'I know I'll never see him again,' I said. 'Our baby will be an orphan.'

'A baby?' the driver said. He was a large, hairy man; he resembled a bear. '*Mazel tov!*' He didn't ask me for an address; he had been told in advance where to take me.

'Yes, a baby orphan.'

'My wife is exactly the same,' he said. 'Every time I leave for reserve duty, it's the same thing – "If only you didn't have to go, what will I do without you for a whole month?" Only in her case it's a big act.' He chuckled. 'She can't wait to hop into bed with her lover.'

'Her lover?'

'She thinks I don't know. She thinks I don't have a nose.'

'I assume you also have someone.'

'Maybe.'

'Are you with them?'

'Who?'

'The other driver.'

'Me? No way, I'm just a taxi driver.'

'Who are they?'

'How should I know? I don't ask and I don't know.'

'Don't take me home,' I said suddenly.

'Oh?'

'I don't want to go home.'

'Uh-huh,' he said insinuatingly.

'Don't be an idiot.'

'Well, where do you want to go?'

I wanted to visit someone, tell someone I was pregnant. I considered taking up Dr Grubach on her offer and visiting her in the Old City, but I couldn't drop in on her unannounced, and I had no idea whether she had a phone or how to find her number; only home owners were listed in the phone book. Bracha would feed me and make a fuss: I didn't feel up to her attentions. And I wasn't in the right mood for Mary Jo and Ibrahim. I finally decided to try Sheila. I didn't know whether she'd be at Bar Ilan, because she was on holiday too, and she had an endless supply of relatives all over the country who were constantly urging her to stay with them. On the other hand, she was usually behind with her work, and there was a chance she was still at the university catching up on overdue essays. She was studying psychology.

'Take me to Bar Ilan,' I said.

'Bar Ilan. Interesting.'

I ignored the driver after that, and he didn't say anything either. But as he pulled up in front of the gate at Bar Ilan, he said, 'I was just kidding, yes? No hard feelings?' I could see he was worried he'd get into trouble with the people who had hired him to drive me.

'I'll think about it,' I said.

The guard at the gate asked me suspiciously who I wanted to see. He was an old man, white-haired, with beady eyes and a nasty mouth. 'Are you a human or a beast?' he asked, referring to the low cut of my leotard top, which left more skin exposed than he thought appropriate for the species.

'I'm a satyr,' I said.

'Huh?'

'A transsexual satyr.'

'Who are you here for?' He'd given up trying to understand me.

'Shlomit Weiss.' Sheila used her Hebrew name now that she was in Israel. 'In the new halls.'

'I'll take you,' he said. 'Follow me.' He didn't want to let me loose on campus.

He led me to Sheila's room, knocked loudly on the door and called, 'Someone here to see Shlomit.' Sheila's roommate opened the door. The rooms at Bar Ilan were a lot larger than the ones on Mount Scopus, and the door opened on to a small partitioned foyer in order to protect the privacy of the people inside.

'Someone here to see Shlomit,' the guard repeated.

'Oh, hi!' The roommate smiled at me. She had dimples and a halo of curly hair, and she was holding a paperback on Zen Buddhism, with which she waved away the guard. 'Pain in the arse,' she said, apparently not worried that the guard would hear her. 'Shlomit's at a party in Ramat Gan. Here, I'll give you the address. I was going to go, but I got my period and I feel like hell. Come in. Do you want some orange juice?'

'No, thanks. What happened to Sheila's old roommate?'

'Got married. And I took the first opportunity to switch rooms. My roommate was a total head case. Stayed up all night picking her toenails. What a nightmare. Shlomit is great. Sheila, I mean. I love her. Here's the address. Eleven Nordau Street. Listen, maybe I can find you a lift.'

'It's OK, I'll take a taxi. Is there a phone I can use?'

'Sure, I'll call you one.' She led me to a phone in the hallway, and waited with me for the taxi. 'Say hi to Shlomit for me,' she said when the taxi arrived. 'Tell her to be good.'

The taxi smelled of coconut sun lotion, and all at once I was transported back in time to a camping trip I went on with my family. The camping site was near a lake, and I had wandered off and met the manager's son, who offered to take me on his raft. I couldn't swim, but I knew I would be in good hands. The entire scene came back to me: tiny insects swirling in the water, the cloudless sky, my hand on the curved logs of the raft as we drifted towards deep water, far from the shore, the caravans and tents growing smaller and smaller. The boy wore shorts and a white sleeveless top, and his shoulder blades smelt of coconut sun lotion. I was excited by the adventure, but when I returned from my little voyage my father was angry: he thought I'd drowned.

'Where you from?' The driver woke me from my trance.

'Lethe.'

'Where's that?'

'Near Hades.'

'Never heard of it.'

'We don't get a lot of visitors, these days.'

'You go to Bar Ilan?'

'No.'

'I didn't think so. What's your name, sweetheart?'

'Penelope.'

'You're one hell of a gorgeous chick. Want a good time? You won't regret it, you'll thank your stars you met me.' He turned round to exhibit his handsome face and show me what I'd be getting if we fucked. 'I'm Tal. Nice to meet you.' *Tal* means 'dew'. It always amazed me how many Israeli men had delicate, feminine names.

I didn't reply to Tal's greeting and he was offended. 'I said, nice to meet you,' he tried again.

'I heard you,' I said.

He was too offended to say any more. But as I was paying for the ride, he said, 'I apologize. I didn't realize you were religious. My apologies. I wish you good health and all the best.'

'It's OK,' I said. It seemed to be my day for contrite taxi drivers.

The door to the building on Nordau Street had been left

open, and I could hear loud music coming from upstairs. The party was on the second floor. A sign in English had been taped next to the peephole: 'Sex, drugs, rock & role. To enter at your own risk.'

I opened the door and walked in. The place was packed, and the energetic South American music blasting from two gigantic speakers urged its optimism upon all who entered.

I wove through the bodies in search of Sheila. I found her on the balcony. It was cool outside, and she was wearing the jersey I liked best, white with tiny pearl beads on the collar; it had belonged to her grandmother in Poland. The jersey suited her china-doll face, and she looked like someone transported to the present not only from another era but possibly from a more innocent world. She shrieked when she saw me. 'Lily! What are you doing here?'

'Your roommate gave me the address.'

'Great! What's going on? Come and meet everyone. Where have you been?'

'London, actually.' Suddenly I remembered the woman we were supposed to meet at the bar. 'Oh, no — I need a phone. Is there one here? I'll pay.'

'Sure.' I followed her to the bedroom. Several people were sitting on the bed, eating crisps and peanuts from plastic bowls. Despite the warning on the door, the party-goers on the bed were neat and contained, protected by identical, carefully constructed forts of coded behaviour. The girls wore loose tops with long sleeves and expansive skirts, and they pretended not to notice that the boys were leaning boldly against their arms. They were all making a mess, however. There were crumbs everywhere, and I felt bits of food disintegrating under my shoes.

I placed fifty lirot on the bedside table, shut the door against the music, and phoned the hotel. The connection was poor and I had to shout to make myself heard. I asked the hotel receptionist to tell Ms Rose that we had had to leave suddenly, an emergency, and I left our phone number. When the man at the other end realized who I was his tone changed. I was surprised that he recognized my name, but word of the dismantled phone and our mysterious departure must have circulated. In a sombre voice he said, 'Your message will be passed on.'

'So, what's going on?' Sheila asked.

'It's so noisy here.'

'I know. Let's go back to the balcony.'

Most of the space on the balcony was taken up by two fat male students who were sitting Buddha-style on the tiled floor and eating sunflower seeds. They were surrounded by mounds of husks. Sheila and I squeezed into a corner. 'Nice bag, where'd you get it?' She ran her fingers along the carved flowers of my leather handbag.

'London.'

'Very nice.'

'You can have it. Here, take it. I can get another one any time.'

Sheila tried to resist, but I insisted. I gave her the bag, keeping only my wallet and ID, which I slid into my back pocket.

'You're mad,' Sheila said, 'but thanks. What were you doing in London?'

'I went there with my new boyfriend, Ami.'

'Great, for how long?'

'Well, it was supposed to be for a week, but he was called back by the army on the second day. There was some emergency.'

'Really! He works for the army?'

'Yes.'

'So, where did you stay?'

'The Savoy, for a treat.'

'The Savoy! How could you afford that?'

'He has a pretty good income.'

'Oh, yeah? He must be doing important stuff.'

'I guess.'

'People who work for the Mossad aren't even allowed to tell their wives.'

'He's definitely not with the Mossad. They'd never take someone like him. He has Palestinian friends.'

'That's probably just a cover-up. And what's this Palestinian business?'

'Well, you know . . .' I said hesitantly. I was a little afraid of Sheila. She could be quite bossy.

The fat students turned towards us, interested. 'What's that you're talking about?' one said. They continued to crack sunflower seeds as they spoke.

'Palestinians!' Sheila said, and they all burst out laughing.

'No such thing,' one of the students said. 'It's just geography, it's not a race or a nation. They lost their land, they lost it because of their own stubborn refusal to compromise. They lost it because they can't stop hating us.'

'You'd hate us too, if you were them,' I said.

'What have we done? We gave them every chance to work things out. And they didn't take it. They could have changed their lives a million times over. They have only themselves to blame, their own backward culture. Look at what the Jews did here in such a short time. All they can think of is where to throw the next bomb. Why don't other Arab countries help them out? The Arabs just don't care about each other.'

I felt a wave of depression sweeping over me, like a soft wind from hell. Sheila saw at once that something was wrong. We had once been very close. 'What is it? Are you OK?'

'Yes, I'm fine.'

'You seem down.'

'No, I'm fine. I'm pregnant.'

'Oh, no!'

'No, no, we're in love. We're getting married.'

'Wow! Since when?'

'It just happened fast.'

'*Mazel tov!*' Everyone on the balcony began congratulating me.

'Hey, you gonna have Palestinians at your wedding?' one of the students said. He started laughing, but his laughter turned into a cough; he seemed to be choking on one of the sunflower seeds.

'How can you laugh?' I said, my voice unsteady with the fear of fighting back. 'Don't you know how most Arabs live? How they're treated? How can you not care?'

'I do care,' the student who wasn't choking said. 'I feel bad for them, but it isn't our responsibility.'

'It is. We run this country now, we're responsible for everyone here.'

'You're so naïve. Don't you know that they want to take over this country? They don't want us here. And if we don't restrict them, they will take over. They'll arm themselves and they'll try to wipe us out.' His eyes widened as he imagined the gruesome details of this catastrophe. 'They don't want to be our friends. They want us to go back to the countries we came from.'

'Oh, who cares?'

No one spoke. Someone had changed the music to the songs of Naomi Shemer, and the students began to sing along loudly and off-key to '*Lu yehi*'. If only, if only.

'I need a toilet,' I said.

I made my way to the bathroom and locked the door. There were cigarette ends in the sink and rust stains in the toilet. A man's razor, sticky with hair and dried shaving soap, lay by the sink.

I ran out of the bathroom, out of the flat, out of the building. I ran down street after street. It was dark now, and cold. Finally I had to stop to catch my breath. I leaned against a hoarding and tried to do up my brown corduroy jacket, but the zip jammed. Ami had tried to persuade me several times to buy a winter coat, but I was attached to this jacket, which I had found in a flea-market in Jericho.

A man my age, perhaps a year or two older, came up to me and asked me for matches. He had red hair and freckles, and large eyes that looked at me searchingly through dark-framed glasses.

'Sorry, I don't smoke. Do you know the way to the sea?'

'You can't walk from here, it's too far.'

'Just point me in the right direction.'

'I guess you could take Arlozorov Street the whole way. But don't get confused, it turns into Jabotinsky Street at the station. Just keep going, and you'll get back on to Arlozorov Street.'

'Thanks. Can I ask you something?'

'Yes.'

'What are we doing here?'

'What everyone does everywhere,' he said. 'Trying to survive.'

'Trying to survive . . .'

'With a bit of luck. Because I wouldn't count on brains.'

'Why not?'

'Because people are too emotional. There are seven hundred Greek tragedies taking place inside everyone. And another three hundred stories by Kafka.'

'Yes. Well . . . thanks for the directions.'

'Take care of yourself, Girl-with-jacket-looking-for-the-sea.' He took a notebook out of his pocket and began writing by the dim light of the street-lamp. He waved goodbye without looking up: he didn't want to break the flow of inspiration that had suddenly come to him.

I began walking towards the sea. The streets were nearly deserted, and the square concrete buildings seemed alien, shutting me out, shutting out anyone who wasn't safely at home. I was too unsettled to care, or to long for home. I reached the beach finally and continued north along the shore. Here and there lone men called out to me, but I ignored them and walked on, my eyes drawn to the inky waves.

I had come to a stone barrier, and was starting to walk round it when I heard voices: a woman pleading, a man shouting. On the other side of the barrier a man was holding a knife to a woman's face; with his other hand he held her wrists. The woman was sobbing. I backed away, terrified. 'I'll teach you a lesson you'll never forget,' the man was saying. 'Every time you look in the mirror you'll remember.'

I looked around frantically for someone who might be able to help, but this part of the beach was deserted. 'Excuse me,' I called. I waved politely. The man instinctively lowered his knife. 'Excuse me,' I said, coming closer, 'I was just wondering what time it was.'

He looked at me carefully and finally decided I was a stupid tourist. He was quite short, possibly even shorter than me, and the woman towered over him. In spite of this, they looked a little like twins, because they were both wearing identical black leather jackets and the woman's white suede skirt matched the man's white sailor's trousers.

The man checked his watch. 'Half past eleven,' he said.

'Thanks,' I said. 'Which way to Ramat Aviv, do you know?'

'You need the number six bus,' the woman said. 'It's a bit of a walk from here.'

'Go on, show her the way,' the man said. 'You're a lucky bitch,' he added.

The woman took my arm and steered me towards the street. Her suede skirt was fringed at the edge, and so short it looked more like a wide belt than a skirt. I wondered whether she was cold.

'I hate that fucking bastard,' she said, as soon as the man was out of earshot. 'Never trust a man. Never ever trust a man. Fucking liars.'

I tried to breathe deeply so that my heart would stop pounding so wildly.

She showed me to the bus stop. 'I hope the bus is still running.' She drew a packet of cigarettes out of her handbag and offered me one. 'Thanks,' I said. I took a cigarette and we lit up. I'd never smoked an ordinary cigarette before.

'You have a boyfriend?' she asked.

'Yeah, but he's away in Jenin.'

'Career?'

'Uh-huh.'

'What's he like?'

'He has an irregular schedule.'

She laughed. 'You're lucky if that's the worst of it.'

'Was he really going to use that knife?'

'Oh, you saw that?' She seemed embarrassed. 'What the hell,' she shrugged. 'Well, I'd better get going, the night's still young. Good luck, hey? You're a sweet kid . . . you wouldn't happen to have an extra ten lirot? That bastard took every last *agura* I had.'

I gave her a hundred-lirot note. She looked at the money with surprise and was about to say something, but changed her mind. 'Thanks. You're a sweet kid,' she repeated. Then she left.

A taxi slowed down and honked, but I didn't feel like talking to another taxi driver. Finally the bus arrived. A mad woman in the back seat kept saying over and over, '*Sheh-yamutu, sheh-yamutu.*' May they die, may they die. Everyone was relieved when she got off.

∽ —∾

My daughter left me a letter inside her pillowcase. I suppose she thought I would change the sheets at once, and I did, but I left her pillowcase on; I wanted to breathe in the fragrance of her apple-scented shampoo as I slept. So I didn't find the letter until today.

She wrote:

Mum, I'm sorry I pretended not to know what you were talking about all those times when I came to your bed. It was horrible of me. Sometimes I miss Dad, and that's why I was crying. I talked to K about it today at the park and I see now that I blamed you, and I wanted you to know how unhappy you'd made me and to make you feel bad, that's why I came to your bed and then pretended I didn't. That was very childish of me. I know it didn't make any sense to blame you, but I was being an idiot. I suppose I also wanted you to feel sorry for me. Well, I am really sorry. Remember how I never let you read me anything with a sad ending? I'm going to start trying to be less afraid of sad endings, and K says I should read the newspaper now and then too. You see? He's a very good influence on me. Love and apologies, your A.

◦﹏◦

I was surprised to find Ami at home. Not only was he back earlier than I'd expected, he wasn't exhausted. In fact, he seemed to be in high spirits. 'Where were you, love?' he asked. 'I was worried. I called three times, but there wasn't any answer.'

'I went out,' I said. I sank down on to the sofa, but nervous energy held back my fatigue. 'I went to visit Sheila. But she was at a party in Ramat Gan. I went there, but I left. Then I walked along the beach. And I saw a man holding a knife to a woman's face. So I interrupted him, I asked him the time.'

Ami stared at me.

'And she walked me to the bus stop. And now I'm home. And I don't care what you think.'

'What's going on, Lily?'

'Nothing. Nothing.'

'You almost got yourself raped or killed. Or both.'

'No, I could tell he wasn't the type.'

'What were you doing wandering along the beach?'

'I like the sea.'

'Where's your new bag?'

'I gave it to Sheila.'

He didn't say anything. He just looked at me.

'I didn't want to come home to an empty house.'

'You approached a man with a knife.'

'Yes. What would you have done?'

'It's different, Lily. I'm trained.'

'You should be complimenting me on my courage.'

'It wasn't courageous, it was stupid. And I'm angry that you took a chance like that.'

'Fine, think what you like.'

'I'm sorry about London, Lily.'

'How come you're back so soon?'

'I got lucky.'

'Did anyone say anything about the bugs?'

'No, no one said anything. I just put them on the table. I said, "Here's a present for you." They had other things on their mind.'

'Yup.'

'Lily, I really think you should call your parents, tell them you're pregnant. They deserve to know.'

'I can decide that for myself.'

'Imagine how they'll feel if they find out from Bracha.'

'They won't care. I told you that already.'

He didn't answer. He began looking for his cigarettes but he couldn't find them.

'We're so far apart now,' I said.

'Yes, you've moved away.'

'Are you sad?'

'Of course I'm sad.'

'I left a message for that Rose woman. I gave her our number here.'

He smiled. 'I don't think she's going to follow us to Israel,' he said.

'I had an awful evening!' I said. But when he came over and tried to put his arm round me, I shook him off.

I got up and walked to the kitchen. The stone floor was cool under my bare feet. 'Do you want a drink?' I asked, opening the fridge.

'OK.'

I took out a carton of grapefruit juice and two glasses. But instead of pouring the juice, as I'd planned to do, I picked up the glasses and smashed them on the floor. I bent down and began picking up the shards with my right hand, placing them in my left hand. I saw that my left hand had closed on the glass. I was vaguely aware that I was sobbing. Ami was prising my fingers apart, removing the pieces of glass. He wrapped my hand in a towel. 'I think we need to get you to hospital,' he said.

'No, I won't go,' I said. He lifted me above the sea of glass and blood, and I rested my head on his shoulder. '"Diamonds and Rust",' I said, looking at the floor. 'I saw her live. Joan Baez. That was before she wrote that song. She didn't want to perform here.'

He carried me to the bed.

'She didn't mean it personally. She just wanted us to think

about what we're doing. How wrong it is. I love that line, "Speaking strictly for me, we both could have died then and there".'

'I don't know it.'

'You do, you've heard it, you just forgot. The one she wrote for Dylan. He came and he went. And she said, "Speaking strictly for me, we both could have died then and there". Because she loved him so much. My hand hurts. It didn't hurt before. Suddenly. It does.'

'We have to go to hospital. There's no choice.'

'No. I won't go.'

He touched my cheeks with his wrists, felt my pulse. 'All right, I'll call Hillman, he's our family doctor. I'll see what he says.'

'He'll be angry with me.'

'He won't be angry. He's not that type of person.' He dialled Dr Hillman's number. I didn't listen to the conversation. 'OK, he's on his way. I think I woke him.'

'You hate me.'

'No,' he said.

'Yes, yes, you do. I don't care.'

He looked at me, he looked into my eyes. I started crying.

'No crying allowed, my love,' he said, moving my hair away from my forehead. 'There's a tear tax in these parts, haven't you heard?'

'I don't want to see a doctor.'

'You know, when my brother was seven and his appendix burst, Hillman went with him in the ambulance and sang him funny songs all the way there. That's the sort of man he is.'

'What songs?'

'I think they were drinking songs, very silly.'

The doorbell rang. Dr Hillman lived only a few minutes away, in Ramat Aviv. He was a brisk, athletic man with smiling eyes, very bright and blue, and he wore a tie-dye shirt, pink and orange and lime green. He checked my pulse, then asked me, in South African English, 'Any health problems, Lily?'

I shook my head.

'What's this all about?'

'I don't know.'

'This entire country's gone mad.' He sighed, and unwound the towel from my hand. 'What a mess.' He inserted a needle in my upper arm, then pulled a chair next to the bed and sat down. 'Ami, go to the other side of the bed and keep Lily company. Lily, you keep your eyes on Ami.'

'You don't have to worry, I'm not squeamish. Things like this don't bother me.'

'Be a good girl, Suzie Q, and don't argue. This is hard enough as it is.' He opened a case of medical instruments and waited for the drug to take effect. Ami stretched out next to me on the other side of the bed, and I shut my eyes. I felt as if I was floating, and I was reminded of a childhood song about a bed that turned into a ship. From what seemed like a distant place I heard Dr Hillman telling Ami about various bureaucratic hassles he was having, the endless red tape, the Catch-22s. Then he talked about the bureaucratic hassles his wife, who was also a doctor, was having. 'OK, I think we can start,' he said. 'What a mess,' he repeated, and sighed again.

I was aware of pain but, like the conversation about Dr Hillman's problems with various government agencies, it seemed distant and unimportant. Ami told me about a camping trip he'd taken in his childhood, a cave he and his friends had discovered, the baby rabbits they had saved.

'That should do it,' Dr Hillman said. 'Ring me if you have swelling or a raised temperature or anything out of the ordinary. Here's a prescription for antibiotics. Ami, could you give us a few minutes alone, please?'

Ami left the room and Dr Hillman leaned back in his chair and looked at me. 'So, Suzie Q, what's going on?' he asked.

'I don't know. It happened suddenly. I didn't plan it.'

'What was going on just before?'

'Nothing. I'm pregnant. Ami said I should phone my parents. I didn't want to.'

'You're pregnant, and neither of you told me?'

'I'm sorry. Does it matter?'

'When was your last period?'

'Beginning of November. Oh God, will that drug harm the baby?'

'Luckily, no. Next time mention small details like pregnancy, OK? So, you didn't want to call your parents. Because?'

'Because they won't care. They'll only pretend.'

'You have siblings?'

'An older sister.'

'Are you close?'

'No, I hardly know her. She's a marine biologist.'

'So, another perfect family. Did you read *The Bobbsey Twins* as a child?'

'Yes, I think so.'

'I used to love those books. In real life my father was a tyrant and we were all terrified of him until he died of a heart-attack when I was ten. I used to have fantasies about shooting him with one of his hunting rifles. Here's my advice. Get Ami to ring your parents and tell them. What else is bothering you?'

'I don't know. I'm happy.'

'What was your day like?'

'I went to Bar Ilan to visit a friend. A girl I was friends with at school, in Canada. She was at a party in Ramat Gan, so I went there, but I left.'

'You had a fight with her?'

'No, I just didn't see eye to eye with the people there.'

'You're aware that the political situation in Israel isn't your fault? They were going to consult you, but they forgot.' He got up. 'I'll be back next week,' he said. 'Look after yourself in the meantime.'

I was too groggy to move and I felt myself drifting off into a drugged sleep. Ami came back, lay down next to me and sang a line from a popular song: 'The judge was very lenient, he only gave me twenty years.' I smiled and fell asleep.

⌒—⌒

The Bible is full of frightened people. Practically on every page someone is afraid. And even though the Bible is not big on synonyms, it has five different words for fear.

The first people to be afraid are Adam and Eve, after they've eaten the forbidden fruit. They hear God's spirit wandering in the garden and hide rather pitifully behind some trees. And God says to Adam, 'Where are you?' although, of course, He knows perfectly well where Adam is. And Adam, in panic, rambles incoherently, 'I was afraid, because I was naked, and I hid myself.' It's always hard to be naked when you feel vulnerable. And easier to feel ashamed. It looks as though Adam is on the right track, ready to own up to what he did, but then he loses his courage and, in what can only be called a desperate move, he tries to shift responsibility to God and Eve: 'The woman You gave me, she gave me the fruit, and I ate it.'

But it isn't only God who gives rise to fear. Just as frequently it's humans who create panic, especially human armies. When the Philistines approach with thirty thousand chariots and six thousand horsemen and troops as numerous as the sand on the seashore, everyone runs for cover: '. . . the people hid in caves and holes and rocks and tombs and cisterns'. Shortly afterwards, when Jonathan and his armour-bearer, in a daring mood, decide to enter enemy territory and manage to kill twenty Philistines, it's the Philistines who flee: 'There was panic in the camp, in the field, and among all the people; the garrison, and even the raiders trembled; the earth quaked; there was a very great panic.'

Early this morning a child phoned in to a Tel Aviv-based radio show. I was listening to the show on the Net. The child was talking about a splendid weapons display he'd seen on Independence Day. He wanted to go and see it again the following day but, he said, 'because of all the wars and the explosions we couldn't'. He was referring to the daily eruptions of violence since the second *intifada* began. He then informed the radio announcers that in the old days people were given weapons without being told how to use them. 'If you give people weapons at least teach them how to use them,' he said.

He sounded anxious, and the announcers said, 'Listen to him, he's really angry.'

And the boy said, 'Yes, I'm afraid, because if, heaven forbid, there's another war and they don't teach me how to use the weapons, I won't know what to do.'

❦

When I woke up Ami was sitting in bed beside me, reading a novel.
'Hello there,' he said.

'What day is it?'

'Monday. You've been asleep for sixteen hours.'

'Were you here the whole time?'

'I went into work for a few hours.'

'You're not exhausted.'

'I had all kids today, they're easy.'

'How old?'

'Fifteen, sixteen. I've brought you some cheesecake.'

'Great, I'm starving.'

We had tea and cake on the bed. I reclined on my side and stuffed myself with the delicious cheesecake. I was famished.

'How are you feeling, Lily?'

'I'm back to myself. I'm so sorry I was rude and horrible. I'm sorry I was stupid on the beach.'

'You were heroic on the beach.'

'And I'm sorry about the glass. You must think I'm mad.'

'That's the last thing I think.'

'Most people don't do things like that.'

'Really? I haven't met those people. Of course, we all

have our own unique style. The varieties of self-destructive behaviour motivated by guilt and anger are endless.'

'I'm embarrassed now.'

'Don't be. Because anything we do in life we do because we're part of the human race. You can try to understand what you do and you can evaluate what you do but it doesn't make sense to feel embarrassed.'

'Yeah, well, Israelis never feel embarrassed. Have you ever met an Israeli who was embarrassed about anything?'

'You're right, we're far too arrogant.'

'What are you thinking?'

'I'm thinking the same thing I've thought since I met you. That I love you. And I'm worried about you, of course.'

'I'm OK. Obviously insane, but otherwise OK.'

'You're obviously sane, but maybe not entirely OK.'

'You never told me why you came home so early after London.'

'It turned out to be an easy case,' he said. 'We smoked together.'

'Who?'

'Me and the prisoner.'

'You smoked together!'

'We hit it off. I told him about you.'

'Me?'

'Yes, how much I loved you and that you were pregnant and how excited I was about being a father. And even though he's a lot younger than me he has three kids and he started talking about them. So then I asked him about labour and he told me about his experiences. In fact, he helped deliver the last baby because it arrived unexpectedly. We were smoking cigarettes and he said he wished the cigarette was a joint, so I took a break and called my supplier and I arranged to get some grass. The people listening in nearly had a fit, especially the ones who want me discharged. I came back and we smoked together. We got high, both of us, we were laughing and talking about things that had happened to us. And he spilled the beans. He didn't care. It wasn't because he was stoned, it was because . . . Well, in any case, he was a goldmine of information, they were practically dancing the *hora* out there in the hall. And that was it.'

'But how come it was such an emergency?'

'Because of the information he had. They'd just caught him and they needed that information right away.'

'What'll happen to him now?'

'Life in prison, I guess.'

'Oh! He's killed someone . . .'

'Yes, several people. He's been involved in all sorts of things.'

'How can you not get freaked out?'

'He's just a person.'

'Do you sometimes fail? Are there times when your interrogations don't work?'

'Yes, there are people I can't interrogate. Sometimes they send me someone who's beyond the point of no return. And I tell them, "Look, I can't work with this person, he's practically autistic". At first they used to pass him on to our star interrogator, Gabi. Even the other interrogators are terrified of this guy — they call him Gunther behind his back. He's the only one apart from me who works on his own, likes to do everything himself. There are all sorts of stories about him . . . Anyway, this Gabi would give it a shot and, of course, he wouldn't be able to do anything either, and they'd end up having to pull him off the prisoner, so they stopped doing that. Now when I say it's hopeless they usually accept it. And once . . .'

'What?'

He paused. 'This is really sensitive.'

'OK.'

'Well, once they called me in for a big case. I had misgivings from the start, when they gave me the rundown. This person had nothing to do with the Middle East, he was just attracted to the idea of killing some Jews, and the interrogation was going to be in English. I was reluctant, but they put a lot of pressure on me. But, you know, I walked into the room, took one look at him and walked out. I said, "I'm not working with that person, he's a Nazi, I can't do it". I didn't care what happened to him, or what they did with him.'

'What did they do with him?'

'I don't know, I never asked.'

'Why did they call you for him? Didn't they feel the same?'

Ami burst out laughing. 'You think they call me for humanitarian reasons? You're such an innocent, Lily.'

'Who wants you discharged?'

'People who hate my attitude. But they can't help liking the results I get. Your turn, Lily. What exactly happened after you left the airfield?'

I told him about the taxi drivers, the party in Ramat Gan, the walk on the beach.

He sighed. 'The best our country has to offer, all in one evening.'

'Those guys on the balcony, their fear was real,' I said.

'Yes, fear is real. The fear that Jews were poisoning wells was real. The fear that we were killing Christian children to make our matzas was real. The fear that we were taking over the world was real.'

'But we really do get bombs exploding, we really do get rhetoric.'

'That isn't what's scaring those people, you know. What's scaring them is the vision of the mad, wild-eyed Arab running amok with his knife, leering under his *keffiyeh*. That's what the word Arab means to them. That's all it means to them.'

'What's the solution?'

'To racism? I don't know – a lobotomy, maybe.'

'Does my hand disgust you?'

He laughed. 'I've seen worse things and lived.'

'I don't know what came over me.'

'You know, my guess is that you were re-enacting a scene in your life. So that this time you could change the plot.'

'You mean . . . with Dalia?'

'I don't know. But look how quickly you made that connection. That must mean something.'

'That would be really weird.'

'What were you missing, then?'

'Someone to save her. Not me, I couldn't do it. I was just a child. I needed an adult. My parents.'

Ami didn't say anything. I said, 'That's just too neat.'

'You're right, it's never simple. I think it might also have something to do with being pregnant, with wanting to protect your baby, I'm not sure how. Maybe it's this idea you got when you were watching Dalia and Boaz that someone has to get hurt so that another person won't be. And you wanted to be the one, so it wouldn't be our baby. Does that make sense?'

'You should be a shrink, Ami.'

'A lot has happened to you in a short time. Sometimes we just get overwhelmed.'

'Dr Hillman says you should phone my parents.'

'That's probably a good idea.'

'I'll listen in on the extension.'

'Do you want me to call now?'

'Might as well. What time is it in Canada?'

'Around eleven in the morning.'

'I think my mother will be in. My father's probably at work.'

'You haven't even told me what he does.'

'He works in the Jewish community . . .' I said vaguely.

Ami went to the kitchen to dial, and when the phone rang I picked up the extension in the bedroom.

My mother answered.

'Hello, Leah?' Ami said.

'Yes?'

'This is Lily's friend, Ami, calling from Israel.'

'Oh, yes, Ami! Bracha wrote us about you. How nice to hear from you.'

'We have some good news.'

'Oh?'

'We've decided to get married.'

'How wonderful! When?'

'We don't have the exact date yet.'

'Well, keep us informed. How's Lily?'

'She's fine. She wants me to let you know she's pregnant.'

'Hi, Mum,' I said.

'Oh, Lily, there you are! What great news! I'll tell Dad as soon as he gets home. We're having a small dinner party tonight, there's lots to do.'

'I'm due around August,' I said.

'I hope it's a boy, I'd love to have a grandson. How's university?'

'Fine. I missed a day, though. I got some glass in my hand, I had to have stitches.'

'Oh, that's too bad. Is there something you need us to send you?'

'No, no, I have everything.'

'Well, good luck, honey.'

'Thanks,' I said.

'Goodbye, Ami. *Lehitra'ot,*' she added flirtatiously. *Au revoir.*

'*Lehitra'ot,* Leah.'

''Bye, Mum.'

''Bye, honey. Thanks for calling with the exciting news.'

There were a few more goodbyes and then the three of us hung up.

Ami came back to the bedroom. 'Well, that really was something.'

'I told you.'

'It's like you're a remote acquaintance.'

'It's just the way they are,' I said. 'Maybe they had to distance themselves on the kibbutz. My mother says she cried for days when she first had to leave me in the Children's House. So maybe she just forced herself to be detached. But my father said he loved the arrangement. He liked having my mother all to himself in the evening. I bet the whole idea of segregating the children was the men's idea.'

'I don't think so. Fathers are proud of their kids, they like having them around.'

'Well, who knows why they did it, then?'

'It was an experiment in Utopia. That's the nature of experiments, they don't always work.'

'Still, imagine leaving children alone all night, right from birth. It goes against instinct, reason, everything. We were at the mercy of anybody and everybody, not to mention each other. Golding must have visited a kibbutz before he wrote *Lord of the Flies*.'

Ami laughed. 'That bad?'

'Well, not most of the time. Most of the time we were OK. But we definitely had our *Lord of the Flies* days.'

'I can't get over that phone call. You deserve more.'

'Everyone deserves more than they get. Except me. Right now I have more than I deserve.'

'There's no such thing. Especially not in your case, Lily.'

'Yeah, but when life is suddenly great, you feel morally obliged to live up to your good luck. It's a lot of pressure.'

Ami laughed again. 'And if you have bad luck you're allowed to be nasty?'

'A little.'

'I'll keep that in mind . . . She didn't even ask you about the glass,' he said, shaking his head.

'She didn't really hear me. She blocks out anything she doesn't want to confront.'

'We had some pretty unusual parents in our neighbourhood, but no one quite like her. I feel so sad for you, Lily.'

'A lot of people have worse parents.'

'What's worse than neglect? And what about your sister? When I was a child we all fought a lot, me and my brothers and my sister, but we were very close underneath. It's hard for me to imagine not having that.'

'My sister was popular – she had a very active social life and she wasn't at home much. She imitated my parents – they were always having parties too, almost every weekend, with all these literary and arty people . . . Once . . .' I hesitated.

Ami waited.

'You said you didn't want to hear about things like this.'

'I think this is a different category altogether.'

'Well, my mother was the administrative director of a theatre school for a while. And she used to invite all these really cool people over, young students and directors – they were like the ultimate in cool. I just stayed in my room, I hated those parties because my mother flirted with the men and my father flirted with the women. It's not the sort of thing you like to see your parents doing. So I used to hide. But once I came in to the kitchen during one of the parties and there was this guy there, he was a really famous director – they'd brought him from London to direct a production. He had shoulder-length hair, he was just incredibly sexy and charming. Well, I was only fourteen, I was so naïve. He started talking to me, and he acted as though I was the most amazing person he'd ever met. That's how they operate, these guys. They make you believe they've fallen in love with you, that as far as they're concerned you just dropped down from heaven for them, or maybe they really do feel that at the time, who knows? Anyway, we ended up in the bathroom together. I hadn't even kissed a guy before, and I was so flattered and excited. And before I knew what was happening he was trying to get inside me. I let him – I even helped him. But then he changed his mind. Maybe he hadn't realized I was a virgin and he was scared, so he just went down on me and then he came on my stomach.'

Neither of us said anything for a few minutes.

'Anyway, of course I never saw him again. A few days later I went to see the production of the play he'd directed. It was some nineteenth-century German play and, really, the directing was so brilliant, you can't imagine. There were these cages on the stage, and the actors were dressed in sort of ropes and they ran back and forth from cage to cage in this frantic way. I thought it was the greatest play, but then I read it and realized it was dated and melodramatic, but he had transformed it into something great. *Spring Awakening*, that was its title. I've forgotten who wrote it. Sort of ironic, that title. He really was a genius, and also a schmuck.'

'And your parents never knew.'

'They couldn't not know. I kept asking about him, I asked for his address, I wrote him letters, I waited every day for the post, I hardly ate for two weeks. Finally my father said, "He's never going to write to you, and if you make yourself cheap no one will be interested in you." My father only acted cool. Basically he was very conservative.'

'You didn't tell me any of this before.'

'I'm just used to the way they are, the way I grew up.'

'And you couldn't confide in your sister?'

'No, she was exactly like them. She was busy with her own life, her friends. She was the most popular girl in her school. We went to different schools, and she was a lot older than me. I went to a private Hebrew school, and she went to an ordinary state school. She asked to go to an ordinary school — she wanted to be like everyone else. She never invited anyone over to our house, you know, and neither did I. Our place was too weird, somehow. I can't explain. It wasn't the way it looked, there were all these nice rugs and paintings and things. It was the way my parents talked to our friends. As if . . . as if they were coming on to them. I know that sounds crazy, but it was a bit like that. It's hard to explain exactly.'

'You know, Lily, I think when we combine your anger with me and your anger with your parents and your guilt about my job and what you went through on the kibbutz, which being pregnant probably brings to the surface, it's surprising you didn't do something more drastic. You're probably sad about your friend Sheila, too.'

'I love you, Ami. And I can't believe I have a child growing inside me. I'm so excited now.'

'It does seem miraculous,' he said, bending down and kissing my stomach. 'Which reminds me, we have to find a good doctor. How about Hillman's wife, Belinda? She's an obstetrician, she's supposed to be excellent.'

'Do you think I should see a private doctor?'

'Yes. You'll get much better service. And you have to start drinking milk.'

'How come you know so much? How come you knew all the symptoms and everything? Have you been in this situation before?'

'No, this is a first for me. But I helped my sister when she was pregnant. Her husband was killed when she was in her second month, so I had to fill in for him.'

'I thought she was married.'

'Yes, she remarried, and her second child is by her second husband.'

'I didn't know.'

'Well, the Yom Kippur war did us in.'

'That's when I got here, you know. In October seventy-three. Five days before war broke out. I thought sitting in bomb shelters was just part of the Israeli experience. I really didn't know anything about Israel. I mean, nothing. In the diaspora you don't get any sense of what it's like. All you get is propaganda. I hated the way they talked about the sixty-seven war in Canada. I hated those postcards of the soldiers at the Wall. I never bought into that, you know. Instinctively. It must have been instinct, because I was the only one. I was the only one who hated all that. I thought I was just weird.'

'You are weird. I told you that at the start.'

'Will our baby be weird?'

'There's a good chance.'

'Are you sure I'm just weird, not mad?'

'Yes.'

'Are you still worried about me?'

'Yes.'

❧

Today I phoned Ibrahim.

'It's Lily,' I said, when he answered, 'calling from London.' There was a lot of noise in the background, and at first he couldn't hear me. I had to repeat my name.

'Lily! God. Let me pick up the phone in the bedroom. We're having a meeting here, hold on.'

I heard Ibrahim saying, 'Ḥevre, I have a long-distance call, keep it down.' The word ḥevre was painful for me to hear. It means a group of friends you hang out with; it's a word that conveys intimacy and trust.

'Lily. I can't believe I'm hearing your voice.'

'I'm still in touch with Mary Jo,' I said.

'I know, I know. We're in touch too.' He chuckled.

'How are you, Ibrahim?'

'What can I say? Welcome to hell. I'm still alive, though. I haven't been blown up yet and I haven't been shot, so that's something. What about you? What's going on?'

'My daughter lives in Belgium, she's a dancer.'

'Far out.'

'Ibrahim, I want to see you.'

'I want to see you too. Are you coming over?'

'I was wondering if you'd like to come here? If I sent you a ticket, would you come?'

'I think I could tear myself away.' He laughed. It was his old laugh: short, loud, unrestrained.

'Do you have a passport?'

'I'll get one. I'm really glad you called, Lily. I've thought about you. I've even dreamed about you.'

'You're still on Edelson Street?'

'Different flat, though. I'm in number seven now.'

Suddenly I couldn't breathe and I couldn't talk. I tried to tell Ibrahim that I had to go, that I would call him back, but the words detached themselves from my body and drifted away, leaving me empty and weak. I put the receiver down on the table, and I heard Ibrahim saying, 'Hello? Hello? Lily, are you there?' and then he said to someone else, 'Something's fucked up with the line,' and I heard clicks and then the dial tone.

I stared at the receiver. I was shivering. I ran to the bedroom and grabbed Ami's quilt and sat on the floor next to the bed and wrapped myself in the quilt but I couldn't warm up. 'Love is as cold as death,' I said aloud.

A thousand memories came rushing at me like leaves in a storm. Crimson and red and yellow leaves, torn at the edges and along the veins, rushing at me and suffocating me.

I was suffocating and I was cold and I couldn't warm up.

I wondered whether it was possible to die of exposure in an ordinary room.

⌒─⌒

I rang Ibrahim and Mary Jo to tell them I was pregnant, and they insisted on taking us out to dinner to celebrate. When Ami came home from work I asked him whether he was up to it.

'Yes, I had an easy day.'

I noticed a stain that looked like blood on the sleeve of his uniform. 'Is that blood?'

Ami unbuttoned his shirt and threw it in the laundry basket. Then he stretched out on the sofa and reached out for me.

'What happened?'

Ami sighed. 'Two prisoners got into a fight and I had to drive one to hospital. I had a boring day, for a change, filling in forms at the hospital, waiting for them to see us, hanging around until he was through.'

'Was it serious?'

'He's OK.'

'Are there Arab hospitals?'

'Of course. Hospitals, doctors, labs, ambulances – amazing how advanced these people are.'

I felt myself blushing. 'I didn't mean it like that. I just thought we took over everything.'

'Not everything. I was only teasing, Lily. Maybe we'll visit Ramallah one of these days so you can see for yourself.'

'Is that where you went? To a hospital in Ramallah?'

'No, we went to Hadassah.'

'Did they know he was a prisoner?'

'Yes.'

'Were the nurses scared?'

'We were the ones who were scared. Have you ever encountered a Hadassah nurse? Even the bravest among us begin to tremble.' And he began imitating the rebukes for which Hadassah nurses were famous ('You think you're the only one who's having a stroke?') until we were both laughing uncontrollably.

At seven we drove to Ibrahim's apartment. Ibrahim slapped Ami on the back and congratulated him. We went to a fish restaurant facing the sea and Ibrahim ordered a bottle of wine and toasted us. He told Mary Jo that she was next, that she should follow my example. 'Children,' he said. 'Children are a good thing.'

'*Le-chayim*,' Mary Jo said.

'*Le-chayim*,' we responded, clinking glasses.

'What happened to your hand?' Mary Jo asked.

'A stupid accident,' I said vaguely, and she was too polite to pry.

While we were waiting for the food to arrive I stared lazily at the sea, lulled by the soft sound of waves falling against the sand. Suddenly Ibrahim said, 'So, Ami, how are my brothers faring there in your prisons?'

Ibrahim's question woke me from my trance. It wasn't a subject I'd heard him bring up before.

'It varies,' Ami said.

'How many do you have?'

'I don't know the exact numbers.'

'All sorts of rumours reach me.'

Ami didn't say anything.

'They need to get organized,' Ibrahim said. 'Nothing can be achieved without some organization. Look at any revolutionary movement. We need Marat, huh, Ami? We need Marat . . .'

'I thought you hated the Communists.' Ami smiled.

'Yeah, well . . .'

'It isn't a question of kicking us out,' Ami said. 'We have to leave. We just have to get up and leave. There's no other way.'

'People don't leave when they're having a good time.'

'Our good time is quickly turning into a very bad time. And it's going to get worse.'

'Worse? How?'

'I don't even want to think about it.'

'At least I can count on you to be a decent human being,' Ibrahim said.

'The whole situation is indecent,' Ami said.

'That's why we need people like him, right, Lily?' he said. He rarely spoke directly to me now that I was Ami's girlfriend.

'Yes,' I said.

'What's a border, I ask you? We're living in a world of mirrors,' Ibrahim said. 'We have no idea who's in, who's out. That's why we build shelters underground. We have a whole underworld of shelters waiting for us.' He downed his wine in one gulp and poured himself another glass. 'But the sea is the sea,' he said happily, looking out at the Mediterranean.

'Yes,' Ami said. 'The sea is the sea.'

Then Ibrahim repeated, 'I hear all sorts of rumours.'

'You know I can't say anything.'

'It's wrong not to say anything,' I said. 'They torture people in those prisons.'

Ami looked stunned, then furious.

Tears began rolling down my cheeks.

'I've just worked something out,' Mary Jo said. We all turned to look at her. 'Iniquity isn't about superficial things.

Even if I ran down the street naked it wouldn't change who I am.'

'Don't try it,' Ibrahim said, and we all laughed.

'I think I'd like some more wine,' Mary Jo said, and Ibrahim ordered another bottle.

By the time we rose to leave Mary Jo found it a little hard to keep her balance. 'I think I've had too much to drink,' she said placidly.

'What am I doing to this woman?' Ibrahim said.

Ami and I didn't speak on the way home. We undressed in silence. When we were both lying in bed I said, 'Are you still angry?'

'No, I understand why you said it. But do you have any idea how helpless you made Ibrahim feel? You're the one in power, you're the one doing these things, it doesn't let you off the hook to say, "This is what we do". It's like you're gloating.'

'But people have to know.'

'He knows, Lily. All Arabs know. They're not the ones you have to tell. And Jews are not going to listen to you.'

'You're wrong, Ami. Ibrahim knows I wasn't gloating. I think he wanted you to say something, to admit what's going on, and he was glad someone was ready to come out and say it.'

'He feels very guilty, Lily. He's safe, he has rights, even if he's a third-class citizen. And in the territories his people have nothing. Imagine how that is for him.'

'Does he have relatives there?'

'No, his family's all here.'

'How many kids does he have?'

'Six.'

'I still think you're wrong. I think you're giving in too easily. You think no one cares, but that isn't true. A lot of people would care if they knew.'

'Yes, *if*. The "if" is the tricky part.'

'Was he right about getting organized?'

'Of course. But they're not allowed to get organized. That's why they get arrested. One of the main reasons, anyway. On the other hand, they're getting organized in prison.'

'So . . . I don't get it.'

'Don't look for logic, Lily.'

'Why does Ibrahim hate the Communists?'

'Oh, I don't know. Sees them as élitist, probably. Or maybe it's personal. Maybe he knows some of them and just doesn't like them.'

'Do you think there will be a Palestinian state in the territories? Do you think we'll ever leave?'

'Yes, one day. Not soon, though. Not without a lot of suffering on both sides first.'

'But what if there's a state and they arm themselves and attack us?'

'Then we'll fight back. But listen, a Palestinian state would mean a whole change of attitude. And, really, I think that's what most of them want.'

'A change of attitude?'

'Yes. People are very simple in some ways. We want simple things. Food, shelter, love, respect, fun. A flag. An apology. A sense of accomplishment.'

'Why can't we just do it, then? Why can't we sit down and sort things out?'

'Because they're angry and we're mad. And several other countries want to keep it like that. By the way, I forgot to tell you, the American woman from London phoned yesterday.'

'I told you so! I told you she'd call. Is she a film producer or something?'

'So she says.'

'Why would she invent something like that? Well, what did you tell her?'

'The same thing I told her at the hotel, that I wasn't interested in acting. She said she might be coming to Israel, though.'

'It can't hurt to see her.'

'I get weird vibes from her, Lily.'

'What do you mean?'

'I don't know. She might be a spy.'

'A spy! For whom?'

'God only knows.'

'You're being totally paranoid, Ami. You just can't believe someone would be interested in you because you're talented.'

'Exactly. How would she know I'm talented?'

'It shows a mile away, Ami. Everyone notices it. Let's at least meet her.'

'If you want, Lily.'

'Yes, I do.'

⌒——⌒

A *miklat* is a bomb shelter, from the root *klt*, which means to hold or absorb or take in. The word *miklat* is used in the Bible in reference to cities of refuge. If you killed someone accidentally, you could hide in the city of refuge (*'ir miklat*) to avoid being killed by a relative seeking vengeance. And you had to stay there until the high priest died. After that you could go back safely to your home. Of course, it wasn't always immediately clear whether the killing was accidental or intentional. In that case you'd go to the city of refuge until a court of law decided whether you were a murderer or not.

The Bible gives some helpful hints to the judges who have to decide whether a killing is intentional or unintentional. If the killer used something made of iron, or a stone, or a weapon made of wood, or stabbed the victim with hatred, or lay in wait for the victim, then threw something at him or beat him to death, it was an intentional murder. But if the killer stabbed someone 'without enmity' (I don't know exactly how that works) or threw something at him without lying in wait, or threw a stone without realizing there was someone there, it's an accidental killing.

And it's important to distinguish between the two, the Bible concludes, because blood pollutes and defiles the land. God doesn't want murderers roaming around; He doesn't want bloodshed in His land; He's insulted by it. 'You shall not defile the land in which you live, in which I dwell,' God says. You live in that land, but I dwell in its midst. And I don't want all this killing going on.

⌒⟋ ⟍⌒

By early March winter was over. I bought a loose Indian print dress, slightly transparent but wonderfully light, to accommodate my expanding stomach. The period of lethargy was over: I now felt energetic and alert. Belinda, my obstetrician, said everything was coming along smoothly and asked me whether I wanted to have a home birth (Ami said no). Ami and I bought Spock and a pregnancy book; we attended a Lamaze class with five other couples. I visited Bracha several times, and she gave me a detailed and only partially reassuring account of her own labour experience ('Several times I called upon my Maker to kill me on the spot'). Apparently Ami had succeeded in getting Noga into the job she wanted, and as a result Bracha now saw him as a demi-god.

Just before the Passover break Ami told me there was someone he needed to see near Akko. Did I want to come?

'I remember Akko!' I said. 'My mother once took me there. When I was six.'

'We can walk around there if you want.'

'We went to the beach and she told me to stay at the edge of the water, on the white foam, and she fell asleep. And she took me to see a Tarzan film. I wonder if that cinema's still there.'

'We'll look for it.'

'I was in love with Tarzan.'

Ami smiled. 'Which one?'

'I didn't care. Who do you have to see?'

'Just someone.'

'Someone important?'

'Someone very unimportant.'

The following morning we drove to an Arab town east of Akko.

'You know,' I said, 'I don't think I've ever been to an Arab town. Except for that time I got stranded. The driver who gave me a lift said he was going to Tel Aviv, but actually he was going to this village to find some workers, and he left me stranded there.'

Ami looked thoroughly disgusted.

'But it turned out fine. These three guys came up to me and asked me whether I was looking for someone. Luckily one spoke Hebrew. Actually, they all seemed to understand Hebrew. When they heard what happened they began running all over the place trying to find a ride for me. They finally found a taxi driver who was going to Tel Aviv but he was already full. So they made one of the guys in the taxi get out to make room for me. And then the driver wouldn't take any money. I was embarrassed – I really wanted to pay, but he wouldn't hear of it.'

'They saw you as their guest.'

'I suppose so. Even though I was just someone who was lost. I have no idea where it was, somewhere in the territories. That was the only time.'

'You mean they never took students from overseas on a guided tour of our Arab villages?' Ami teased.

'Actually I did go to one other Arab city. I went to Jericho, a week after I got here. Because of the song.'

'The song?'

'You know, *Joshua fit the battle of Jericho, Jericho, Jericho. Joshua fit the battle of Jericho and the walls came a-tumblin' down*,' I sang. 'I loved that song when I was little. And I just had to see the city.'

Ami seemed amused. 'Was it like you imagined?'

'Yeah, it was cool.'

'Did you see the refugee camp?'

'Refugee camp? I didn't know there was one there. Too bad, I would have been interested. I just walked around the city, saw some of the ruins, went to the market. Sheila was supposed to come with me but her parents wouldn't let her.'

'There's the town we're going to. Up on that hill,' Ami said, as a cluster of tiny white buildings and terraced gardens appeared in the distance.

'The houses look like they're growing out of the hill. Like they're a part of it. It's so pretty. Architects should come here to get ideas.'

We rode up the sun-washed road, past pink thorns and pale green bushes and oceans of cucumber fields. All around us the mountains of my childhood rose gently against the translucent sky.

'The landscape couldn't care less what we do here,' I said. 'The land doesn't cry out at all. The land is bored by us.'

'Yes. It's seen it all before.'

We parked on the outskirts of the town and walked into a maze of dead ends and unexpected turnings that seemed to lead nowhere. Here, inside the town, the stone houses were crammed together, their various additions and annexes competing for space. Ami asked a man at a vegetable stand for directions and the man sent his child, a boy of ten or eleven, to show us the way. The boy darted through the narrow, winding streets with proprietary confidence. Ami tried to talk to him, but he only smiled and shrugged, pointed out the house we were looking for, and made a quick escape. We knocked on the door and a bulky woman answered, looked at us inquisitively. Ami said something in Arabic and the woman grinned happily and invited us in.

Ami had brought a bottle of olive oil as a gift. The woman took it without much fuss and disappeared into a back room. She returned with tea and plates of food, which she set down in front of us on the carpeted floor. She urged us to eat but I was afraid of the food. I didn't recognize most of the dishes and I didn't like eating things I couldn't identify. On the other hand, it would be extremely rude not to eat. Ami saw that I was uneasy and told the woman I was pregnant and suffering from morning sickness. The woman switched to Hebrew and began congratulating me and giving me advice: sucking tangerines would help, she said, and there was a special tea that was almost miraculous in its power to alleviate morning sickness. She handed me a jar filled with black tea leaves. 'Put one teaspoon in boiling water and brew for half an hour, or even an hour,' she said. 'You won't believe how much better you'll feel.' We chatted about our planned visit to Akko, and then about gardening, and then the woman asked Ami some questions in Arabic and seemed pleased with his answers. Before we left, the woman made us promise to return and meet the rest of her family.

Ami and I walked down the street. We had no idea which

way to turn. 'I once took a course in navigating through a town like this one,' Ami said.

'Does that mean you know where to go?'

'No, it means I know how hopeless it is. We'll have to find another local guide.'

Like a genie summoned from a bottle, the vegetable vendor's son appeared out of nowhere, and showed us to our car.

'Who was that woman?' I asked, as we drove away.

'No one special,' Ami said.

'Ami, there's something weird going on. And you're not telling me. Are we being followed again?'

'No, of course not.'

'What's going on? You're making me nervous.'

'I'm not involved in anything dangerous or strange, Lily. That woman is someone's aunt. I promised I'd visit her and give her news of her nephew, so she could pass it on to his parents. That's all.'

'One of your prisoners?'

'Yes.'

'You're not supposed to be doing this, are you?'

'It's a grey area.'

'Your whole job is a grey area! I hate your job. I hate it, I hate it, I hate it.'

'Yes, I know.'

'You know what else I hate?'

'No.'

'I hate that there are so many things about you I don't know, that I'm not allowed to know. Like Ronny, and the army, and the prostitute.'

'The prostitute?'

'The one you said you ran into on Rabbi Meir Street. When you were seventeen.'

'Oh, her.'

We drove in silence for a while. Then Ami said, 'Would you like to see the Baha'i gardens? They're not far from here.'

'OK.'

We drove to the Baha'i gardens just north of Akko, Persian gardens with carefully cultivated shrubs and trees planted in rows; someone's orderly dream of Paradise.

'So peaceful,' I said. 'I think I'll stay for ever.'

A group of Italian tourists streamed out of the temple at the end of the garden. They huddled around a guide who, as it happened, knew Ami. He left the group and came over to say hello. In a low voice he confided to us that this was his first day on the job and he'd forgotten his notes, so he was making up most of the information. He and Ami cracked up.

We left the misinformed Italians and sat down on the carved benches that lined one of the lush garden squares. 'Is there any religion that doesn't have a holy place in Israel?' I said.

'Luckily, yes.' Then Ami said, 'I was a paratrooper in the army. Army stories aren't interesting, Lily. You're trained to kill people and they're trained to kill you, and then you both have the opportunity to try it out, and things usually go wrong on both sides. People die or they get wounded in horrendous ways. You start off with all sorts of ideas, but when you're in battle your ideas change and you change. Ronny was lovable and talented and he cried when he saw sad films. He wrote songs and he was in a rock band, he played the electric guitar. He grew his hair down to his shoulders and he planned to be a conscientious objector, though he would have gone into the army in the end, they always find some way to accommodate the would-be objectors. They would have probably offered him a job at Army Radio. He was stubborn. He had a pet turtle named Marco Polo that he was crazy about. It made our bedroom smell and kept escaping from its little house.

'Here's what happened with the prostitute. I was seventeen, just before the army, and you know there's this feeling guys get just before they go in, that they should at least get laid once, because they might die and it would be horrible to die without experiencing sex. I wasn't really thinking about it, but when this prostitute came up to me that's what went through my mind. And she was such a sweet little thing. A Yemenite, probably younger than me, big black eyes, little gold earrings. And, like our tourist-guide friend, new at the job. I thought, Why not? I had just been paid, I had a lot of money on me, or at least it seemed like a lot to me then. That was when I was a lab assistant. Anyway, I agreed, but I had this disastrous idea that I had to get to know her a bit first. It seemed mad to fuck just like that. So I suggested we go for an ice-cream. She told me her name was Mercedes, she said she'd given herself that name because she hated her real name. And I realized that I'd made a huge mistake trying to get to know her, because now that I knew her I didn't want to do it with her at all, she wasn't my type. But I couldn't get rid of her, she stuck to me like glue. She finally took me to her place. It was this hole in the wall, a tiny little room, so depressing you can't imagine. I told her I'd changed my mind and she asked me whether I despised her, whether I thought she was ugly. I made up some story about having a broken heart. I think she believed me. She didn't want to take money, but I insisted, I told her it was a loan and she could repay me when she was a big movie star, which was one of her dreams. And that was it.'

'So you didn't get laid before going to the army?'

'Oddly enough, I got laid that very day. I guess it was in the stars. Someone I already knew, we got together at a party and ended up in bed. Her parents' bed. They were in Nahariah for a wedding. It was my first time, and hers too. I think we were both surprised by how much we enjoyed it.'

'You must have had lots of girls after you.'

'Everyone was after everyone. We were all in mating mode back then.'

'Now I feel bad. I feel like I've intruded.'

'I'm glad you told me how you felt. I didn't know you felt like that. I wasn't trying to keep things from you.'

'How come you're so nice to me, Ami?'

'It makes more sense to ask why people aren't nice.'

'I don't feel like going to Akko after all.'

'OK.'

'We're lucky it's so warm today. In Canada it's probably ten below zero now. Once I got stuck in the cold.'

'Stuck in the cold?'

'Yes, there was an extreme cold warning, only somehow I missed it. I was thirteen. And I really loved Bergman. I decided to go to see one of his films in town. *Smiles of a Summer Night*, as it happens. I was OK getting down there, but by the time I came out the temperature had dropped another fifteen degrees, I think. And the street was completely deserted, no taxis, no cars, and I knew if I had to wait for the bus I'd die. I mean literally. I had a hat but my forehead and face were exposed and, anyway, the cold went right through my hat and gloves and boots. I tried to get back into the cinema, but they'd locked the door. Luckily I saw a block of flats not too far off and I ran towards it. It probably only took about two minutes, but I think those were the longest two minutes of my life. The door to the lobby was open, and I waited inside until I saw a taxi pass. It took over an hour. I didn't have any money, so when we got to my house I had to ask the driver to wait while I went inside to get money, and my mother was angry that I'd taken a cab. It must have been twenty below. Fahrenheit. That's like minus thirty Celsius.'

'It's hard for me even to imagine.'

'Well, that's my war story. Battle with the cold. I suppose I'm lucky that that's the worst thing I've had happen to me!'

'You can't quantify unhappiness,' he said. He took a joint out of his pocket and lit it. I was in the mood for a smoke but he wouldn't let me have even one drag. He felt our baby was too young to get into the habit.

'Is grass illegal in Israel?' I asked.

'Of course it's illegal,' Ami said.

'But no one ever gets arrested.'

'They have more important things to worry about. And you can't arrest Arabs for smoking hashish . . . I wonder what those Italians are learning about the Baha'i religion,' Ami said. 'Probably that it's an offshoot of Judaism.'

'How do you know that guy?'

'Dudu? We were on the same basketball team. He was always a joker. Always up to something. Once when we were in the shower he threw everyone's towels and clothes out the window.' He laughed.

'What happened?'

'We had to run out into the street naked to get them. Two old women stopped to watch us, and they began arguing about which of us was handsomest.'

'I'm hungry.'

'I forgot that you didn't eat anything at that house. Too

bad, I'm sure you would have liked those dishes. They were just variations on the usual things. That green dish you were so scared of, it was hummus with parsley.'

'I didn't know. That was the problem, I wanted to know what the food was before I ate it, but I couldn't ask . . . But how come the aunt is Israeli and her nephew isn't?'

'One side of the family left in forty-eight, and the other side didn't. Shall we go and look for a restaurant?'

'Yes, please . . . Is that what you do, bribe your prisoners with promises to visit their relatives?'

'I do whatever works.'

'How do you do it, Ami? How do you get people to confess to you?'

'There are all sorts of techniques.'

'Like what? Can't you just give me an idea?'

'Well, you know, the prisoner's sitting there in a chair and he's expecting the worst. Maybe he's heard rumours about me, or maybe he hasn't, but he's seen enough people returning from interrogation to expect a hard time. Usually he's already had a rough time, he's already exhausted from the arrest and the prison experience. So he's in a certain state of mind when I come in.

'And I take off his handcuffs and offer him water, and then for a while we might sit there and not say anything. Not always, it depends on the prisoner, but a lot of the time that's how we start. We sit there getting used to each other, maybe smoking.

I look into his eyes, he might look back into mine. I wait for him to speak first. That's really crucial. It can take an hour or two hours, you have to be patient. Or it can take ten minutes. Usually he asks me something. And I answer. And then I let him do the interrogating for a while, so to speak. What's going to happen to him, worries about his family, is he going to go to court, will he be allowed to see a lawyer, how long will he be detained, when can he have visitors, will he be deported, can he use the bathroom. Sometimes complaints. He thinks he twisted his ankle. Or he has no sensation in his left arm. And I tell him I'll try to get him a doctor. I might even offer him a hot shower. No one can get used to that, not the prisoners and not the other interrogators. The prisoners think it's a trick and the other interrogators think I'm mad. Then I might ask him about positive memories he has from his past. And he'll be surprised by that question, he might try to resist, but he'll start thinking about it. And most of the time, after one nice memory, other memories, unpleasant ones, come up. Personal things. His father caught him in a lie. Some kids tormented a dog or cat, you wouldn't believe how often that comes up, I'll spare you the details. And eventually we might move to politics and sometimes religion. And it often turns out that there are a lot of things about Jews that he wonders about, that he's always wondered about, and he asks me. And things surprise him. If I'm lucky we start laughing at some point.

'But sometimes it doesn't go like that at all. Sometimes the prisoner starts talking right away, and I take it from there. I let him go on with whatever he's talking about. I let him lead the way. I let him vent his anger, you know. If he's religious he might talk to me about what he believes. Or he might be a Communist, or maybe he just picked things up here and there. And I try to engage him in a theoretical discussion. Or else he might be a common criminal, no conscience, no ideology, just out for himself, and he tries to squeeze some benefit from the situation. It's pretty funny sometimes, sometimes I crack up. But there are times when I can see that the prisoner knows absolutely nothing, is completely uninvolved in anything, and has no idea why he's been arrested. And he's worried about who's going to do the work he was in the middle of doing, look after his family. So I recommend release. I say, "The only thing you'll get out of this guy is how to milk goats or install a pipe". Or else the prisoner's involvement has been totally peripheral, he said *maybe* when his friend asked him to join something, or he delivered some flyers, something like that. And the people I work for know way more about the situation than he does. So I try to get him to sign a confession. I try to get him to write down exactly what he did. At least that way he might get to go to court and maybe pay a fine or serve a one or two-year sentence instead of the whole thing dragging on and on. But if he doesn't want to sign a confession, there's no point pushing it. He has his reasons. You get sad cases too, they offer to help, to collaborate, anything, so they can get back home to their wife and kids and their work. And they ask me to rough them up so that no one will suspect. I send them on to the guys in charge, I don't go on working with them. It's one of the worst parts of my job, sending those prisoners on, but I don't have much choice.

'Those are the routine cases I'm describing. When I get called for big cases, it's a different story. Those guys are less vulnerable. They're shrewd, experienced and proud. And I do different things with them. I challenge them, I try to trick them, I give them the feeling I already know everything. I try to hypnotize them. And since they're expecting to be tortured they get a bit confused. I use that to my advantage. Those guys are usually intelligent and interesting to talk to, and sometimes we get into long debates about things. I'm continually astonished at some of the things they think about us. One guy thought our sex organs were different. How, exactly, I'm not sure. A lot of them think we have strange, secret rituals. One guy who had lived in Egypt and Europe and got arrested the minute he landed here was shocked to discover that we ate Middle Eastern food. He kept listing all these different sorts of food, he was just incredulous. Even shashlik? Even shwarma? Certainly not falafel! He didn't believe me. I had to go out and order those dishes to prove it to him. Some of them are tangled up to their ears in ways they never planned and with people they don't trust. Sometimes they're almost relieved to be out of it. I can't tell you any more, Lily. Well, where do you want to eat?'

'Anywhere, as long as it's close.'

'Akko has some great places. In case you change your mind about going there.'

'Akko's fine. Oh, look, there's Dudu. He's waving.'

We waved back. As we left we could hear Dudu telling the Italians about the trees in the garden. 'Stand under these sweet-smelling trees,' we heard him saying, 'and you'll take home with you the perfume of their leaves.' He was probably getting desperate.

❧

Parsley Hummus Dip (serves 10)
8oz pre-cooked chickpeas, drained
4 tablespoons water
4 tablespoons tahini
juice of 1 lemon
2 tablespoons olive oil
8oz fresh parsley, finely chopped
1 clove garlic
1 teaspoon salt
Purée all the ingredients in a food processor until smooth. Chill and serve with pitta bread.
(from *The Jewish Vegetarian Cookbook*)

꒰ ꒱

I didn't have a class until late afternoon the next day, and I watched Ami lazily from the bed as he ironed his uniform (he never let me do it, he said it would be too depressing a sight) and got ready for work. He said he would be working until Monday, and that he would come straight from work to Freud's flat. I drifted back to sleep, and I dreamed that I gave birth to a baby who spoke at once, right from birth, and this frightened me but also aroused my curiosity. When I woke it was nearly noon. I was just packing my things and getting ready to leave for Jerusalem when Ami returned.

I saw at once that something was wrong. He didn't say anything; he didn't even look at me. He took off his uniform, but instead of dropping it into the laundry basket in the hallway, he stuffed it inside a plastic rubbish bag and tossed it into the broom cupboard. Then he put on jeans and a black T-shirt and made himself coffee.

'What's going on?' I asked.

'Don't ask any questions right now, Lily,' he said.

I was hurt by the tone of his voice, and by the way he seemed not to want me around.

'Fine!' I said. I stomped to the bedroom and slammed the door.

He didn't come after me. I knew I shouldn't have done that, but I didn't care.

I heard the front door open and shut. I came out of the bedroom and ran outside. Ami was already in his car, driving away. I ran after him and he saw me in the mirror and screeched to a stop. 'I'm sorry,' I said. 'Don't go.'

But he didn't soften. He just said, 'Get in.'

We drove up the Haifa–Tel Aviv highway. I stared out at the sea. I wondered how anyone could drive along the Haifa–Tel Aviv highway and not be distracted by the view. But Ami wasn't having any difficulty with it: he wasn't interested in the sea.

Just before we reached Haifa, Ami turned off the highway and took several smaller roads until he reached a gravel path. The path was uneven and narrow, but Ami didn't slow down. I was sure we'd crash if a driver came the other way and I was relieved when he finally slammed on the brakes. He pulled into the paved driveway of a storybook house with a yellow roof and sugar-pink gables. The house was surrounded by orchards, and the sweet smell of lemon and orange trees drifted in through the open windows of the car.

'Who lives here?' I asked.

'Someone I need to see,' Ami said.

'Do you want me to stay in the car?'

'Yes, I won't be long.'

He rang the bell. A short man with greying hair opened

the door, glanced at me, then let Ami in and shut the door.

I left the car and wandered through one of the orchards. Memories from my childhood came rushing at me: the forest in the Galil where we went to celebrate Tu Bishvat, a sea of pine needles on the ground, slippery mushrooms cooking in a frying-pan over a small fire, a mysterious grave in the heart of the forest; Boaz said a baby had been buried there. I held Dalia's sticky hand and we sneaked away to look for wild cyclamens. That night, as a treat, we were allowed to go outside for a night walk in our pyjamas. I ran away from the group and tried to find my father, but he wasn't in his room and he wasn't in the kitchen. Someone told me to look in Shimona's room, but before I could find Shimona's room Miri caught me. She lifted me by the waist and I began to wail and sob hysterically. I remembered my misery, and I wondered whether misery in adult life could be as intense.

I heard something moving and when I turned, I caught a glimpse of a small boy, four or five years old, dodging behind a tree. He reappeared, grinning, and dodged again. I felt he wanted to play hide-and-seek with me, and his energy and playfulness made me realize how hopelessly heavy I felt; how impossible it would be for me to break out of that heaviness, even for a few seconds, even merely to smile at the grinning child.

I returned to the car and curled up on the back seat, waited for Ami.

I waited for over an hour. It was a hot day and I was thirsty but I didn't want to knock at the door and ask for a drink. I walked to the back of the house, and tried the patio door. It was open, and I let myself in quietly. I thought I heard a child's laughter; the grinning boy was probably watching me from his hiding place.

I found a bathroom near the back of the house and I drank cold water from the tap. There were plastic toys in the bath and wet towels on the floor. I knew I was in the house of someone important, and that most people would not see this side of his life, his child's toys, the wet towels on the floor. I heard voices in another room, behind a closed door.

I let myself out of the house. The little boy who had ducked behind the trees in the orchard was waiting for me. He stood in the centre of the back lawn, barefoot, arms folded, wearing red shorts and a sleeveless top. He was a very good-looking boy.

'You're not allowed in the house,' he said. 'You have to ask permission. Bang, bang!' He stretched out his arm and pretended to shoot me.

'You're supposed to fall down,' he said.

'I don't like those kinds of games,' I said. 'They aren't funny.'

'Well, I don't like you. And I'm going to tell my father what you did.'

'Go ahead,' I said. There were several patio chairs on the lawn and I pulled the one that looked most comfortable, a padded *chaise-longue*, to the shade of a tree. I sat down, stretched out my legs and clasped my hands behind my head.

'Don't you know who my father is?'

'I don't know and I don't care.'

'Are you an Arab?'

'Yes.'

'No, you aren't. Liar.'

'Didn't your father teach you any manners?'

'Show me your ID.'

'I'm not going to talk to you. You're too rude for me.'

'I'm not rude. You are.'

I didn't answer. The boy sat down next to me on the grass. He took a stick from the ground and began poking my legs. 'Don't do that,' I said. I was furious.

The boy stopped. 'Why are you here?' he asked.

'Where's your mother?'

'She's not with us any more. Do you want ice-cream?'

'No, thank you. But it's kind of you to ask.'

'What's your name?'

'Lily.'

'Are you really an Arab?'

'Yes.'

'You're blonde.'

'Some Arabs are blonde.'

'You're not Arab. You're Israeli.'

'Some Arabs are Israelis.'

'No, they aren't.'

'Ask your father.'

'Is the man inside an Arab?'

'No. I'm not either. I was just teasing you.'

'I knew that. I'm almost five. And I'm going to be a pilot. And I am going to invent the best tank in the entire universe. And our enemy will surrender immediately. Where were you born?'

'In the north.'

'I won't tell my father on you.'

'You can tell him I drank water from your tap. He won't mind.'

'No, I won't tell him. I like you. Do you want to stay for supper? We're having spaghetti with tomato sauce and mushrooms. And ice-cream.'

'Maybe another time.'

'Your husband is here.'

I turned round and saw Ami standing in the sunlight. 'Let's go,' he said.

'Be good,' I said to the boy. I bent down and kissed him. Then I followed Ami to the car.

He was even more upset than before. He started the car and pressed down hard on the accelerator.

'Ami, please. You're going to get the three of us killed.'

'Sorry,' he said, forcing himself to slow down.

'Who was that man?'

'Someone I needed to see.'

'What's going on?' I was grateful that he was at least talking to me.

'I told you, Lily, not now.' His voice was hard and hostile.

'Don't take it out on me, it's not my fault.'

'No, it's no one's fault. It isn't anyone's fault, that's the whole problem.'

'Well, it's certainly not my fault!'

'Can't you see we're all in this together? Can't you see that?' He was almost shouting at me.

'Don't talk to me like that! I'm not one of your prisoners.'

He stopped the car. I knew I was failing him, but it seemed to me that he was failing me too.

He said, 'I think we both need to cool down.'

I said, 'You're angry, and you're taking it all out on me.'

'I need *you* right now. I don't want you needing me. I need *you*.'

'You're not acting as if you need me. You wanted to drive away without me. And now you're acting like you want me to vanish. Or as if you'd like to hit me.'

'Don't say that, Lily. You're crossing lines you shouldn't be crossing.'

'Sorry, Mr Border Guard.'

'OK, that's it. I'm driving you to Haifa, you can take a taxi home.'

'Good! I can't wait.'

We drove into Haifa and he stopped the car on HaHaganah Street, near the taxis. A pimp walked by and slammed his hand down on the car. He looked like a matador in his green satin shirt and silver trousers. A Jewish matador, ready to take on the world. 'Hello!' he said, in English. He thought we were Americans. 'Cigarette?' We ignored him, and he pounded the car again, this time with his fist, and walked away.

Ami knew I didn't want to go home, and he no longer wanted me to go home either. We sat in the car for a few minutes with the motor running. I didn't move.

He began driving away from Haifa. He was no longer speeding, but he was still angry and his knuckles were white as he gripped the steering-wheel. He drove us to a small guesthouse, half hidden by pine trees. I had no idea where we were and I didn't ask. I followed Ami into the faintly lit lobby and waited while he signed us in. Everything in the lobby had been scrubbed and polished; even the brass bell on the counter gleamed in the dim light. I wondered whether Ami would ask for two rooms, but the man at the desk gave him only one key.

The room had a relaxing effect on both of us. Our window looked out on to the pine forest, and there was something soothing about the clean stone floor and the heavy old furniture and the little lace doilies on the dresser and bedside table. It was as though we'd been transported to eastern Europe, or maybe to Palestine at the turn of the century, to an inn run by an old innkeeper and his wife.

There were twin beds in the room. Ami lay down on the bed closest to the door and covered his eyes with his arm.

'I'm sorry,' I said. 'I didn't mean to say those things.'

I thought he had started laughing, but then I realized he was crying. I had no idea what to do. I knew what women wanted when they cried, but I had no idea what men wanted. I wasn't even sure I'd ever seen a man crying in real life.

I stood by the window and waited. After a few minutes Ami reached into his back pocket, retrieved a crumpled packet of Camels and a book of matches, lit a cigarette, and took his single puff. The ashtray was on the dressing-table, and he extended his hand to me. My fingers touched his when I took the cigarette from him.

'I'm going to lose my mind one of these days,' he said. 'I'm going to join my mother in Ezrat Nashim. They can give me the room next door to hers.'

'Not yet,' I said. 'You have to help me through labour first.'

He shut his eyes and in a few minutes he was asleep. He had fallen into a very deep sleep, so I took off his sandals and pulled the bedspread over his feet.

He slept for a long time. When he woke he seemed not to know for a few seconds where he was. 'What time is it?' he asked.

'Nearly eight.'

He went to the bathroom to wash, then returned to the bed

and sat up, leaning against the headboard. He was more subdued now. He said, 'They're probably going to arrest me.'

'Arrest you?'

'Yes. I left the detention centre and drove to my superior's headquarters and threatened him with a weapon.'

'You mean you pointed a gun at him?'

'Yes. And then I shot a few times at the wall. I just wanted to scare him. And I did.'

'What did he do?'

'Ducked under the desk.'

'Didn't someone grab you?'

'They didn't realize at first who'd been shooting. They burst into the room but I'd thrown my gun on the floor by then, and no one thought it was me. They thought it must have been a terrorist who'd escaped through the window. And before they had time to work it out I drove away.'

'Whose gun was it?'

'Mine, the one from the glove compartment.'

'Why? Why did you do it?'

'I couldn't seem to get him to wake up from the stupor he was in, sitting behind his desk, mumbling. So I pointed my gun at him. I don't know what came over me. I just lost it.'

'Is this the first time you've done something like that?'

'Yes, of course. The army doesn't take well to people shooting at their superiors.'

'I meant losing your temper. I know you've been rude. You swore on the phone, in London.'

He smiled. 'Swearing's allowed, Lily. Anyway, those people in London weren't army people, it didn't matter what I said to them.'

'I suppose you were desperate for a way out . . . Are you hungry?'

'Yes. No. I don't know.'

'Do you want to go for a walk? It looks nice out. We can just stroll around the grounds.'

'Did you lock the door, Lily? At home?'

'No, I just ran out.'

'Is the door closed at least?'

'Yes.'

'You know, lately I've been considering going back into the theatre. Not as an actor, but as a playwright. I'd like to write plays, and maybe direct. I've been thinking about a play I'd like to write.'

'That's such great news.'

'Yes, I even have a title, *Gilgul Nephashot*. I have the whole play in my mind.'

'That would be amazing.'

'We have the house, it's all paid for. And enough to live on for a year. But then we'd be poor.'

'You know I don't care about things like that.'

'The old kibbutz blood.'

'What happened? At the prison.'

'I just decided I'd had it.'

'Someone died,' I said.

'Yes.'

'How?'

'You know, I have a nickname at work. They call me Ha-moreh.'

'Really? You never told me.'

'Yes. The teacher. Because when I'm there they control themselves. Because they feel embarrassed when I'm there, they feel self-conscious, and everything quietens down. For one thing I can't work with constant screaming going on, and they're used to that. The rooms are supposed to be soundproof, but they aren't really, not entirely. In the beginning I just used to barge into the other rooms and tell them to give it a rest. Finally they got used to slowing down when I arrived. I work at one of the smaller detention centres, so I was able to do that. And the people in charge liked it, because they could feel there was a policy, they could pretend they had some control. "Look how disciplined we are here." Then, as soon as I left, all hell would break loose. Last night a few of them got bored, they decided to try to make one of the prisoners walk on all fours and say things that anyone would refuse to say, but for a Muslim are simply impossible. "I want to fuck my mother up her arse." That sort of thing. Well, he refused. So they kicked him until he passed out and he died during the night. And he wasn't even in for anything. He was just picked up for breaking the curfew. They had nothing against him. I don't even know why they sent him to us. He was a kid, he was taking a tape to a friend's house, so they could listen to some music together. A kid with fair hair, almost blond, skinny, tiny for his age, they thought he was eleven or twelve when they picked him up, and he should have told them he was, but he was too scared to lie. A camp kid. Born in one of the camps, and he'd never once in his life been outside that camp. I talked to him for a few minutes when he was first brought in. He seemed OK. He hadn't been beaten, and someone in his cell was looking after him. I was supposed to get him when it was his turn – I usually get the kids because I'm good with them. I was waiting for him this morning, and they went to wake him. And they realized he was dead. And then the story came out. One of the prisoners told me what happened and then the two interrogators admitted it, they defended themselves. They said they were only playing, that he must have been made of glass. They thought that was very witty. They thought it was hilarious. "A glass Arab," they kept saying, laughing their heads off.'

'Yes,' I said. I looked out of the window. 'What will happen now?'

'Nothing. This is the fate of all occupiers. If you want to be an occupier, that's what you sign up for.'

'Is it the first time someone has died?'

'It's not the first time someone's died in detention, but

it hasn't happened before at that detention centre. Although we've come close, because some of these people are in poor health to begin with, and we don't necessarily know about it. Then someone has an asthma attack or something like that, and we have to get him to hospital. But more frequently if they die it's from the after-effects of a particularly brutal interrogation, and it happens at the hospital afterwards.'

'We never hear about it.'

'The government doesn't want to upset the citizens of Israel.'

'Can't you do something? Can't you at least publicize it?'

'You know, I had a schoolfriend, Ya'ir, and three years ago he was patrolling in Gaza. There was a curfew and it was night, and they came across this chubby little guy standing against a wall smoking. You know, the sort of man you see selling olives in the *shuk*. You can get ten or even twenty people living in some of those houses, and maybe it just got too crowded for him. This guy in Ya'ir's unit starts joking, saying, "He looks suspicious to me, very suspicious," and Ya'ir just ignored him, so this guy who was under Ya'ir and not supposed to be operating without orders, shot at the man, just like that. He aimed his Uzi and shot, and there was this man lying there dead, and Ya'ir trying to get help and the family running out and everyone screaming . . . Anyway, Ya'ir spent two years of his life trying to bring the case out, trying to get some sort of justice. He even took it to the Knesset. He couldn't get anywhere. The soldier said he'd thought the guy was about to attack him, the two other soldiers who were there backed him up. Ya'ir finally had a nervous breakdown. Which, right now, is where I'm heading.'

'Write a book about what you know. Write a book about the things we do.'

'Someone already has. An Israeli lawyer wrote a book. No one would publish it so she published it with her own money. Maybe the Communist Party helped her, I don't know. Three bookstores in Israel agreed to stock it. And now whenever she walks down the street people spit at her.'

'Can I meet her?'

'Sure, if you want to. She's probably in the phone book.'

'There are lots of good people in this country. I'm sure they would take up the cause if they knew.'

'No one wants to know.'

'You keep saying that. You're too pessimistic, Ami. You're not even ready to try.'

'It's just that I know what we're up against. This idea that we're the good guys, we're the nice ones, beleaguered, long-suffering, misunderstood – it's ingrained. We're the ones who are advanced, bringing light wherever we go. And for a while there was at least something to hold on to, some good intentions, some sort of real struggle. And whatever didn't fit into that view of ourselves, we ignored. We focused on the good things and we believed we were better than everyone else. Good guys surrounded by bad guys. Well, the occupation finally leaves us without a way out. It proves we're exactly the same as everyone else. Capable of everything and anything. But no one wants to give up the illusion. So they hang on, even when things stare them in the face. It's a huge conspiracy of blindness. Well, the occupation won't last for ever, and one day we'll have to account for everything. We'll have to look back and face it all. And we're going to see then, looking back, that we didn't do it for security, or out of fear, or despair, we did it because we were corrupt and sadistic and out of control. We made people stand with their arms up all night, we made them crawl in the mud, we pissed on them, we spat on them, we threw them against walls, we put out cigarettes on their skin. And we all pretended it wasn't happening.'

'Where is he now? That guy Ya'ir?'

'He's in Canada, as a matter of fact. House-painting.'

I was on the other twin bed, facing Ami. He came over to my bed, lay down beside me. 'I don't know what I'd do without you,' he said. 'I don't know what I did without you.'

'Don't say that. I can't bear that weight. I can't balance out so much bad stuff.'

'Not you, me. My feelings towards you.'

'That's scary too.'

'"Love is as strong as death", you know.'

'Yes, it is. What's going to happen now with the army?'

'They'll probably send me to prison. Anyway, I'm not going back.'

'For how long? How long will you get?'

'I don't know. In theory I could serve five years.'

'Five years!'

'Well, it's unlikely to be that long. They'll take into account my combat record, my brother, your pregnancy, all the work I've done until now.'

'I'm glad you're leaving.'

'It doesn't change anything. Everything will go on as usual, I just won't be there to see it. Well, they're not going to put up with this for ever, the Palestinians. I don't know how they haven't all gone mad by now. I really don't know. It's a mystery to me. A sad mystery.'

'Jews put up with things for centuries.'

'Yes. And we got fed up. And now we're out of control. So, history will repeat itself, the other way round. Then we'll all be out of control, it'll be a battle on the streets. Victims learn fast.'

'You're scaring me.'

'We should be scared. Of ourselves and where we're heading. We had so much to offer! We had so much good to offer, we could have done so much good! But we were in a rush. After everything that happened to us, we didn't want to think about anything – we couldn't. Everyone sat around and let us get slaughtered and gassed and tortured to death. No one gave a shit. So now we weren't going to give a shit either. We were just going to get what we wanted. Well, when you're in that state of mind there's an excellent chance you'll screw up. And we did. We screwed up on such a big scale that it's hard to believe. We're destroying ourselves, that's the worst part. Anyway, I'm out of it. Now I get to watch from the sidelines, I don't have to be in the arena any longer.'

'Why did you do it?'

'I don't know, Lily. I thought I could bring some sanity to that place, and I did manage to help some people. But maybe on a deeper level I just wanted to get away from everything. Just go into the heart of darkness, you know? See what's there, what happens, how you survive. Because I was already there in a way, after my brothers died. I wanted to face angry people and calm them down because I was angry. Maybe I was trying to reach out to that part of myself. But you know, there are so many ways to look at things. Because at the same time I was part of the system, and, look, you suddenly have all the control, all the power in that room. And it sickened me to be in that position. So maybe this is all about masochism, weird as that sounds . . . I told you there was no simple answer.'

'You know what I've noticed, Ami? Israelis are really quite neurotic. Actually, you get two kinds of Israelis. You get get the really neurotic ones, and the kind with the gold chains and open shirts.'

'They're neurotic, too, believe me. I've come to know them intimately. They just don't know it, that's the only difference.

And listen, neurotic is a nice word, but it doesn't excuse anything.'

He got up and walked to the window, stared out at the trees. 'You know,' he said, 'there are things going on behind the scenes that really surprised me. Things I never in my life would have expected or believed.'

'Are you going to write about those things in your play?'

'Of course not, Lily. I'm talking about secret stuff. No one's allowed to know about it.'

'Would you tell anyone? If you thought it could help?'

'No. And I can't imagine a situation in which it would help anyone. On the contrary. Anyway, my loyalty is to my country, you know. It always will be.'

'Yes, I know. Mine too. How come we love our country no matter what?'

'I don't know.'

'It's so deep.'

'Yes, it's very deep.'

'But you are going to write a play?'

'Yes. I'd start now if I had paper on me.'

'I'll get some. Don't move.'

I went out to the front desk and asked for paper, brought it back to the room and watched as Ami began to write his play.

I always thought an Uzi was called an Uzi because *oz* **means strength** and *uzi* means 'my strength'. But in fact the Uzi submachine-gun was named after its inventor, whose first name happened to be Uzi. What if his first name had been David? Or Shlomo? Or Baruch? I suppose we'd have got used to it. 'He killed the demonstrator with his David'; 'He fired his Shlomo into the air'; 'The Baruch has been replaced by an M-16.'

The word *nephesh* means 'soul, spirit, being, human, creature, person'.

The word *gilgul* means 'turning, spinning, moving in a circle, meandering through a series of arbitrary events'.

The phrase *gilgul niphashot* means, literally, 'the cyclical movement of spirits or souls'. That is, reincarnation. But it also brings to mind an image of people spinning and turning and moving back and forth aimlessly, from one place to another.

The word *ha-moreh* means 'the teacher'. You use it as a form of address instead of using a teacher's proper name. 'The teacher, may I please be excused?'; 'The teacher, I forgot to do my homework.' I don't know where that form comes from, with the article tagged on as a sign of respect.

It's the same when you address your superior in the army. Hebrew doesn't have a word for 'sir'. So what you say instead is 'the commander'. 'Yes, the commander'; 'No, the commander'; 'Don't worry, we'll take care of it, the commander.'

～⌒～

No one came to arrest Ami. He sent the army a letter requesting to be released from his contract, but he didn't receive an answer. For five weeks he didn't hear from anyone, and then, in the middle of the night, in Freud's flat, the phone rang. I got up and answered. Ami didn't stir; he was dead to the world.

'Give me Ami,' a man at the other end said.

'He's asleep.'

'Wake him,' the voice ordered.

I tried to wake Ami. It took quite a bit of shaking. 'The phone's for you,' I whispered.

'Not a chance,' he said groggily.

I picked up the receiver. 'He doesn't want to come to the phone,' I said.

'Tell him he doesn't have a choice.'

'He says you don't have a choice.'

'Tell him to go to hell.'

'He says to tell you . . . he's not interested.'

The man was getting exasperated. 'Be a good girl, Lily, and put Ami on the phone. *Yalla*, I don't have all night.'

Ami stumbled out of bed with a curse, took the phone and said, 'What does it take to get through to you?' He hung up and we returned to our curtained fortress. Under the flannel sheets Ami took my hand, clasped it on his chest and fell asleep. I could feel his heartbeat and it frightened me, but I didn't move.

A few minutes later a sound startled me and woke Ami. It was the buzzer to Freud's flat: someone was holding it down steadily and not letting go.

'Don't get it,' Ami said.

Buzzing was replaced by pounding. The pounding went on and on. I wondered what our neighbours thought, whether they were scared, whether they would phone the police. 'Open up. This is an order,' a voice said.

'You can't refuse an order!' I said. Even I knew that.

'Watch me.'

The pounding stopped and the phone rang again. Ami put a pillow over his head. Finally he got up and picked up the phone. 'What's going on?' he said.

There was a reply at the other end. Then Ami said, 'Fine, let them. Let them blow us out of existence. It's your problem, not mine.'

The person Ami was talking to said something. Ami cupped the phone. 'They're offering me ten thousand lirot.'

'Say no.'

'I've consulted with my financial adviser,' Ami said. 'She feels it's a bad investment.'

I could hear the voice of the man at the other end rising in fury, threatening Ami with dire consequences.

Ami hung up.

'Aren't you scared?' I asked him.

'Of what? What can they do? Deport me to Jordan? The worst they can do is send me to jail.'

'How come they're so desperate?' I asked him.

'It's a huge thing.'

'Where do they get that kind of money?'

'They have a big budget.'

'But, Ami, are you sure it's right to refuse? Is someone planning some huge terrorist act?'

'Not you too, Lily, please. You're my last hope.'

'I just don't want to have a guilty conscience.'

'I thought you were a pacifist.'

'Your interrogations aren't violent.'

'I told you a million times, Lily, that's not the point. I'm not participating in this farce any longer.'

'What will they do?'

'They have their own interrogators. I'm not the only interrogator in the country. Let's go back to sleep. You've really expanded in the last week, you know. Look at this belly.' He drew up my nightgown to get a better look.

'Yes, but it's surprisingly solid. I used to think pregnant

women were really fragile and delicate, but it's the opposite. You get stronger than ever.'

'Hello there, baby.' He spoke to my belly. 'How's it going?' Then he drew down the nightgown and covered me with the blanket.

'I feel so relieved,' he said. 'I feel like a seven-ton weight has been removed from my shoulders. I'm finally free.'

I kissed him. We kissed for a long time; almost the entire night.

∾ — ⌒

Despite the long name and historically significant life of Sir Edmund Henry Hynman Allenby Allenby, Field Marshal the Viscount of Megiddo and Felixstowe, in certain circles the name 'Allenby' does not bring to mind a person, Allenby, but rather an event, deportation. This is because deportations of Palestinians from occupied Palestine to Jordan used to take place at the Allenby Bridge. When a Palestinian thought of 'Allenby' he thought of the possibility that he would be woken in the middle of the night, taken to the Allenby Bridge and told to cross over to Jordan, which in Christian mythology can refer to Paradise ('The river of Jordan is muddy and cold/Well, it chills the body but not the soul'), but which in real life is mostly arid land with very few trees, poor pastures, and lots of wolves, jackals and wild mountain goats.

The word for 'deportation' in Hebrew is *geyrush*, which is a harsh word (it means 'cast out, get rid of, divorce, expel, dismiss, throw out of a place') but far less harsh for Jews than the English word 'deportation', which conjures images of Jews being sent to be gassed and burnt and buried alive.

The concept of *geyrush* has been replaced, in recent years, by the concept of *transfer*. 'Transfer' has become a Hebrew word and refers specifically to the transfer of Palestinians out of the occupied territories. The idea behind *transfer* is that instead of deporting individuals, you can deport an entire population. How exactly this is to be done is never spelt out by the proponents of *transfer*.

At one time *transfer* was a shocking word in Israel, a taboo word that only fanatic extremists used. But *transfer* has become an ordinary word, thanks to the tireless efforts of its proponents, who never cease to say the word and write the word and discuss the word, and who have printed hundreds of thousands of posters and bumper stickers using the word. Which proves that people can get used to anything.

＿◌◌＿◌

Ami wrote the play in two weeks.

He worked from early afternoon until late at night, and he was in a very good mood. He liked having the radio on, and all day we listened to Abie Natan's pirate station, the Voice of Peace, broadcasting the latest music from a ship on the Mediterranean.

I was on my three-week Passover break, and getting more pregnant all the time. I told Bracha that Ami had left his job and that he was writing a play.

'We're drawn to the theatre like bees to honey in this country,' she said. 'It's easier to see things on stage than on the news. You can imagine you have some control.' Sometimes Bracha surprised me.

After two weeks, when the play was finished, Ami's sister typed it up and I read it.

'This is superb,' I told Ami. 'You're going to be famous.'

He laughed. 'Famous in Tel Aviv, anyway. And Natanya.'

Ami invited some of his friends over to discuss putting on the play as an independent production. The meeting wasn't supposed to be an audition but in the end a lot of the casting was done too. There were seven characters: three interrogators, an off-stage prisoner, a teenage girl who has been brought in for questioning, a putative informer, a Jewish beggar.

Ibrahim was going to be the off-stage prisoner, who was being interrogated. He gave a demonstration of his vocal abilities and we were all impressed.

The putative informer, Sami, was going to be played by an Arab too, a friend of Ami's from his acting-school days. His name was Masoud but everyone called him Susu. He was in his fifties and he hadn't acted for a while; he was pleased to be in a play again.

A new graduate from the drama department, Nili, was cast as the girl brought in for questioning. She didn't speak Arabic, but she was dark and looked the part and, anyway, she didn't have a lot of lines. The few lines she did have were in Hebrew, and Ami said he'd work with her on her accent. Nili was relieved to discover that she wasn't involved in any sex scenes — she would not have been able to accept the part; her family would never have allowed it. As it was they had practically disowned her for studying drama.

The only parts that remained to be cast at the end of the meeting were the interrogators, and everyone had suggestions about who could be approached. Alex was going to be in charge of music, and he assured us that his brother, who was away on reserve duty, could be recruited as stage manager when he returned. Rita, a tense woman who informed us that she was in therapy and on Valium, agreed to be in charge of publicity.

Ami opened a bottle of champagne and brought out a large square of hashish, and there was a lot of cheering. Several people felt the censorship board was going to have a fit when they read the play, but Ami said he'd been careful: he didn't think there would be a problem.

During the evening Alex got very stoned and made a long speech about Job and the leviathan. Then he was sick from the champagne (he was the only one who had drunk more than half a glass) and I took him to the bedroom so that he could lie down. He stretched out on the bed and I pressed a wet towel to his forehead and he told me I was the Virgin Mary (or, in Hebrew, St Miriam).

Later, after everyone had left, I asked Ami whether the attitude of the interrogators in the play towards the girl (they don't plan to use physical force) reflected the way things really were. He said yes. He said women were treated differently from men, and in real life they wouldn't even be in the same interrogation wing as the men; they'd be interrogated separately, with another woman present. That's why he had decided on a female prisoner for his play: he wanted to focus more on the psychology of interrogation, on the way the power structure affected the participants.

I asked him why women were never raped by soldiers in other circumstances.

He said rape went entirely against Israeli army culture, as a rule.

Besides, the women were almost all Muslim. Even the biggest morons wouldn't dare.

◦~ ~◦

This is the history of Ami's play: opened 18 July 1977; closed by the censorship board, 20 July 1977; ignored, 1977–88; revived 3 October 1988, following the report of the Landau Commission (which found that the use of torture by the Shin Bet was widespread) in November 1987 and the outbreak of the first *intifada* two weeks later; won seven prizes, 1989–93; became part of standard repertory.

I have settled on a date with Ibrahim. He will be here in two weeks' time. It turns out there are several people he wants to see here, journalists and writers with whom he's been in touch and will now finally be able to meet in person.

'I'm so happy you called,' he said.

'I'm writing a book.'

'Really? Excellent.'

'I've written other books, about language, but they weren't personal.'

'I knew you'd go far, Lily.'

'I haven't gone anywhere.'

'Well, don't go anywhere now. Stay put, so I can find you.'

'I'll meet you at the airport.'

'I'll be wearing a black and yellow anorak.'

'I'll know you,' I said.

'Yes, you will.'

⌒‿⌒

Ami and his sister didn't celebrate Passover, but they had a tradition of inviting people over for dinner on Passover night. They alternated homes; this year the dinner would be at Ami's sister's house. There would be eleven people altogether: Ami's sister, her husband Tzvi'ka, their three-year-old son Eitan, their two-year-old daughter Tali, me, Ami, his mother, Ibrahim, Mary Jo, Susu and Shoshi, a psychiatrist from Argentina who had no family in Israel and was a close friend of Ami's sister.

Ami's sister and her husband lived in a flat in Yad Eliyahu. On the way to her place we passed graffiti that said, '*Avadim hayinu ve-akhshav bnei zonot.*' It was a play on the Passover text, 'Once we were slaves, now we are the sons of free men.' The graffiti said, 'Once we were slaves, now we are the sons of bitches.'

'It's the writing on the wall,' Ami said, in English.

Ami's sister's flat was luxurious by Israeli standards: a dining room as well as a kitchen, four bedrooms, a view of the skyline from the balcony's wide glass doors. Ami and I arrived early to help prepare. The only indication that it was Passover was a plate of matza on the table, sitting next to a plate of pitta bread.

And though there was not going to be a traditional *haggada* reading, Ami's sister had asked everyone to bring a poem or a passage to read aloud before the meal started.

Ami's sister didn't say hello when we walked in but she kissed us, Israeli-style, on the lips. And she surprised me by looking at Ami and saying, 'What a *ḥatikh*!' Which can be translated as dishy or sexy, but really has a meaning all its own.

I followed Ami's sister to the kitchen to help with last-minute food preparation while Ami and Tzvi'ka gathered chairs to set around the table. Tzvi'ka was a skinny little man, balding, with glasses; he looked bookish and shy. He had about seven jobs, most of them related to writing, editing and translation.

Ami's sister took a noodle kugel out of the oven. 'I made lots of vegetarian dishes . . . You know, Lily, I don't know when I last saw Ami looking so happy. And I can't believe he's gone back to the theatre. You're the best thing that could have happened to him. Here, taste, see if it's hot enough.' She cut a small corner of the kugel, lifted it out of the casserole with her fingers and fed it to me hand to mouth, the way you'd feed a small child. Bracha did that too sometimes. Even Ami fed me now and then, when he wanted me to taste an olive or a stuffed vine leaf he found particularly delicious.

'Perfect,' I said. 'Yes, he's on really good form, and he hasn't even been smoking. And there's this Hollywood producer who's after him.'

'Really?'

'Yes, she spotted him in London, at the hotel. She phoned us when we got back, and she says she's coming on the opening night to see the play. Ami says she's a spy, but he's just being paranoid. And modest. He can't believe anyone would come all the way to Israel just to try to get him to be in a film. He says he won't act again, but you never know, maybe he'll change his mind. But I'm still a little nervous about the way he left his job.' I told her about the gun and about the scene in Freud's flat: the phone call in the middle of the night, the pounding on the door, the threats of the man on the phone.

She stopped attending to the food and stared at me intently as I spoke. 'That's bad,' she said. 'He threatened an officer . . . and he walked out of the job. Now they've got two things against him. Three things. Threatening an officer with a weapon, leaving without permission and insubordination. He's in huge trouble.'

'What can they do?'

'There has to be a formal release of some sort. I thought there was one.'

'Not so far.'

'I'm worried now, too.'

'Will they court-martial him?'

'Yes, they'll have to. But don't worry, sweetie, they won't give him a long sentence, I'm sure of it. A few months in jail at the most. Poor guy. Strange, though, that they haven't arrested him yet. I don't understand it. They never answered his request to be released?'

'No.'

'Very strange.'

'He saw someone high up, someone who lives near Haifa. But it didn't help.'

'He should never have agreed to work for them in the first place,' she said angrily, taking the lid off a pot of vegetable and lentil stew and lowering the heat. 'Ami, of all people. We were shocked when he told us — no one could believe it. He couldn't wait to leave the army! And he was totally traumatized in seventy-three. Almost everyone in his unit was killed. I was sure he'd leave after that, but he went on. It makes me furious just to think about it.'

'He never talks about that stuff. The army, I mean.'

'No, no one talks about war experiences in this country. People just go quietly insane.'

'Did he ever tell you about his job? In interrogation, I mean.'

'He didn't have to say anything, I could see the toll it

was taking. What an environment to work in! Let's hope it's really over.'

'He's not going back, no matter what. He's decided.'

'Yes . . .'

The doorbell rang. It was Shoshi and Ami's mother, Rachel. Shoshi had brought her from Jerusalem.

Ami's sister kissed Shoshi but only placed her hand on her mother's arm. 'How are you, Rachel?' she asked.

'"*Hanukka, Hanukka, ḥag yapheh kol kakh*'," Rachel sang.

'It's Passover, not Hanukka,' Ami's sister said.

The two children ran over to see their grandmother.

'*Safta! Safta!*' they said, tugging at her sweater.

'"*Ner li, ner li, ner li daqiq*",' Rachel sang, switching to another Hanukka song.

The children tumbled over each other, then Susu and Ibrahim and Mary Jo arrived, and after a few moments of chaos as everyone greeted everyone else, we all sat down in the living room to watch the news, a daily ritual in everyone's household except mine and Ami's.

'"*Sevivon sov sov sov*",' Rachel sang.

'*Safta*, be quiet!' Eitan said. 'Can't you see there's news going on here?'

It was 2 April 1977. The news report was only fifteen minutes long and had been recorded because it was a holiday. When it was over, Tzvi'ka turned off the television, we sat down at the table and Ami's sister welcomed everyone.

Then we all had to get up again to fetch our readings from handbags and pockets and, in Tzvi'ka's case, an initially elusive location.

Tzvi'ka went first. He read a passionate love poem by Alterman, which he dedicated to his wife. It was a little hard picturing Tzvi'ka in the throes of passion, but Ami's sister didn't seem at all surprised.

Her turn came next, but she passed. She said she hadn't had time to look for anything because she had been too busy all day with the kids and cooking.

Eitan and Tali sang the first few lines of the Passover questions, which they'd learned at nursery, and we all applauded.

Rachel said, 'I once had a camera.'

Ami read a comic passage from some play or comedy sketch, a monologue in which an old woman sitting on a balcony watches and comments on her neighbours. We were all in hysterics.

I recited a Hebrew children's rhyme I'd liked when I was a child. 'Come to me, sweet butterfly/Come and sit upon my hand/Sit and rest and do not fear/Then rise and fly away again!'

Eitan and Tali applauded.

Mary Jo read the passage from the Bible about the coming of spring: 'For lo the winter is past, the rain is over and gone. The flowers appear on the earth, the time of singing has come, and the voice of the turtle dove is heard in our land. The fig tree puts forth its figs and the vines are in blossom, they give forth fragrance. Arise, my love, my fair one, and come away.'

Ibrahim said, 'Next year in Jerusalem. *Our* Jerusalem,' he added.

Susu read 'Song of the Strange Woman' by Lea Goldberg.

Shoshi said, 'I hope, Ibrahim, you'll let us into your Jerusalem.'

Ibrahim laughed. 'If you behave yourselves,' he said.

Shoshi said she had nothing to read because, by an amazing coincidence, she'd planned to read the same passage Mary Jo had chosen. She made a little speech instead. She said she was honoured to be a guest among such fine company and she wished Ami enormous success in his new venture, and Ami and me great joy in our joint venture, and she hoped all of us would soon have whatever our hearts most desired.

Then we dug into the dozen or so dishes that Ami's sister had prepared.

Half-way through the meal we all became aware of a strong smell of urine. Ami and his sister looked at each other. They went over to their mother and helped her up. 'Oops!' she said, as they led her away. 'I forgot to ask permission to go.' Tzvi'ka took her folding chair to the balcony and poured water and disinfectant over it. The children giggled. Tzvi'ka dried the chair with a rag and brought it back. Then he cleaned the floor.

We could all hear Ami and his sister and their mother in

the bathroom. Ami was saying, 'Come on, Rachel, be a good girl, in you go, everyone's waiting.' Eitan and Tali ran to the bathroom hoping to get a peek, but the door was locked.

After a few minutes Ami and his sister returned with Rachel, who was now wearing a pair of her daughter's corduroy slacks and a T-shirt with the words 'Born To Be Wild' printed in English. She sat down and said, 'Once we *all* had a camera.'

After the meal Susu and Tzvi'ka had a long political discussion about the status and future of Israeli Arabs. Tzvi'ka was pessimistic. He said Begin was probably going to win the elections, and in that case we might as well dress in black and go into mourning, because it would be the end of even a glimmer of hope for real democracy. Susu, on the other hand, was optimistic. He said progress was a natural phenomenon and Begin probably wouldn't win because he was too vocal in his support for settlement in the territories. Susu said that most Israelis wanted peace and they knew that settlement growth meant never-ending conflict.

They took a break to listen to Mary Jo, who had brought her guitar. She sang 'Bridge Over Troubled Water' in her gentle, placid voice, and everyone applauded. After many urgings and pleas, Ami's sister agreed to take the guitar and sing 'I Saw a Bird of Great Beauty', and Ibrahim and I cried. Then Susu and Tzvi'ka went to wash up and continue their discussion. Ami and I reclined lazily on the sofa and Eitan and Tali took the opportunity to climb on to their uncle. Eitan sat on Ami's shoulders and Tali perched herself on his knees. 'My real father died in the last war,' Eitan confided to me, resting his cheek on Ami's hair. 'But I love my new Abba as much. *And* my Uncle Ami.'

Then he turned his attention to my belly and asked us how the baby was going to get out and, more important, how it had got there in the first place. 'How long does it take?' he wanted to know.

'One and nine-thirteenths of a second,' Ami said.

'How does it feel?'

'Sort of like eating chocolate ice cream on a very, very hot day.'

'Do you have to practise?'

'Yes, for at least three years.'

'Then does your mother have to give you permission?'

'Yes.'

'Can you show us how you do it one day?'

'Demonstrations aren't allowed.'

'How come?'

'It's the law.'

'Oh! But what if I can't work out *how* exactly?'

'At that point, you can give me a ring.'

Tali wasn't interested in this conversation. Instead, she wanted to know whether I had any milk. She had only recently been weaned, and she kept asking me whether she could try to squeeze a few drops from my breasts. She whined and nagged

('Why not, why not, why not?') until finally Shoshi suggested I let her see for herself, so we went to the bedroom and I sat on the bed and Tali tried without success to suck milk from my nipples. '*Esek bish!*' she said, sliding off the bed. '*Ani legamri meyu'eshet.*' Meaning: 'This is useless! I'm so frustrated.'

Ami and I stayed after everyone left so Ami could help his sister put their mother to bed in the guest room. The two of them debated for some time whether to lock the door from the outside: on previous occasions there had been incidents during the night. Rachel finally solved the problem for them: 'Lock, lock,' she said. 'The Messiah isn't coming tonight in any case.'

~⌒~

The news that day included the following items:

King Hussein of Jordan was ready to negotiate for peace but demanded full withdrawal to the pre-1967 lines and a shared-jurisdiction compromise on Jerusalem. He was ready to accept some military presence in the West Bank. Labour planned to respond after the elections.

Kuwait and the Soviet Union signed a large-scale arms deal.

The parents of Brigitte Schultz, one of five terrorists (two German, three Palestinian), being held for an attempt to bring down an El Al plane the previous year, visited their daughter.

Begin was in hospital with chest pains and nervous exhaustion, a slight setback for the Likud election campaign.

Security forces had found a loaded 32mm mortar trained on the settlement in Hebron. The mortar was an old type and did not work.

Anwar Sadat began a tour of Germany, France and the US.

Israeli lawyer Felicia Langer, who represented Palestinians in court, was disqualified from acting in military cases because she was privy to military files and at the same time in contact with the enemy. She was planning to appeal.

PLO forces were fortifying their positions in the southern Lebanese town of Bint J'bail in order to block mounting attacks by right-wing Christian militia. The PLO claimed the militia were backed by Israel. Of Bint J'bail's thirty thousand residents, only two thousand remained. The rest had fled.

A hot wind was blowing in from the desert, causing temperatures to rise to the high twenties.

❧

It took some time to get married. Ami was too busy with the play, and neither of us was looking forward to a close encounter with the Rabbinate. Ami phoned a rabbi who was known to be less strict, but his wife said he had gall-bladder problems and wasn't doing any weddings. We considered going to Cyprus, but we didn't really feel like going to all that trouble, especially since the play was in rehearsal. Besides, we were now living on Ami's savings, and we wanted them to last as long as possible.

In the end we took the usual route. I told Ami I really didn't mind going to the *miqveh*, the ritual bath: it would be interesting to see what it was like. And it would be funny, too, going through a purification ritual in my sixth month of pregnancy. But Ami was repelled by the idea of a *miqveh* and furious that I was being forced to do it. It turned out that he never even had a *bar mitzvah*. His mother had been in favour of a *bar mitzvah* but he and his father had talked her out of it.

Ami was very gloomy driving to the Rabbinate and even gloomier once we arrived. We sat on a bench in the hallway to wait our turn. The building was old and run-down and packed with people. I watched a couple getting married in the midst of the bustle; it was a free ceremony, which meant a five-minute ritual in the hallway. The father of the bride tried to inject a festive spirit into what must have been for him a humiliating display of his poverty: with desperate enthusiasm he passed round slices of pale yellow cake. 'Take, take,' he urged the five or six guests who were sitting on a bench next to us. He did not succeed in rousing his wife, who had sunk into passivity. She had draped a strip of thin purple gauze over her shoulders for the occasion, but seemed otherwise oblivious to her surroundings. The whole scene was very depressing.

Finally my name was called. They didn't need Ami, they only needed me: the date of our marriage was to be determined by my menstrual cycle.

'When are you expecting your next period?' the woman at the desk asked me. She looked like a character in a *shtetl* story, with her *shtetl* kerchief and small, wizened face.

'After I give birth,' I said. 'Probably in the autumn. But I'd like to get married as soon as possible.'

'You're pregnant?'

'Yes. As you can see.'

She glanced at my stomach. 'Mmm,' she said. 'What month?'

'Sixth.'

'Why did you wait so long?'

'I was hoping to get married in Cyprus, but it didn't work out.'

'What?' She wrinkled her small face in confusion.

'Anyway, here I am.'

'Yes. Throwing caution to the wind. Breaking your parents' hearts. Behaving like one of the Akum.' Akum is an acronym for idolaters.

'I *am* an idolater,' I said childishly.

She ignored me. 'You can get married next Tuesday, God willing, at eleven o'clock. You need to go to the *miqveh* the night before. They'll give you a slip of blue paper. Without that slip you're not getting married.'

Then she handed me a tattered newspaper clipping that reported the results of a study on sex during menstruation. It had found that women who had intercourse during their periods were more likely to get uterine cancer. 'You must place a hand kerchief on your finger when you finish your period and insert it to make sure it comes out clean.'

'OK,' I said. 'I'll bear that in mind.'

'Now you and your groom have to attend an information meeting with a few other couples,' she said. 'Room twelve.'

Ami refused to come with me, so I had to go without him. I told them my groom was deaf, and that I'd transmit the information to him by sign language. The meeting wasn't too long, but there were ten of us packed into a room the size of a cupboard and we could barely move. It was unbearably hot and stuffy and everyone seemed depressed. No one paid any attention to the rabbi, who was droning on about something or other; we were all waiting to be released.

On the night before the ceremony, we drove to the German

synagogue for my ritual bath. Bracha had recommended the German synagogue; she said it had a reputation for cleanliness.

She was right: the room I was taken to looked like a bathroom in a five-star hotel. Apart from a bath and wash-basin, it had a small rectangular pool in one corner.

'Wash yourself,' a plump, cheerful woman in a stiff blonde wig instructed me. She handed me a comb. 'Then comb your hair. All your hair. Your hair everywhere, all over your body,' she said, and I felt myself blushing. I couldn't help feeling that this was going too far, even though I knew that 1,700 years ago it had probably all made perfect sense.

'Ring the buzzer when you're ready.'

I took my time. I undressed and had a long shower. At Ami's I never felt comfortable taking long showers because hot water was so expensive. But here I didn't care.

Suddenly I heard hysterical screams coming from the next room. 'No, no, no!' a woman shrieked in terror. 'Get me out, get me out! Nazis! Nazis!' After that she shifted to Yiddish and Polish, so I couldn't understand what she was saying. I heard the soft voices of women trying to pacify her, but they didn't succeed.

I only understood what was going on when my own turn came. I had to step into the miniature pool and immerse myself. I had to go in all the way, without holding on to the sides, and recite a complicated prayer. Each time I tried it turned out that I hadn't done it properly: the top of my head was showing, or my elbow had touched the side, and I had to try again. I needed three correct immersions in all, but it took about nine tries until I managed three correct ones.

The water was warm and clean, and the woman in the blonde wig was pleasant, but I could see how if you were afraid of water or of being forced to immerse yourself in it while you were naked, it might be hard for you. Letting go of the sides and then sinking all the way under would be the hard part. And if you didn't like being naked in front of strangers, if it reminded you of being naked in a concentration camp, for example it would be unbearable. I wondered whether they had let the terrified woman go without three perfect immersions, in the same spirit that they were ignoring my tangled hair.

After the immersions I had another shower. Then I dressed and came out of the synagogue, waving my blue slip like a winning lottery ticket. 'You can fuck me now,' I told Ami. 'I'm pure.'

But Ami wasn't amused. 'Medieval,' he said in disgust. 'Let's go and eat. I'm in the mood for bacon.'

The next day we got married in the hallway. We didn't bring any witnesses, so the caretakers who worked at the Rabbinate had to be fetched. They were in the middle of a paint job and they rushed downstairs in their paint-splattered overalls, muttering and complaining that they couldn't just leave things in the middle, the whole job would be ruined. They were so anxious that they could barely stand still. But it only took five minutes to get married to Ami, who looked ready to kill everyone in the room, including the four caretakers who were holding the canopy. He had to wear a *kippah*, of course, and I thought he looked funny with the big gold *kippah* flopping like a forlorn pancake on his curly hair, but he didn't think it was funny at all. I had a head covering too, a white *keffiyeh* that Ami had found in his underwear drawer.

The ceremony included a question about money. Ami had to say how much he'd give me if we divorced. I wondered whether any other religion in the world inserted terms of divorce into the marriage ceremony.

'Nothing,' Ami said. 'She'll have to starve.'

'Just say anything,' I started saying, but the rabbis frantically hushed me; apparently I wasn't allowed to speak during the ceremony.

'Fine. Five lirot,' Ami said.

The rabbis paid no attention. They were used to dealing with seculars.

Apart from the question about alimony, Ami only had to say, 'You are hereby blessed unto me with this ring according to the law of Moses and Israel.' I extended my finger for the ring, the canopy vanished, and the caretakers hurried away with their buckets. We went to another room to sign the contract. While we were waiting, someone came over to Ami and explained that a tip was expected.

Ami said, 'Thanks for the information.'

Finally we were free to go, marriage contract in hand. I looked at it. In the blank space reserved for the alimony arrangement the rabbis had written 'five thousand' instead of 'five'.

'They tricked you, Ami. They've signed you up for five *thousand* lirot.'

'With the current rate of inflation, in eight months it'll come to the same thing.' He was still fuming.

'Well, at least it's over and done with,' I said.

'Yes, it was really fun.'

I pulled off the ring and slid it on to Ami's little finger. 'With this ring you are blessed to me, according to the laws of Love and Eros,' I said. We kissed passionately on the pavement, and then Ami drove me to Central station because I had to go to Jerusalem to do an exam, and he returned to his rehearsal.

⌒──⌒

My daughter phoned, in tears, ready to leave Piesas and come home. The story was hard to follow, but one of the other dancers had upset her and no one was on her side. No one was on the other dancer's side either. My daughter and the other girl had been told to sort it out themselves.

'But it was Bobo's fault,' my daughter sobbed. 'I didn't do anything to her. I don't know why she's so nasty.'

'Does she have a smaller role?'

'No, a bigger one. She's practically the star. I think she fancies Keys.'

'Oh . . .'

'It's not as if they ever went out with each other, or anything. It's not my fault. What am I supposed to do? Drop him because she likes him? He can't stand her!' she said triumphantly.

'Really?'

'Yes. He says she's self-absorbed and shallow.' My daughter began to perk up.

'Oh?'

'Yes. And now I'm sure she's planning something for the opening night, I can just tell. She's going to steal my costume. Or something.'

'If you're really worried about that, talk to Line.'

'I did. I told Line. She said I was being paranoid. I hate her!'

'I'm sorry, honey.'

'Oh, it's all my fault. I was boasting about Keys. And Bobo was there. I shouldn't have done that.'

'You were boasting?'

'Yes, about how great he was and how we're getting engaged. Oh, yes, I forgot to tell you, Mum, we're engaged!'

'You're engaged!'

'Yes. We're in love. He's so perfect. He's the most perfect person in the world. After you.'

'Did he propose?'

'No, I did. I could tell he wanted to, but he was scared. So I did . . . I think Bobo's jealous.'

'It's possible.'

'Mum, I'm going to ask her out for dinner. Bobo, I mean. I'm going to make it up with her. Isn't that what Dad would have done?'

'Yes.'

'I'm going to go over to her flat right now with chocolates. As soon as I get off the phone.'

'Sounds good, honey. You'll keep me informed of any more developments? Between you and Keys, I mean.'

'Of course.'

And then she told me about Keys and his parents and brothers and sisters and their many cousins and what she and Keys had decided about when to have children and how to bring them up (as 'lovers of humankind').

'You'll come and meet everyone,' she said. 'They live just outside Stockholm.'

'I'd love to,' I said.

'You'll have a big family, Mum. You'll have a million new relatives.'

And because she was so excited, I didn't explain that the new big family would be hers, not mine. I let her think that I was willing to be swept into Keys's entire clan of brothers, sisters and innumerable cousins.

⌒ ⌒

Ami's birthday was on 20 April, which fell that year three days before Independence Day. He didn't want to celebrate, but I bought him a shirt and baked a cake. We spent the day organizing the baby's room. We had to clear out either the study or the storage room. Ami had no idea what to do with all the boxes and furniture in the storage room (his brothers' things, his mother's things) so we bought bookshelves for the living room and began to empty the study. We moved all the books and took out the desk. Then we painted the room and put up lace curtains over the blackout shutters and Ami made a bird mobile and hung it from the ceiling. We decided to wait with the rest of the furniture: Ami said we'd have to see the baby first, get a sense of what he or she wanted.

When we moved the desk one of the drawers slid open and its contents spilled on to the floor: pens, coins, phone tokens, ancient erasers, glue, rubber bands, envelopes, airmail paper, broken watch straps, a snow globe of the Eiffel Tower. Also what appeared to be two medals.

'What are these?' I asked.

'Nothing,' he said.

'Are they medals?'

Ami didn't say anything.

'What did you get them for?'

'I don't know. The first seemed to make sense at the time, even though trying to save your friends doesn't seem like an extraordinary act to me. I never understood the second. All I did was manage to stay alive while everyone around me died.'

'You must have done something.'

'Yes, I tried to hold on to my life. Just stick them back in the drawer, Lily.'

Another thing we found in the desk was a diary Ami had kept when he was fourteen. It included detailed descriptions of his lust for Miss Hinterbush, his chemistry teacher, and what he would do if he could get her alone; plans for a talking clock; an explanation of the rules for masturbation contests with his friends Shimi (now head of a major Israeli bank) and Yossi (now running a falafel kiosk); and ridiculous family arguments quoted verbatim.

On the eve of Independence Day we stayed at home. We didn't join in with any of the celebrations; we didn't even turn on the radio or television. We lay on the floor and listened to Billie Holiday and the New York Rock and Roll Ensemble. At one point I got up to go to the lavatory. When I returned Ami was standing in front of the patio doors, looking out at the dark garden. He said, 'Beloved country, where are you?'

It was warm out, and at midnight we went for a walk. We walked away from civilization, towards Afeka, where the skeletal structures of buildings still under construction surrounded new luxury high-rises. We walked down the recently named streets: Rekanati and Abba Ahimeyer and Meir Feinstein and Shlomo ben Yosef and Magshimim. No one was around; everyone was away celebrating Independence Day, or indoors.

I have nothing of importance to record about that walk, except that it was quiet and peaceful and we were happy.

⌒⌒

Nouns in Hebrew are either masculine or feminine.

The word for 'country' happens to be feminine. The question, 'Beloved country, where are you?' sounds sadder in Hebrew than in English, because you use the words you'd use if you were addressing a woman. 'Where are you, beloved? Where have you gone? Were you ever really there?'

⌒⌒

They tried one last time to get Ami back.

He was washing the dishes when the doorbell rang. It was Emil, the man with the pretty wife who had taken us to the revue. 'Hello, Ami!' he said cheerfully. Ami didn't answer but he dried his hands and sat down at the table. Emil sat down opposite him.

He said they'd accepted Ami's decision. They were going to allow him to leave and they would overlook his recent behaviour. All they wanted now was that he give a one-week training course for interrogators somewhere in the Negev. He'd be well paid. They wanted him to do some sample interrogations – mock interrogations, he added quickly – and they wanted to film them for future use.

Ami said he wasn't interested. He said he'd cut himself off entirely from that world, and he didn't want to get into it again, not even for a week. Besides, he had nothing to teach anyone; he had no idea how he operated. As for filming him, they had hundreds – thousands – of hours of his interrogations on tape; what more did they need?

Emil said he'd fought hard to get this deal for Ami. And if he didn't take it, he'd end up with a court-martial.

'I don't mind a court-martial,' Ami said.

Emil told Ami to think about it. He said Ami had a lot to offer. He was well known for his non-violent strategies, and he could make a difference, set a tone. He could be responsible for the implementation of new policies. And, with a child on the way, surely he could use the money: no one could make a living in the theatre.

After he left Ami said, 'I don't know what to do. In theory they could give me a long sentence. You'd be on your own, although my sister would help you. And, of course, the play would have to be postponed.'

'What would jail be like?'

'Nothing unmanageable.'

'Can't you just say you had a nervous breakdown?'

'I can try, but I doubt they'd believe me, seeing as I'm putting on a play.'

'I don't know. Whatever you decide is OK with me. If you go to jail I'll be OK, I'll visit you. I'm allowed to visit?'

'Of course I'd be able to see you. Even if I got a long sentence, they'd let me out for the birth. We wouldn't have to worry about that part.'

'Emil seems so nice.'

'He is nice.'

'How can that be?'

'He's been fighting the system for years.'

'But he's in it?'

'Yes, he has a lot of power.'

'It's cruel to punish you after all the work you've done.'

'In any other army in the world I'd have been in deep shit years ago. We get away with a lot in our army.'

'I thought the army was really tough. Someone told me IDF training was one of the hardest anywhere.'

'It has nothing to do with being tough. It has to do with equality. We used to watch these American war movies. Two officers would be talking to each other – yes, sir, no, sir, will that be all, sir? – and we'd crack up. Because, you know, we're such a small country, everyone knows everyone else, it creates a certain intimacy. Your commander could be the guy who sold you an air-conditioner last week, or the father of the kids you babysat for five years. And you know how Israelis are, everyone has to have a say. Before an operation even ordinary soldiers make suggestions about how to proceed . . . You know, Lily, I just can't believe how big your breasts have become. How can such a tiny person suddenly have such big breasts?'

'I know, it's weird! Did I tell you Bracha lent me two bras?'

'Do you mind that I like it?'

'No, as long as you're not too disappointed when they go back to their usual miniature size.'

'Variety is good. And also . . . also you have a new smell,' he said, lifting my maternity dress.

'A smell! What sort of smell?'

'One I like a lot. Here, lie on your side. That way I'll be at a very good angle for holding on to these new breasts.'

'Ami! Whatever happened to two hours of foreplay?'

'I don't think I'm familiar with that word.'

'And what's this *holding on to*? Like I'm a pole on the bus.'

'No, more like fruit on a branch.'

'Fine, fine, go ahead. I see I'm dealing with a teenager now.'

'Thank you. Oh, what's this? Noah's flood?'

'I can't keep anything from you.'

'No, you can't.'

Later that evening he told me he'd decided to reject the man's offer and take his chances on a light sentence. Prison wasn't so bad, especially if he got sent to Athlit. He only hoped the play would proceed according to schedule; if he was arrested the next day, the actors would have some difficulties, but Alex could take over, and if he was allowed weekend visits he could help them.

The next day he phoned Emil and informed him of his decision. We thought he'd be arrested that afternoon, and we went to Mandy's to have our last meal together. But no one came.

～～

Ibrahim arrived yesterday morning.

He hasn't changed much; he looks like a wearier version of his younger self, slightly creased, eyes more deeply set.

He spotted me first and called out my name, rushed over and lifted me off the ground as he hugged me. Then he took my face in both his hands. 'You haven't changed at all,' he said. 'I would have known you anywhere. Amazing. Amazing.'

'You look the same, too,' I said.

'Yeah, well, my hair's thinner.'

'Where's your luggage?' I asked. He wasn't carrying anything, not even a knapsack.

'I didn't bother with luggage.'

'You don't have anything at all?'

'I have big pockets.'

'OK, we can buy whatever you need.'

'What do I need? I'm here, I'm with you, that's all I need.
I can hardly believe it.'

We drove to my flat in silence. Ibrahim stared out happily
at the city.

I prepared the bedroom for him; once again I am exiled to
my study.

We had lunch at my small kitchen table. Ibrahim commented
on the view out of the window ('exotic'), on the tea, teapot and
tea cosy ('cute'), on the picture of my daughter ('a jewel'). He
took a CD from the inside pocket of his jacket. 'For you,' he
said. 'Yehuda Poliker's latest.'

'Just what I wanted!' I said. 'I know all the words to the
first song.'

'You're pretty up to date.'

'I listen to the radio. You know, on the Net. Thanks,
Ibrahim.'

After lunch we walked down to the market and I insisted on
buying him socks, an extra T-shirt and a pair of warm slippers.
'She's looking after me,' Ibrahim told the vendors.

He wanted to ride in a double-decker bus, so we took the

first one that came and ended up in Oxford Street. Ibrahim was delighted with everything. 'My God, it's so peaceful here,' he kept saying. 'I forgot what it's like to walk down the street without worrying about losing several limbs. No bag inspection, even. I feel I'm on another planet.'

'Are you still working at the garage?'

'The garage!' He smiled. 'That was another life . . . No, I do computer maintenance. I'm in even higher demand than when I fixed cars.'

'What's with Tufiq?'

'We'll talk about that later, Lily. I need some postcards, and stamps. I have to change my money, though. Unless they take Visa.'

'I'll pay for them – you can take me out for dinner tonight. They'll take Visa at the restaurant.' We bought postcards and stamps and several souvenirs.

We didn't have dinner until ten. We went back to my place first, and Ibrahim showered, then spent two hours trying to fix my broken shower head and my leaky toilet and my loose kitchen tap. He borrowed tools from the elderly man next door, but he needed more things, he said. He said he'd go to the hardware shop tomorrow and get a washer and some other items so he could finish the job.

We drove to a quiet Indian restaurant I know. Ibrahim ordered a bottle of wine.

'How have you been, Lily?' he asked me.

359

'Well, occupied with bringing up my daughter, and my studies, my work.'

'How do you live?'

'I teach usually. I'm off this year. I want to tell you I'm sorry I ran away and I'm sorry I haven't been in touch.'

'I don't think you have any reason to be sorry.'

'Do you believe in forgiveness?'

'Of course.'

'I don't. I lost the skill. I just forgot how to do it.'

'Is that why you asked me here? To give you lessons?' He smiled. 'I'm out of practice myself, these days.'

'I know.'

'It's complicated, Lily. It isn't just something you can pull out of a hat, like a rabbit.'

'Or a dove.'

'There has to be a context.'

'I don't know what to do. I don't know what to do next.'

'We'll talk about that, I have some ideas. But not right now. Right now let's eat. Indian food, far out. You're way too thin, by the way.'

'I haven't been hungry since I started my book.'

'It has nothing to do with hunger.' He tore the naan bread into two and handed me half. 'Be a good girl,' he said.

'Remember you said we were all good?'

'Did I? I don't remember. I must have been stoned.'

'You were, actually.'

He burst out laughing. 'Yes, that definitely explains it,' he said.

'Whatever happened with Mary Jo? Why did you break up?'

'You didn't hear?'

'No.'

'I can't believe she didn't tell you.'

'No, all she wrote was "Back in the States".'

'Her parents paid us a surprise visit. Either they really wanted to surprise her, or else they were checking up, I don't know. The neighbours directed them to my flat, and I answered the door in a towel. Mary Jo was asleep. They assumed we'd married secretly, and Mary Jo had to explain the situation. Well, that was the end of it. They took her home.'

'She never returned?'

Ibrahim smiled. 'She returns all the time, she comes to visit every year. But she agreed with her parents. Not that she'd done anything wrong, but that if she wanted kids she had to find someone she could marry. But it never happened – well, you know that part.'

'Do you think it's because she never got over you?'

He shook his head. 'She just never met the right person. What about you, Lily?'

'Hard to replace someone like Ami.'

'I think Ami was the loneliest person I ever knew.'

'Lonely?' I said, startled.

'Yes. Outside of our small circle, who saw things the way he did back then? Fifteen people? Sixteen? Jews, I mean. Now it's half the country.'

'Well, not quite half.'

'Believe me, Lily, Israelis are getting almost as sick of the occupation as the Palestinians. Remember Nili? She teaches first years now. The first ten minutes of the class all the children use their cellphones to tell their parents they're alive. One boy rings his parents to make sure they're alive. Who can live like that? In the Haifa bomb two women lost their husbands and both their children. I can't even imagine what that's like.' He shook his head. 'God, you're a stubborn people.'

'Unlike Palestinians,' I said.

Ibrahim smiled. It was a new smile, one I hadn't seen when he was younger, or maybe it wasn't the smile that was new, but the expression in his eyes when he smiled: penetrating and weary.

'What meeting were you at when I phoned?' I asked.

'I couldn't possibly remember. All I do these days is attend meetings. My whole life is one big meeting. Soldiers refusing to serve, lawyers fighting expulsions, people organizing convoys . . . We're trying to pull ourselves out of this mess, Lily. We need your help. No one on the outside is going to help us, they only want to push us deeper in. We're the only ones who can do it.'

'It's hard.'

'Yes, it's hard.'

'What happened with Tufiq?'

'Another time, Lily.'

The car was parked at a fair distance from the restaurant, and after the meal, as we walked down the quiet, dimly lit street, Ibrahim took my hand. Then he let go and put his arm round my shoulders.

We didn't talk. We were too sad.

◊⁓◊

That's the end of the story. I met Ami, we fell in love, I got pregnant, he left his job, he started rehearsing his play, he turned thirty, we took a walk on Independence Day. Seven months of my life, seven months of his.

The Angel of Death, disguised as two men, descended upon us on a Saturday at the end of May.

We were at rehearsal in a dusty warehouse in Tel Aviv. Everyone was there, the actors, the stage manager, a few friends who had come to help out. I was sitting in a rocking chair, watching Ami direct.

Two men in uniform burst into the warehouse. They said, 'Ami, Ibrahim, we need to see you alone, fast.'

The four of them went to a cloakroom that was separated from the warehouse by a curtain. Everyone else left the warehouse, but I stayed behind and listened.

One of the men said, 'Ibrahim, your son's taken a hostage, a soldier. Ami, he's asked to see you.'

Ibrahim said something under his breath I didn't catch. Then he said, 'Don't go, Ami. Don't go. I'll handle this.'

'It's out of the question,' the man said.

'All I have to do is talk to him. Just give me five minutes with him.'

'There's no time to discuss this. We have to move.'

Ami said, 'It's OK, Ibrahim. I'll take care of it. Did Tufiq say why?'

'He and the soldier got into an argument. We don't have all the details. We'll brief you in the car about what we do know. Let's go.'

They came out. The men were too rushed to notice me, but Ami stopped and smiled at me. 'I'll be back soon,' he said. 'Alex will take you home. Don't forget to lock the door, Lily.'

Those were his last words to me: 'Don't forget to lock the door, Lily.'

◦~──◦

Last night I had the numberplate dream again, but this time it was different. This time as I ran after Ami he waved at me from a car. He was sitting in the passenger's seat and he waved at me and smiled, and he seemed to be saying that he'd left the numberplate behind intentionally, he'd left it for me, and I didn't need him to interpret it, because it was mine now. It was no longer his.

⌒ — ⌒

When an Israeli soldier dies in the line of duty, three officers come to your house and sit in your living room and tell you about it. Imagine how many times that scene has been played out in Israeli living rooms. A hundred times: that's something you can imagine, you can imagine a hundred living rooms if you try, a hundred different homes. And the officers, three hundred officers, though some of them are the same ones, the same officers. They don't just come and go, they stay. So that you have time to think about the living rooms. Flowered sofas. Striped sofas. Folding chairs. Pictures on the wall. Bare walls. Little china dolls, or clay plates.

Two hundred times, that's harder. You start forgetting. The rooms blend together. But you can still try. You can try to imagine three hundred rooms and even four hundred or five hundred or six hundred or seven hundred rooms.

After that the rooms become very small. Just boxes. Tiny boxes. Eight hundred, nine hundred, one thousand boxes. Eleven hundred, one on top of the other. Twelve hundred, thirteen hundred, fourteen hundred, fifteen hundred.

The officers use spoons to stir their coffee. Sixteen hundred spoons. Seventeen hundred spoons. Eighteen hundred, nineteen hundred, two thousand spoons. Twenty-one hundred cups. Twenty-two hundred sugar cubes. Twenty-three hundred drops of coffee spilling on the table. Twenty-four hundred drops. Twenty-five hundred drops. Twenty-six hundred windows. Do you open the window? Or do you shut it because it's suddenly too bright in the house? Do you look out of the window, or do you stare at the officers with pity and hatred?

Twenty-seven hundred shutters coming down or going up. Twenty-eight hundred shutters. Twenty-nine hundred hands fiddling with the shutters. Three thousand hands. Thirty-one hundred hands. Thirty-two hundred hands. Thirty-three hundred hands.

They are in uniform. They wear boots. They are huge. Thirty-four hundred huge trios of officers. Thirty-five hundred uniforms. Thirty-six hundred uniforms. Thirty-seven hundred shoulder loops with insignia. Thirty-eight hundred shoulder loops. And fingernails. Perfectly trimmed, except for one, who bites his nails, surprisingly. Thirty-nine hundred knuckles. Four thousand, forty-one hundred, forty-two hundred, forty-three hundred, forty-four hundred knuckles. You choose one. You ignore the other two. You choose one and that's the one you listen to. And they notice your preference and let him speak. They hate this part of their work. One, the one you're listening to, is crying.

Not in any obvious way, but you can tell. Swallowing,

sniffing, wiping his eyes. Forty-five hundred swallows. Forty-six hundred, forty-seven hundred. Forty-eight hundred. Forty-nine hundred. Five thousand swallows. Fifty-one hundred swallows. You offer your hand, and he takes it. Fifty-two hundred taking of hands. Fifty-three hundred, fifty-four hundred. Fifty-five hundred cups. Fifty-six hundred kettles. Fifty-seven hundred chairs. Fifty-eight hundred people vomiting in the lavatory. Fifty-nine hundred people holding on to something. Six thousand walls. Sixty-one hundred, sixty-two hundred, sixty-three hundred walls. Sixty-four hundred walls. Sixty-five hundred lavatories. Sixty-six hundred bathrooms. Sixty-seven hundred medical officers following you to the bathroom. Sixty-eight hundred medical officers seeing this again, fuck, again.

Sixty-nine hundred nods. Seven thousand nods. Seventy-one thousand nods. Seventy-two hundred frozen stares. Seventy-three hundred people too stunned to move. Seventy-four hundred frozen people. Seventy-five hundred thoughts of suicide. Seventy-six hundred endings to one part of life. Seventy-seven hundred beginnings of something different. Seventy-eight hundred changed lives. Seventy-nine hundred, eight thousand, eighty-one hundred, eighty-two hundred, eighty-three hundred, eighty-four hundred changed lives.

Eighty-five hundred stories. Eighty-six hundred stories. Eighty-seven hundred detailed stories. Eighty-eight hundred telephones. If there is a phone. Nowadays there's always a phone but in the fifties and sixties and seventies there wasn't always a phone. Eighty-nine hundred explanations. Nine thousand explanations. Ninety-one hundred fathers. Ninety-two hundred mothers. Ninety-three hundred sons. Ninety-four hundred, ninety-five hundred, ninety-six hundred daughters. Ninety-seven hundred sisters. Ninety-eight hundred brothers. Ninety-nine hundred unborn children. Ten thousand lovers.

Ten thousand one hundred sensations of something very dark behind your eyes. Ten thousand two hundred steel rods rising from the floor. Ten thousand three hundred steel rods coming up from the floor and stiffening you. Ten thousand four hundred, ten thousand five hundred, ten thousand six hundred hearts pounding harder. Ten thousand seven hundred cups of coffee. Ten thousand eight hundred promises to be there always. Ten thousand nine hundred reassurances. Eleven thousand refusals to believe. Eleven thousand one hundred refusals. Eleven thousand two hundred refusals. Eleven thousand three hundred visions of death. Eleven thousand four hundred visions of slow death. Eleven thousand five hundred visions of quick death. Eleven thousand six hundred references to combat. Eleven thousand seven hundred visions of combat. Eleven thousand eight hundred bodies. Eleven thousand nine hundred bodies losing life. Twelve thousand bodies. Twelve thousand one hundred bodies. Twelve thousand two hundred bodies. Twelve thousand three hundred sugar cubes. Twelve thousand four hundred hands. Twelve thousand five hundred boots. Twelve thousand six hundred hands on the window.

Twelve thousand seven hundred toilets. Twelve thousand eight hundred wrists with watches on them. Twelve thousand nine hundred hands on your forehead.

Thirteen thousand.

Fourteen thousand.

Fifteen thousand.

Sixteen thousand.

Seventeen thousand.

Eighteen thousand.

Nineteen thousand.

Nineteen thousand and one.

You sit quietly and listen. The sentences are clear and precise, so that they can be imprinted in your memory for ever. A commando unit surrounded the house. Ami went in. He was in there for an hour and ten minutes. The soldiers were ready to move in if things didn't work out. The snipers had a description of Tufiq. A red *keffiyeh*, jeans, denim jacket. They were ready to shoot to save the soldier and to save Ami. They had a deflector on them, to blind Tufiq if he appeared at the window or the doorway. Ami came out of the house carrying the soldier's Uzi and wearing Tufiq's *keffiyeh* round his neck. The deflector interfered with the vision of the commanding officer. And it was twilight. And Ami was wearing jeans. The sniper had to act fast, there was no time to think, and the officer gave the order to shoot. The sniper shot right on target: Ami died at once, he was not in pain. They don't know why Ami was wearing the *keffiyeh*. Maybe it was part of some arrangement with Tufiq. Tufiq has been arrested. He will be tried and sentenced; he will be in prison for a long time. It was a tragic accident. Everyone is heartbroken. The boy who shot Ami is heartbroken.

At first you're calm. They ask you who you want to call and you say Ibrahim. They look at each other, they think you're in shock. They think you're confused because you're in shock. They want you to call your parents, they want you to call Ami's sister and her husband, who are also being notified. But you insist. You insist and they hesitate and you keep insisting, and in the end they obey you because you are the bereaved person. Then they promise to be there for you always, to help you, to help your child. You can turn to them, they are there for you, anything you need you have only to ask. They give you a list of phone numbers, printed out on a sheet of cheap, rough paper, the kind they use at the university. They make coffee. The medical officer helps you when you run to the bathroom. He wears a watch exactly like Ami's on his wrist.

They don't leave when Ibrahim comes, they don't want to leave you alone with him. They call in a nurse and a social worker, and when the nurse and the social worker arrive the messengers leave. The nurse and the social worker try to talk to you, they try to convince you to lie down. They can't give you drugs because you're pregnant. They try to convince you to call your parents. You don't think about anything while they're there, you just wait for them to leave, but they don't want to leave you alone with Ibrahim so they phone Ami's sister and Tzvi'ka comes over and sits on the sofa, motionless and mute. Then Tzvi'ka goes away too and you try to die, you try to swallow pain-killers, but Ibrahim catches you and throws them down the drain and talks to you. 'Ami wants you to have his child,' he says. He uses the present tense. And you try to escape from him so you can try something else but he won't let you go. 'Don't let them kill you too, it's not what Ami wants,' he says. He doesn't say anything about what happened. You hit him with your fists because he won't let you go and he cries and you scream, and this goes on all night until finally at daybreak you collapse on the sofa and sleep.

He wakes you for the funeral, a big military funeral with the flag of Israel draped over the coffin and wreaths of flowers and soldiers in formation. And everyone comes, all the important people, all the army people, all the government people, all the intelligence people. And they make speeches about the incredible contribution this person who has died made and the debt we all owe him, and everyone thinks the person who has died was a person who was way up there, way up in Intelligence, doing all kinds of important, secret, brave, dangerous things that have saved many lives. They use words like sacrifice and heroism and they say how much he'll be missed.

Ibrahim and Ami's sister support you through it: hold you up, you and the foetus inside you. Everyone wears sunglasses.

Then everything is sold; Emil and his wife look after everything. Ami's sister doesn't want any of it, and you take the money and move to London and you give birth.

And you go back to your studies, eventually, in London, and you expand your field of research to include Hebrew and Arabic, and your daughter, whose name is Amit, has an English accent and you don't remarry. Every summer Ami's sister visits you with her two, then three, then four children. You don't talk about politics, you don't talk about the past. You go with her to the museum and you look at the *Bathers at Asnières* and you don't mention Lebanon or the *intifadas* or the failed peace talks or the new shopping malls in Tel Aviv. But you follow the news from Israel and Palestine, year by year, slaughter by slaughter.

In the back of your mind, you plan one day to return.

ᵔ—ᵔ

The sacrifice of children was a common practice in ancient times. At a certain point, though, it no longer seemed the right thing to do. This emerging view is taken up by the Bible, which stipulates that the sacrifice of children will no longer be permitted.

To make its point, the Bible presents a morality play, an enactment of this new Thou Shalt Not. That way you can actually see the prohibition acted out, you have a story to help you understand it and remember it and internalize it. You don't just get a statement, as you do with all the other laws, because this thing (unlike lying and murdering and coveting) is the one thing (the Bible seems to be saying) you really can stop doing.

In the story God tells Abraham to sacrifice his child and Abraham gets ready to obey: he builds an altar, he ties up his child, he puts his child on the altar, and he raises his hand to slay his child.

But an angel of God calls to him from heaven and says: 'Do not bring down your hand on the child.'

Here it is. You can see it: it's very clear. A child on the altar, a knife in the air, an angel saying no.

Do not bring down your hand on the child.

אל תשלח ידך אל הנער

You can buy any of these other **Review** titles from your bookshop or *direct from the publisher*.

FREE P&P AND UK DELIVERY
(Overseas and Ireland £3.50 per book)

Summertime	Raffaella Barker	£6.99
Baggage	Emily Barr	£6.99
Infidelity for First-Time Fathers	Mark Barrowcliffe	£6.99
The Last Hope of Girls	Susie Boyt	£6.99
Cranberry Queen	Kathleen de Marco	£6.99
The Woman Who Painted Her Dreams	Isla Dewar	£6.99
Startling Moon	Liu Hong	£6.99
Fruit of the Lemon	Andrea Levy	£6.99
Living with Saints	Mary O'Connell	£6.99
My Lover's Lover	Maggie O'Farrell	£6.99
Dumping Hilary?	Paul Reizin	£6.99
Kissing in Manhattan	David Schickler	£6.99

TO ORDER SIMPLY CALL THIS NUMBER

01235 400 414

or visit our website: www.madaboutbooks.com

Prices and availability subject to change without notice.